AN INDIE NEXT SELECTION, A *NEW YORK TIMES BOOK REVIEW*
EDITORS' CHOICE, AND AN AMAZON AND *ELLE MAGAZINE*
BEST BOOK OF THE MONTH

"Addictive, moving and risk-taking."
—*SAN FRANCISCO CHRONICLE*

"Charges from the gate . . . Gay seems to be saying . . .
Are you prepared?"—*GLOBE AND MAIL* (CANADA)

"Roxane Gay seems to have a knack for fearlessly telling the truth."
—GABOUREY SIDIBE, *NEW YORK TIMES BOOK REVIEW* ("BY THE BOOK")

**ROXANE GAY** is also the *New York Times*—bestselling author of the memoir *Hunger*; the novel *An Untamed State*, which was a finalist for the Dayton Literary Peace Prize; the book of essays *Bad Feminist*; *Ayiti*, a collection; and several comic books in Marvel's *Black Panther: World of Wakanda* series. She divides her time between Indiana and Los Angeles.

"Signature dry wit and piercing psychological depth."
—*HARPER'S BAZAAR*

"Gay's writing is unparalleled."
—*FORBES*

"Deftly and terrifyingly underscores the absurdity of a
society tacitly ordered by skin color."—*NEW REPUBLIC*

"Solidifies Gay's place as one of the voices of our age."
—*NATIONAL POST* (CANADA)

roxanegay.com
🐦 @rgay
roxanegay.tumblr.com

mundaneness when relationships start to fail . . . One of the most important writers in contemporary English literature."

—*Sydney Morning Herald* (Australia)

"Like Joyce Carol Oates' *Where Are You Going, Where Have You Been?* or Shirley Jackson's *We Have Always Lived in the Castle,* this is fiction pressed through a sieve, leaving only the canniest truths behind . . . Addictive, moving and risk-taking."

—*San Francisco Chronicle*

"The women in *Difficult Women* are all deliciously complex, and their relationships are just as multifaceted."

—*Baltimore City Paper*

"Gay brings the powerful voice that flows through her work as a novelist and cultural critic to [these] 21 short stories . . . Gay's 'difficult women' are unforgettable."     —BBC.com

"Her pitch-perfect insights to these female archetypes are so Gay—candid, observant, concise, stirring."     —*Ms.*

"Gay is at her best when merging vivid yet straightforward language with stories that contain an element of folklore . . . Refreshing yet intricate, in the vein of Clarence Major's *Chicago Heat and Other Stories.*"

—*Library Journal* (starred review)

"Unequivocally excellent . . . roughly urgent and skillfully timeless . . . Gay's voice is lyrical throughout, mesmeric and unflinching. This collection shocks, despairs and triumphs."

—*Bookreporter*

"This collection begs for a slow, serious reading."

—*Minneapolis Star Tribune*

"In so many ways, Gay's *Difficult Women* feel simultaneously fictitious and like they could (and probably do) live right down the street. Perhaps they even live inside of our coworkers, our friends, our sisters and ourselves . . . Gay's writing is unparalleled."                                          —*Forbes*

"The titular subjects in the literary star's short-story collection are strippers and engineers, participating in fight clubs and elite suburban dramas. Each one is compelling, thanks to Gay's illuminating prose."                          —*Entertainment Weekly*

"Intimate and powerful . . . an unforgettable story of modern American womanhood. A compelling collection that will stick with you long after you finish the last page."          —Bustle.com

"Women's lives have been Gay's most consistent subject . . . In these stories, she writes fearlessly and with insight about love and power between men and women, about the horror of sexual violence and its inescapable aftershocks, about the fierce and flawed tenderness of mothers for their children."
                                                    —*Tampa Bay Times*

"A powerful collection of short stories about difficult, troubled, headstrong, and unconventional women . . . challenging, quirky, and memorable."                          —*Publishers Weekly*

"Incredible . . . These stories are so lovely the book is best parceled out into multiple readings, so the reader doesn't miss the nuance and the dark beauty of each tale."
                                              —*Charleston Gazette-Mail*

"Haunting and powerful stories which run the gamut between real and surreal . . . Rendered with great specificity and empathy, Gay's characters are unforgettable—and certainly, in their own ways, are difficult women, but also real human beings in whom we may all find ourselves reflected." —*Buzzfeed*

"*Difficult Women* . . . deftly and terrifyingly underscores the absurdity of a society tacitly ordered by skin color and the privileges accrued by those who have ended up at the winning end, circled and watched by those who have not . . . Gay peels it all back, exposing the raw, the enraged and the perversely beautiful."
—*New Republic*

"Astonishing, arresting, and staggering." —*Book Riot*

"The collection is often dark and disturbing, but also deeply empathetic . . . In her deliberate and often exquisite attention to detail, she crafts stories that will haunt the reader long after the book has been put away."
—*Washington Independent Review of Books*

"Gay tells intimate, deep, wry tales . . . Be they writer, scientist, or stripper, Gay's women suffer grave abuses, mourn unfathomable losses, love hard, and work harder." —*Booklist*

"Roxane Gay is a force. . . These are stories about women, in all of the difficult, glorious, inexplicable forms that we take."
—*Rumpus*

"Gay's writing encompasses so much—simultaneously direct, funny, whipsmart, sometimes painful, and always thought-provoking." —*Chicago Review of Books*

"Unified in theme—the struggles of women claiming independence for themselves—but wide-ranging in conception and form . . . Gay is an admirable risk-taker in her exploration of women's lives and new ways to tell their stories."
—*Kirkus Reviews*

"Gay's work is as varied as women's experiences. Each story feels fresh and new, a blanket of snow you both want and don't want to muddy with a footprint. *Difficult Women* . . . solidifies Gay's place as one of the voices of our age."

—*National Post* (Canada)

"Gay is a master of memoir, personal essay, creative nonfiction and lyrical prose, which gives her writing a smart, modern edge that's hard to look away from." —*FUSE*

"When Roxane Gay picks up a label, she'll play with it, rip it apart a little, break it down, and finally embrace it . . . [These] stories celebrate the condition of being difficult in the face of a world that is determined to hurt you." —Vox.com

"[Gay's] goodness cuts to the quick of human experience. Her work returns again and again to issues of power, the body, desire, trauma, survival, truth." —*Brooklyn Magazine*

"The stories in *Difficult Women* . . . are both edgy and bold. But they are also witty, nuanced and extraordinarily affecting . . . Gay is an experience, each of her tales eye-opening— and memorable." —*Buffalo News*

"Realistic storylines and hard themes like the effects of abuse, body insecurities, and trauma are present, but there's also an element of playfulness steeped in fairytales and magical realism . . . Gay revels in stereotypes and . . . shatters and rebuilds these tropes into new and more interesting forms."

—*Miami Rail*

"Gay's characters seem extraordinarily real . . . Enthralling and extraordinarily well-written . . . *Difficult Women* . . . leaves readers hopeful." —*Fairfield Mirror*

"While we'll admit that we would read anything that Roxane Gay writes, from her groundbreaking essay collection *Bad Feminist* to a scribbled grocery list, her latest release is especially intoxicating . . . Our rec? Just let this whole book wash over you."              —*Refinery 29*

"With beauty and realism, *Difficult Women* is an incisive look at the many different experiences of womanhood and the haunting, healing moments that define relationships between women of all ages and backgrounds."              —*City Weekend* (China)

"*Difficult Women* is full of stories that are all too familiar . . . Her stories are heartbreaking and touching, and draw you in."
                                                          —*Brock Press*

# DIFFICULT
# WOMEN

Also by Roxane Gay

*Ayiti*

*An Untamed State*

*Bad Feminist: Essays*

# DIFFICULT WOMEN

# ROXANE GAY

Grove Press

*New York*

*Published simultaneously in Canada*
*Printed in the United States of America*

First Grove Atlantic hardcover edition: January 2017
First Grove Atlantic paperback edition: November 2017

ISBN 978-0-8021-2737-2
eISBN 978-0-8021-8964-6

Library of Congress Cataloging-in-Publication data is available for this title.

Grove Press
an imprint of Grove Atlantic
154 West 14th Street
New York, NY 10011

Distributed by Publishers Group West

groveatlantic.com

17 18 19 20    10 9 8 7 6 5 4 3 2 1

*For difficult women,*
*who should be celebrated for their very nature*

# CONTENTS

# I Will Follow You

My sister decided we had to go see her estranged husband in Reno. When she told me, I was in a mood. I said, "What does that have to do with me?"

Carolina married when she was nineteen. Darryl, her husband, was a decade older but he had a full head of hair and she thought that meant something. They lived with us for the first year. My mom called it *getting on their feet* but they spent most of their time in bed so I assumed *getting on their feet* was a euphemism for sex. When they finally moved out, Carolina and Darryl lived in a crappy apartment with pea-green wallpaper and a balcony where the railing was loose like a rotting tooth. I'd visit them after my classes at the local university. Carolina usually wasn't home from her volunteer job yet so I'd wait for her and watch television and drink warm beer while Darryl, who couldn't seem to find work, stared at me, telling me I was a pretty girl. When I told my sister she laughed and shook her head. She said, "There's not much you can do with men but he won't mess with you, I promise." She was right.

Darryl decided to move to Nevada, better prospects he said, and told Carolina she was his wife, had to go with him. He didn't need to work being married to my sister but he was inconsistently old-fashioned about the strangest things. Carolina doesn't like to be told what to do and she wasn't going to leave me. I didn't want to go to Nevada so she stayed and they remained married but lived completely apart.

I was asleep, my boyfriend Spencer's arm heavy and hot across my chest, when Carolina knocked. My relationship with Spencer left a lot to be desired for many reasons, not the least of which is that he spoke only in movie lines, thinking this made him more credible as a cinephile. He shook me but I groaned and rolled away. When we didn't answer, Carolina let herself in, barged into our bedroom, and crawled in next to me. Her skin was damp and strangely cool, like she had been running in winter. She smelled like hair spray and perfume.

Carolina kissed the back of my neck. "It's time to go, Savvie," she whispered.

"I really do not want to go."

Spencer covered his face with a pillow and mumbled something we couldn't understand.

"Don't make me go alone," Carolina said, her voice breaking. "Don't make me stay here, not again."

An hour later, we were on the interstate, heading east. I curled into the door, pressing my cheek against the glass. As we crossed the California border, I sat up and said, "I really hate you," but I held on to my sister's arm, too.

★  ★  ★

The Blue Desert Inn looked abandoned, forgotten. Mold patterns covered the stucco walls in dark green and black formations. The neon VAC N Y sign crackled as it struggled to stay illuminated. There were only a few cars in the parking lot.

"This is exactly where I expected your husband to end up," I said as we pulled into the parking lot. "If you sleep with him here, I will be so disappointed."

Darryl answered the door in a loose pair of boxers and a T-shirt from our high school. His hair fell in his eyes and his lips were chapped.

He scratched his chin. "I always knew you'd come back to me."

Carolina rubbed her thumb against the stubble. "Be nice."

She pushed past him and I followed, slowly. His room was small but cleaner than I expected. The queen-size bed in the middle of the room sagged. Next to the bed were a small table and two chairs. Across from the bed, an oak dresser covered with used Styrofoam coffee cups, one bearing a lipstick stain.

I pointed to the large tube television. "I didn't know they still made those."

Darryl's upper lip curled. He nodded toward the door leading to the next room. "You should see if the room next door is available." He patted the bed and threw himself at the mattress, which groaned softly when he landed. "Me and your sister are going to be busy."

In the office, an older man with a large gut and thick head of red hair leaned against the counter, tapping a map of the hotel, explaining the merits of each of the available rooms. I pointed to the room adjacent to Darryl's.

"Tell me about this room."

The motel clerk scratched his stomach, then cracked his knuckles. "That there is a fine room. There's a bit of a leak in the bathroom ceiling but if you're in the shower, you're already getting wet."

I swallowed. "I'll take it."

He looked me up and down. "Will you be needing two keys or will you be needing company?"

I slid three twenties across the counter. "Neither."

"Suit yourself," the clerk said. "Suit yourself."

The air in my room was thick and dank. The bed carried a familiar sag as if the same person had gone from room to room, leaving the weight of memory behind. After a thorough inspection, I pressed my ear to the door separating my room from Darryl's. Carolina and her husband were surprisingly quiet. I closed my eyes. My breathing slowed. I don't know how long I stood there but a loud knock startled me.

"I know you're listening, Savvie."

I pulled my door open and glared at my sister, standing in the doorway, hands on her hips. Darryl lay on his bed, still dressed, his ankles crossed. He nodded and grinned widely.

"Looking good, little sis."

Before I could say anything, Carolina covered my mouth. "Darryl's taking us out to dinner, at a casino even."

I looked down at my outfit—faded jeans with a frayed hole where the left knee used to be and a white wifebeater. "I'm not changing."

The Paradise Deluxe was loud in every way—the carpets were an unfortunate explosion of red and orange and green and purple; classic rock blared from speakers in the ceiling. The casino floor was littered with bright slot machines, each emitting a

high-pitched series of sounds that in no way resembled a dis-
cernible tune, and at most of the machines drunk people loudly
brayed as they pushed the SPIN REELS button over and over. As we
walked through the casino, single file—Darryl, Carolina, me—he
nodded every few steps like he owned the place.

The restaurant was dark and empty. Our waiter, a tall skinny
kid whose hair hung greasily in his face, handed us menus encased
in dirty plastic and ignored us for the next twenty minutes.

Darryl leaned back, stretching his arms, wrapping one around
Carolina's shoulders. "This," he said, "is paradise. They serve the
best steak in Reno here—meat so tender and juicy a knife cuts
through it like butter."

I pretended to be deeply absorbed in the menu and its array
of cheap meats and fried food.

Darryl kicked me beneath the table.

I set my menu down. "Must you?"

He slapped the table. "The gang's together again."

While we waited, Carolina idly rubbed her hand along Darryl's
thigh. He did weird things with his face and started smoking,
ashing his cigarette on the table.

"I don't think you're allowed to do that," I said.

Darryl shrugged. "I've got pull here. They're not gonna say
anything."

I stared at the small mound of ashes he was creating. "We are
going to eat at this table."

He exhaled a perfect stream of smoke.

Carolina touched my elbow lightly and looked across the table.
"Leave her alone," she said.

Darryl and my sister married at the justice of the peace. I stood
by her side, wearing my best dress—yellow, sleeveless, empire

waist—and pink Converse high-tops. His brother, Dennis, stood up for him. Dennis couldn't even bother to wear pants and hovered next to Darryl and my sister in a pair of khaki shorts. While the justice droned about loving and obeying, I stared at Dennis's pale knees, how they bulged. Our parents and brothers stood in a stiff line next to Darryl's mother, who chewed gum loudly. She always needs a cigarette in her mouth. After ten minutes without one, she was hurting real bad.

After they exchanged vows, we stepped into the busy hall filled with people going to traffic court and renewing their driver's licenses and seeking justice. We had been in the courthouse three years earlier seeking something but we didn't speak of it that day. We pretended we had every reason to celebrate. Dennis reached into a backpack and pulled out two warm beers. He and Darryl cracked them open right there. Carolina laughed. A cop whose gut hung over his pants watched them through heavy-lidded eyes, then looked down at his shoes. Everyone started slowly shuffling toward the parking lot but Carolina and I stayed behind.

She pressed her forehead against mine.

Something wet and heavy caught in my throat. "Why him?"

"I'd be no good to a really good man and Darryl isn't really a bad man."

I knew exactly what she meant.

Darryl worked nights managing a small airfield on the edge of Reno, the kind frequented by gamblers and other cash-rich miscreants who appreciated discretion where their travels were concerned. It was a mystery how he had fallen into the job. He knew little about managing, aviation, or work. He invited us to join him like he was afraid if he let Carolina out of his sight she might disappear. A friend of his, Cooper, was going to bring beer and some weed. As we drove to the airfield, I sat in the backseat, staring at the freckles on his neck pointing toward his spine from his hairline in a wide V. When Carolina leaned into him like they had never separated, I looked away.

"Don't you have actual work to do?"

He turned around and grinned at me. "Not as much with you ladies here to help me."

"You could just take me back to the motel."

Carolina turned around. "If you go back I go back," she said, sharply. "You know the deal."

"Are you two still joined like those freaky twins, those what you call 'em, you know, like the cats?"

I picked at a hole in the back of the driver's seat. "Siamese?"

Darryl slapped the steering wheel and hooted. "Siamese, yeah, that's it."

I nodded and Carolina turned back around. "We're something like that."

We were young once.

Where Carolina went, I followed. We are only a year apart, no time at all. Our parents moved out of Los Angeles after I was born. With two daughters, it seemed more appropriate to live somewhere quieter, safer. We ended up near Carmel in a development of large Spanish casitas surrounded by tall oaks.

I was ten and Carolina was eleven. We were in the small parking lot adjacent to the park near our neighborhood. There was a van, with a night sky painted on the side—brilliant blues filled with perfect dots of white light, so pretty. I wanted to touch the bright stars stretching from the front of the van all the way to the back. Carolina's friend, Jessie Schachter, walked up to us and they started talking. The van was warm against the palm of my hand, so warm. I had always imagined stars were cold. The stars started moving and the door was flung open. A man, older like my father, crouched in the opening, staring, a strange smile hanging from his thin lips.

He grabbed me by the straps of my overalls and pulled me into the van. I tried to scream but he covered my mouth. His hand was sweaty, tasted like motor oil. Carolina heard how I tried to swallow the air around me. Instead of running away, she ran right toward the van, threw her little body in beside us, her face screwed with concentration. The man's name was Mr. Peter. He quickly closed the door and bound our wrists and ankles.

"Don't you make a sound," he said, "or I will kill your parents and every friend you've ever had." His finger punctuated every word.

Mr. Peter left us at a hospital near home six weeks later. We stood near the emergency room entrance and watched as he drove away, the shiny stars of his van disappearing. I clutched Carolina's hand as we walked to a counter with a sign that said REGISTRATION. We were barely tall enough to see over it. I was silent, would be for a long time. Carolina quietly told the lady our names. She knew who we were, even showed us a flyer with our pictures and our names and the color of our eyes and hair, what we were wearing when we were last seen. I swayed dizzily and threw up all over the counter. Carolina pulled me closer. "We need medical attention," she said.

Later, our parents ran into the emergency room, calling our names frantically. They tried to hold us and we refused. They said we looked so thin. They sat between our hospital beds so they were near both of us. Our parents asked Carolina why she jumped into the van instead of running for help. She said, "I couldn't leave my sister alone."

When we were released, detectives took us to a room with little tables, little chairs, coloring books, and crayons, as if we needed children's things.

On the first day back at school, three months had passed. I sat in homeroom and waited until Mrs. Sewell took attendance. When she was done, I walked out of the classroom, Mrs. Sewell calling after me. I went to Carolina's classroom and sat on the floor next to her desk, resting my head against her thigh. Her teacher paused for a moment, then kept talking. No matter what anyone said or did, I went to Carolina's classes with her. The teachers didn't know what to do so eventually the school let me skip ahead. My sister was the only place that made any sense.

At the airfield, we followed Darryl into the tiny terminal. A long window looked onto the tarmac. He pointed to a small seating area—three benches in a U-shape. "That's the VIP area," he said, laughing. He showed us a cramped office, filled with dusty paper, bright orange traffic cones, some kind of headset, and a pile of junk I couldn't make sense of. Carolina and I sat in the seating area while Darryl did who knows what. A few minutes later he said, "Go to the window. I'm going to show you something." As we stood, I leaned forward. Suddenly, the entire airfield was illuminated in long rows of blue lights. I gasped. It was nice to be surrounded by such unexpected beauty.

Darryl crept up behind us and pulled us into a hug. "Ain't this a beautiful sight, ladies?"

A while later, a heavy-duty truck pulled up in front of the window.

Darryl started jumping up and down, flapping his arms. "My buddy Cooper's here. Now we're going to party." He ran out to greet his friend. They hugged, pounding each other's backs in the violent way men show affection. They jumped onto the hood of the truck and cracked open beers.

I turned to my sister. "What the hell are we doing here, Carolina?"

She traced Darryl's animated outline against the glass. "I know who he is. I know exactly who he is. I need to be around someone I understand completely." She pulled her hair out of her face.

Carolina was lying but she wasn't going to tell me the truth until she was ready.

She ran to the truck and the guys slid apart so she could sit between them. I watched as she opened a beer and it foamed in her face. She tossed her head back and laughed. I envied her. I didn't understand a single thing about Spencer, not even after nearly two years. I wanted to know how he felt about that. He answered on the first ring.

"I don't understand you," I said. "I need to be with a man I understand."

Spencer cleared his throat. "Pay strict attention to what I say because I choose my words carefully and I never repeat myself. I've told you my name: that's the who."

I couldn't take his arrested development for one moment longer. "You know what, Spencer? Goodbye."

I hung up before I had to listen to him say another stupid thing.

I joined my sister and Darryl and his friend on the tarmac. Carolina grinned and threw me a beer. "How's the video clerk?"

"We're through."

Carolina threw her arms over her head and crowed. Then she was crawling up the windshield and standing on top of the cab and shouting for me to join her. Cooper reached into the truck and turned up the volume on the radio. We drank and danced on the top of that truck while the boys passed a joint back and forth below us. The night grew darker but we didn't stop dancing. Eventually, we grew tired, and climbed down into the truck bed. We stared up at the stars, the night still warm. I wanted to cry.

Carolina turned toward me. "Don't cry," she said.

"We're not going home, are we?"

She held my face in her hands.

I woke up and blinked. My eyes were dry and my mouth was dry. My face was dry, the skin stretched tightly. The desert was all in me. I sat up, slowly, and looked around. I was back in my motel room—the dank smell was unbearable. I grabbed my chest. I was still dressed. The door to Darryl's room was open and Darryl was asleep, sprawled on his stomach, one of his long arms hanging over the edge of the bed. Carolina was sitting against the headboard, doing a crossword, her glasses perched on the tip of her nose.

"You didn't sleep long."

"How long have we been here?"

She looked at the clock on the nightstand. "A couple hours." Carolina set her crossword down and led me back to my room. She helped me out of my jeans and pulled a clean T-shirt over my head. She washed my face with a cool washcloth and crawled into bed with me.

I turned to face her. "You should sleep."

She nodded and I pulled the comforter up around us. "You keep watch," she whispered.

My chest tightened. "Hush," I said. "Hush."

I stared at the ceiling, brown with age and water damage. Carolina started to snore softly. When I grew bored, I turned on the television and listened to a documentary about manatees off the coast of Florida, how they were on average nine feet long and how most manatee deaths were human related. When the scientist said this, the interviewer paused. "Man always gets in the way," the interviewer said, ponderously.

We were young once and then we weren't.

Mr. Peter drove for a long time. We were so little and so scared. That was enough to keep us quiet. When we stopped, we weren't anywhere we recognized. He didn't say very much, his hands clamping our necks as he steered us from the van into a house. He took us to a bedroom with two twin beds. The wallpaper was covered with little bears wearing blue bow ties and had a bright blue border. There were no windows. There was nothing in that room but the beds and the walls, our bodies and our fear. He left us for a minute, locking the door. Carolina and I sat on the edge of the bed farthest from the door. We were silent, our skinny legs touching, shaking. When Mr. Peter returned, he threw a length of rope at me.

"Tie her up," he said. I hesitated and he squeezed my shoulder, hard. "Don't make me wait."

"I'm sorry," I whispered, as I looped the rope around Carolina's wrists, loosely.

Mr. Peter nudged me with his foot. "Tighter."

Carolina started babbling, her voice quickly rising in pitch as I pulled the rope tighter. Her lips wet with tears, spit, spite.

"Take me," she begged. "Just take me." He refused. When I was done, he tugged on the rope. Satisfied, he pulled me by my shirt. Carolina stood and held my hands. Her fingertips were bright red, knuckles white. As Mr. Peter dragged me out of the room, Carolina tightened her grip until he finally shoved her away. My eyes widened as the door closed. My sister went crazy. She yelled and threw her body against the door over and over.

Mr. Peter took me into another bedroom with a bed as big as my parents'. There was a dresser, bare, no pictures, nothing. Carolina was still yelling and hitting the door, sound from a faraway place.

"We can be friends or we can be enemies," Mr. Peter said.

I didn't understand but I did; there was the way he looked at me, how he licked his lips over and over.

"Are you going to hurt my sister?"

He smiled. "Not if we're friends."

He pulled me toward him, rubbing his thumb across my lips. I wanted to look away. His eyes weren't normal, didn't look like eyes. I did not look away. He forced his thumb into my mouth. I thought about biting down. I thought about screaming. I thought about my sister, alone in a faraway room, her wrists bound and what he would do to her, to me, to us. I did not understand why his finger was in my mouth. My jaw trembled. I did not bite down.

Mr. Peter arched an eyebrow. "Friends," he said. He pulled me to him. My body became nothing.

Later, he took me back to the other room. Carolina was slumped against the far wall. When she saw us, she rushed at him, barreling into his knees.

He laughed and kicked her away. "Don't make trouble. Me and your sister are going to be good friends."

"Like hell," Carolina said, rushing at him again.

He swatted her away and tossed a box of Fruit Roll-Ups on the floor and left us alone. After we heard him walk away, Carolina told me to untie her. I stood in the corner, wanted to wrap the walls around us.

My sister studied me for a long time. "What did he do?"

I looked at my shoes.

"Oh no," she said quietly, so quietly.

We fell into a routine—we'd explore Reno during the day and go to the airfield at night with Darryl. Sometimes, he let us play with equipment we had no business touching. As planes landed, we stood on the edge of the runway, arms high in the air like we were trying to grab the wings. After planes touched down, we chased after them like we could catch their wind.

Spencer never called, made no grand gesture to win me back. I didn't care. Our parents were long accustomed to Carolina and me chasing after each other. Once they were assured we were safe, they sent us text messages every few days to remind us they loved us, to call if we needed anything. They didn't understand us. They did not know the girls who came home after Mr. Peter.

One morning, I couldn't sleep, and found Darryl, in bed, watching over Carolina, who was asleep. I crawled in next to her and he looked at me over my sister's narrow frame.

It's like he knew exactly what I was thinking. "I'm not that guy anymore," he said. "I'm all grown up and I aim to be true." He kissed my sister's shoulder. I nodded and closed my eyes.

Every day, Mr. Peter came and made me tie up my sister. He took me to the other room. He took what he wanted from my body.

Carolina went mad, always trying to reach me, always trying to make me tell her what happened. I couldn't.

It was worse for her until Mr. Peter made her tie me up. I screamed until my throat bled. I spit blood at his feet. "We were supposed to be friends," I said. "You promised."

He laughed. "Your sister is going to be my friend, too, little girl."

While she was gone, I threw myself against the door, bruising my body with rage, calling out her name. I knew too much. When he brought her back she limped over to me and untied my wrists. We sat on the floor. She said, "It's better this way, more fair," but she was crying and I was crying and we didn't know how to stop.

After that, Mr. Peter came for us every day, sometimes more than once a day. Sometimes there were other men. Sometimes we lay next to each other on his big bed and stared at each other and we would never look away, no matter what they did to us. We'd move our lips and say things only we could hear. He bathed us in a little bathroom with a sea-green tub where we sat facing each other, our knees pulled to our chests. He wouldn't even leave us alone to clean ourselves. He made our whole world the windowless rooms in his house, always filled by him.

The smell of the Blue Desert Inn was driving me crazy. The air was moldy and too thick. It covered my skin and my clothes and my teeth. One morning I saw a cockroach lazily ambling across the television screen and snapped. I stomped into Darryl's room and found my sister curled up in his arms while he smoothed her hair. I looked away, my face growing warm. I hadn't considered that such intimacy was possible between them.

"I am not staying here for one more day."

Carolina sat up. "I don't want to go home." The edge in her voice made my heart contract.

I was ready to argue but she looked so tired. "We can stay somewhere nicer." I waved around the room. "But we're not going to live like this."

She poked Darryl's chest. "What about him?"

"Aren't you guys playing house right now?"

Carolina grinned. Darryl gave me a thumbs-up.

As we pulled out of the parking lot of the Blue Desert Inn, the sign read VAC    Y.

The police caught Mr. Peter when we were fifteen and sixteen. His name was Peter James Iversen. His wife and two sons lived in the house in front of the house where he kept us. The authorities found videotapes. We didn't know. Two detectives came to our house. Carolina and I sat on the couch. The detectives talked. We did not blink. They told us about the tapes; they had watched. I leaned forward, my forehead against my knees. Carolina put her hand in the small of my back. Our parents stood to the side, slowly shaking their heads. When I sat up, I couldn't hear anything. The detectives kept talking but all I could think was *people have seen videotapes*. I stood and walked out of the room. I walked out of the house. Carolina followed. I stopped at the end of the driveway. We watched the traffic.

"Well," she finally said. "This sucks."

A convertible sped by. There was a woman in the passenger seat and her red hair filled the air around her face. She was smiling, all white teeth.

"That bastard," I said.

We went back into the house and said we wanted to see the tapes. At first the detectives and our parents protested, but eventually we got our way. A few days later, my sister and I sat next to each other in a small windowless room with a TV and VCR on a cart. Concerned adults hovered over us—a detective, some kind of social worker, a lawyer.

"Our parents can never see these," Carolina said. "Not ever."

The detective nodded.

We watched hours of black-and-white videos of the girls we used to be and what we were turned into. I held my hand over my mouth to keep any sound from escaping. After a particularly disturbing scene, the detective said, "I think that's enough." Carolina said, "Being there was worse." When we were done I asked if the tapes could be destroyed. That was the one thing we wanted. No one would look us in the eye. *Evidence*, they said. As we walked out of the police station my legs threatened to give out. Carolina did not let me fall.

The criminal trial went quickly. There was too much *evidence*. Mr. Peter was sentenced to life in prison. There was a civil trial because he had money and our parents decided his money should be ours. We both testified. I went first. I tried not to look at him, sitting next to his lawyer, the two of them in their blue suits and neat haircuts. My words rotted on my tongue. Carolina testified. Between the two of us, we told as much of the story as we were ever going to tell. When she finished she looked at me, her eyes flashing worriedly. She stared at her hands, fidgeted. The courtroom was quiet, only the occasional shuffling of paper or a body shifting in the gallery. The judge excused her but Carolina wouldn't move from the stand. She shook her head and gripped the rail in front of her. Her lower lip trembled and I stood. The judge leaned toward my sister, looked down, then coughed and cleared the courtroom. I went to my sister. I smelled something sharp, her fear, something more. I looked down, saw a wet pattern on her skirt, stretching along her thigh. She had wet herself. She was shaking.

I took her hand, squeezed. "This is not a problem. We can fix this."

"Come with me," the judge said. We froze. I stood in front of my sister and she buried her face in my back, her trembling arms wrapped around my waist. I did not let her fall. The judge's face flushed. "Not like that," he stammered. "There's a bathroom in my chambers."

We followed, warily. In the bathroom Carolina wouldn't move, wouldn't speak. I helped her out of her skirt and her underwear. I washed her clean as best I could with dispenser soap and paper towels.

A while later, a knock, our mother, whispering. "Girls," she said. "I've brought a change of clothes."

I opened the door, just a crack. My mother stood in her Sunday suit, a strand of pearls encircling her neck. I reached for the plastic bag and as she handed it to me, she grabbed my wrist gently.

"Can I help?"

I shook my head and pulled away. I closed the door. I dressed my sister. I washed her face. Our foreheads met and I whispered the soft words I give her when she locks up.

On the drive home, we sat in the backseat. Our parents looked straight ahead. As we turned onto our street, our father cleared his throat and tried to sound happy. "At least this is over."

An ugly sound came out of Carolina's mouth.

My father gripped the steering wheel tighter.

The new hotel was much nicer. There was room service and daily maid service and many *amenities*. While Darryl strutted around their room, Carolina and I sat on my bed, poring over a thick leather portfolio detailing the benefits of the hotel. There was a pool, Jacuzzi, and sauna.

While we studied the room service menu, I bumped Carolina's arm gently. "What's really going on here? No more bullshit."

"I just woke up one day and realized we never left that town, and for what?"

"They have French toast." I pointed to a bright picture of thick French toast, covered with powdered sugar.

Carolina reached for her purse and pulled out an envelope, the words DEPARTMENT OF CORRECTIONS in the upper left corner. She smoothed the letter out.

"No," I said, but it sounded like three words.

Her hands shook until she closed her fingers into tight fists. I started reading and then I grabbed the letter and jumped off the bed, kept reading, turned the letter over.

"Don't freak out," Carolina said.

I kicked the air. I set the letter on the nightstand and started banging my head against the wall until a dull throb shot through the bone of my skull.

Carolina closed the distance between us and grabbed my shoulders. "Look at me."

I bit my lip.

She shook me, hard. "Look at me."

I finally lifted my chin. I have spent the best and worst moments of my life looking my sister in the eye. "You brought us here to hide," I said. "You should have told me the truth."

Carolina leaned down and dried my tears with her hair. She sat next to me and I saw her at eleven years old, throwing herself into the mouth of something terrible so I would not be alone. "This is the truth—he knows my address and he sent this letter and that means he can find us. I don't want to ever go back there," she whispered. "I don't ever want him to find us again."

The jury awarded us a lot of money, so much money we would never have to work or want. For a long time, we refused to spend it. Every night, I went online and checked my account balances and thought, *This is what my life was worth.*

My sister and I went to work with Darryl. We sat in the backseat as he drove.

"You girls are awful quiet," he said, as we pulled up to the airfield.

I held his gaze in the rearview mirror. I wanted to say something but my voice locked. Carolina handed him the letter from Mr. Peter. As he read it, Darryl muttered under his breath.

When he was done, he turned to look at us. "I may not seem like much of a man, but that SOB isn't gonna hurt you here, and won't find you, either."

He carefully folded the letter and handed it back to Carolina. Right then I knew why she found her way back to him.

While he worked, my sister and I lay on the runway between two parallel lines of flashing blue lights. The pavement was still warm and the ground held us steady. Our bodies practically glowed.

Mr. Peter was up for parole and Mr. Peter was a changed man. Mr. Peter needed to prove he was a changed man and to prove that Mr. Peter needed our help. Mr. Peter found God. Mr. Peter wanted our forgiveness. Mr. Peter needed our forgiveness so he could get parole. Mr. Peter was sorry for every terrible thing he did to us. Mr. Peter couldn't resist two beautiful little girls. Mr. Peter wanted us so bad he couldn't help himself. Mr. Peter was an old man now, could never hurt another little girl. Mr. Peter begged for our forgiveness.

We were young once.

I was ten and Carolina was eleven. We begged Mr. Peter for everything—food, fresh air, a moment alone with hot water. We begged him for mercy, to give our bodies a break before they were broken completely. He ignored us. We learned to stop begging. He would, too, or he wouldn't. It did not matter.

Carolina pulled the letter out of her pocket and held the corner to the open flame of a lighter before tossing the burning letter into the air. We lay down on the runway, holding hands. The flame burned white, then extinguished. The ashes slowly fell to the ground, drifting onto our clothes, our faces, our deaf ears, our silent tongues.

# Water, All Its Weight

Water and its damage followed Bianca. Every time she looked up. Everywhere she looked up. Water stains, in darkening whorls, curling across the drywall or fiberglass panels, filling them with rot and mold. Fat droplets of water fell on her forearm, her neck, her forehead, her lower lip.

In the gym, one of the fiberglass panels over the free weights had finally broken. The dissolved mush lay in a neat pile on the floor. There was a ladder beneath the empty space, an open toolbox. No repairman was in sight. She got on the treadmill, started running. Bianca's muscles stretched away from her bones and she fell into a comfortable gait. A droplet of water on the back of her neck, then another. She looked up, held her stride. A new stain slowly spread across the panel. She continued running.

Later, at work, Bianca sat at her desk and ate a sensible lunch—a turkey sandwich with mustard, lettuce, and tomato. Above her, the ceiling panels had long since rotted into something dark and unrecognizable. Her small office was filled with a dank smell that clung to her clothes for hours after she left work each night. Fortunately, Bianca was very good at her job. She worked efficiently. She worked fast. She was lovely to look at, wore the wet look well. After she finished her sandwich, she wiped the crumbs from her hands and turned to face her computer monitor. Bianca typed and typed and typed, her fingers making quick work. She ignored the picture of her ex-husband on the corner of her desk. She should have removed it months ago but she wasn't going to let his countenance get off that easily.

They went to the Sahara Desert for their honeymoon, to do something good, Bianca said when Dean, her now ex-husband, asked why they should go to the end of the earth. From village to village, dancing children ran to greet them, held their fingers to the rain that suddenly appeared. Dark people with white bright teeth formed tight circles around Bianca. They painted her face, lifted her up on their shoulders. They said she was a god. When she left, there were high-pitched wails of sorrow. Then, the rain was gone and Dean and Bianca began their lives as a married couple.

On the drive home, Bianca opened the sunroof, looked into the setting sun. Long after she pulled into her assigned space, she sat in her car looking up at angry rain clouds forming, following. For dinner, she ate pasta with a little butter and cheese, had three glasses of red wine. Above her, the ceilings groaned, swollen with the weight of water. Some nights she lay on her couch and stared up, studying the concatenations of water stains, the new forms her ceiling was taking, the way the panels undulated when her upstairs neighbors crossed from one room to another. When she grew tired, she crawled into her empty bed, lay on her side, traced the slight indentation where her ex-husband used to sleep. "This is my life," she said to the empty room. "I am grateful." Then she tried to master faith.

Dean couldn't handle the watery rot that followed Bianca. It was too much, the falling water, the decay everywhere. On their last night, as they made love, Dean on his back, holding Bianca's ass in his hands, enjoying the way her body curved into him, as she rocked against him and moaned softly, as he said the final I love you he would ever say, he suddenly opened his eyes and could only see past his beloved wife, past the flat of her stomach and the gentle rise of her breasts and the lustrous black hair framing her face, to the decomposing darkness above them. His cock immediately grew limp. He felt all the strength he had ever possessed seep from his pores. Bianca moaned louder, stopped moving, planted her hands against his chest. "What's wrong?" she asked. She kissed his chin, nipped at his lower lip with her teeth, tickled his neck. He pushed her away. Even though he had no strength left, he was not gentle. She fell off the bed onto the damp floor. The next morning, Dean was gone. He took nothing with him but the mold spores growing in his lungs. If she were prone to the maudlin, Bianca would admit that he also took her heart.

When Bianca was only three days old, her mother noticed a small water stain in the corner of the nursery, just above the crib. She thought nothing of it. She held her beautiful baby with a thick head of black hair and clear blue eyes, swaying side to side, singing silly songs. She kissed the soft spot of Bianca's head and inhaled the sweetness. The older Bianca got, the more the stain grew, until it had consumed the entire ceiling in a mural of black mold. A contractor was called. Her parents explained that there was a leak, that there was something unknown somewhere. An exhaustive search for the source of the damage was conducted. Nothing was found. The ceiling was replaced.

Bianca continued to grow, and new stains formed, traveling across the nursery ceiling late at night in deep arcs. After the third time they replaced the ceiling, her parents gave up. It was their daughter or their sanity, their marriage. They took Bianca to the orphanage on the edge of town, left her on the concrete steps with a note tucked inside her sweater. Bianca cried for four days after they left; not a soul could console her. The only picture Bianca has from her childhood is one the nuns took on her second day at the orphanage. In the picture, she's three years old. Sister Mary Angelica is holding her. Her chubby arms stretch out at angles, her tiny fingers curled into tight fists. Her cheeks are bright with anger, slick with tears. Her eyes and mouth are red, wide open.

Bianca agreed to go on a date with Dean, who worked in the law firm a few floors below her office, only after he began leaving her handwritten notes on her desk each morning. He wrote her lovely, whimsical things. He had perfect penmanship. He told her all the things he loved about her and he used that word—*love*—without any self-consciousness. When she finally gave in to his advances, she suggested an outdoor café. As they ate and smiled at each other dark clouds circled above their table. She could feel raindrops on her shoulders. In the near distance, there was sunlight. "That's the damnedest thing I've ever seen," Dean said.

By the end of the meal, they were teasing each other with their feet. He traced the fine knuckles of her hand with his fingers and smiled, never looked away. He asked if they might retire to her place for an after-dinner drink. Bianca paled and Dean stammered an apology for being so forward. "No," Bianca said. "It's not that. My place is a mess." As he drove her home, they passed a park. She squeezed his shoulder. "Pull over here." Dean grinned and pulled into the empty parking lot. Bianca slipped out of her shoes and ran across the wide expanse of grass to the merry-go-round.

There had been a playground at the orphanage. She often played there, alone. The other children were frightened of her, as were most of the nuns who tried to love her as one of God's children but failed. Priests from far away were brought in to examine her, to anoint her with holy water. They all said the same thing. Whatever plagued her was the work of the devil and his demons. Whatever possessed her was more powerful than their God. Sermons were delivered about her, about this child who was followed by water and decay. Bianca still managed to grow up a happy child. She would grab hold of a metal rail on the merry-go-round and run as fast as she could. She would run until the ground moved with her and the wind would start whipping the clouds. As the raindrops started to fall, she'd jump onto the merry-go-round and work her way to the middle. She would sit in the middle and throw her arms back, her face open to the wet sky.

"I haven't been on one of these in years," Bianca said, walking around the contraption slowly, touching each of the handrails. Carefully, she climbed into the center. Dean began turning her around and around. She closed her eyes, reached up into the cool night breeze. When his arms grew sore, Dean stopped spinning and climbed onto the metal platform, still turning slowly. He knelt between Bianca's thighs and she began unbuttoning his shirt. When they were both naked, Bianca lay back, enjoying the sensation of the metal grooves against her skin. Dean kissed her forehead and her eyelids and her lips. He tasted like wine and salt and he smelled clean. He marveled at the dampness of her skin, and licked droplets of water from the hollow of her neck. Then he was inside her, and he was her first and his mouth was hot against her ear, whispering all the lovely things he had written in his letters. He said I love you for the first time. She said it back. A warm rain began to fall on their naked bodies. Dean held Bianca's face between his hands, gently moved the long strands of her hair aside. As she looked into his eyes, and her body opened to him completely, she hoped.

# The Mark of Cain

My husband is not a kind man and with him, I am not a good person.

Sometimes I wake up in the middle of the night and he, Caleb, is kneeling over me, his fingers tracing my neck. I place my hands over his, the rough skin, the swollen knuckles. I squeeze.

I wear heavy eyeliner and dark lipstick because my husband once said that he always wants me to look the way I did the night we met in a bar, drunk and numb, looking for trouble before it found us. He can't stand to see me any other way, he said. He wasn't being nostalgic.

I worry about the day when he leaves me, torn apart on our bed, waiting for him to put me back together again.

My husband has an identical twin, Jacob. Sometimes they switch places for days at a time. They think I don't know. I am the kind of woman who doesn't mind indulging the deception.

My husbands have a father who was neither a good father nor a kind man. When he died, shot in the head by a woman he had beaten one time too many, Jacob and Caleb, then fifteen, immediately forgave their father his trespasses—the drinking, his meaty fists against their young bodies, the way he rid them of their mother. With each passing year, the brothers rewrote their past until they had beatified their father's memory. They each have a tattoo of their father's likeness on their back. The ink, Caleb told me on our first date, was mixed with their father's ashes so he would always be with them.

It is nearly impossible to tell Caleb and Jacob apart. They have the same physique, the same haircut, the same mannerisms. Neither of them snores. They are both left-handed. They have dark hair, blue eyes, long, sharp faces, high cheekbones. My husbands work together at the architecture firm they started, so whether it is Caleb or Jacob who comes home, they have the same story to tell me about their day. I married Caleb but I prefer Jacob's company. When Jacob and I make love, there is a sorrowful kindness to his touch. I never worry about being left asunder.

Jacob has a girlfriend, Cassie, who is really Caleb's girlfriend. She is unaware of the distinction. The four of us are at dinner. Jacob, pretending to be Caleb, and I are holding hands. Caleb, pretending to be Jacob, and Cassie are holding hands. There is a light in his eyes that isn't there when he looks at me. My husbands are finishing each other's sentences, regaling Cassie and me with stories about a particularly difficult client. Jacob orders another bottle of wine, and we continue to drink and talk and practice being normal. His arm is heavy across my shoulders and every once in a while, he leans in and brushes his wet lips against the spot on my neck that makes my back arch sharply. Then he smiles at his brother and his brother smiles back. This is when they are at their best—when they are together, sharing the same moment. There is safety, for them, in the number two.

Cassie is a graduate student in museum studies. Caleb told me this in bed after she and Jacob first started dating. He told me about how Cassie plans to curate modern art exhibits, how she has a unique aesthetic, how he thinks she may be the one for Jacob, but what he's really telling me is that she's the one for him. I lay next to Caleb, let him talk, traced his father's image with my fingernails. I told him I was happy for Jacob but I was really happy for him.

When it's time to settle the check, Cassie and I go to the bathroom and we eye each other in the mirror as we freshen our lipstick. "It must be hard being married to a twin," she says. I start to think that she may be smarter than I thought. I say, "It's like being married to two men."

Jacob takes me home while Caleb takes Cassie to Jacob's house, five houses down from ours. In the middle of the night, they will switch places and I will know because Caleb will smell like another woman. Cassie won't notice because she is the kind of woman who doesn't pay attention to details or who chooses not to pay attention to details. On the drive home, I trace Jacob's knuckles and the tiny scars on his fingers, all from architecture school, making miniature models of grand ideas with sharp knives. I tell him how I wish every night could be like this night. He nods and says, "Let's go for a drive." I lean back in my seat, kick off my heels. Jacob takes me to the site of a project he's working on, and we take the construction elevator to the top floor, his arms wrapped tightly around me as the hoist slowly creaks upward. There's no ceiling yet on the top floor, so when we get out of the elevator, it is disorienting, seeing the city sprawling around us and nothing keeping us from falling into it.

I hold on to Jacob to steady myself and then I laugh and pull him into a slow waltz, staring up into the night sky. When we stop, the world keeps spinning, so we drop to the concrete floor and sit with our knees pulled against our chests. What I want to say is that I know who he is and that I would choose him, I would always forever choose him, but I also know his first love is his brother, so I say nothing. I pull my shirt over my head and slide out of my skirt and I lie back on the cold floor, gritty with dirt and sawdust. I reach for Jacob and sigh when he lies on top of me. We kiss, softly, and he closes his eyes, blowing air along my neck, across my shoulders. Then I'm tearing off his shirt, pulling him against me, opening myself to him the way he wants me to. I tell him the only true thing I can. I say, "I love you."

When Caleb drinks too much, where too much is anything more than one drink, he forgets the new history he and his brother have cobbled from their memories of their father. After he and Jacob have switched places, Caleb climbs into bed reeking of wine and cigarette smoke. He barks at me to wake up. I pull the sheets over my head because I am thinking about Jacob and the freedom of tall buildings, and falling into stars while the husband I love most is moving over and in me. Caleb pulls the sheets away, turns on the lights. I sit up, shivering, alone with the husband I do not love most.

He starts telling me a story about himself and his brother sitting in the backseat of their father's Cadillac while the old man got a blowjob from a woman who was not their mother, and how their father had that woman give his sons blowjobs as well. As he tells me this story, his voice grows coarser. His features become less recognizable. Caleb grabs me by my waist, straddles me, and slaps my face. "Don't ever do something like that," he says. "Don't be a fucking whore." Then he's flipping me onto my stomach, his unkind hand planted against my skull, holding me to the bed, treating me like the whore he doesn't want me to be. I think about Caleb's cock, slick with Jacob's seed. I think about how much I hate and therefore love the husband I'm with because I pity him and maybe I pity myself. I come immoderately. Caleb falls asleep lying on top of me. His body is heavy and damp, his smell unfamiliar.

In the morning, Caleb and I avoid making eye contact. He showers, pretends he's going to work, goes to his brother's house, sends Jacob back to me. I am at my dressing table, trying to mask the angry purpling bruise spreading across my face. Jacob stands in the doorway and smiles so kindly that I become nauseated. "What are you doing?" he asks. Then he notices the arc of broken blood vessels beneath my eye. His hands clench into tight fists as he approaches me. When he places soft kisses along the edges of the hurt, my face starts to ache more deeply than it ever did beneath Caleb's fist. "I'm so sorry," Jacob says, shouldering the burden of his brother's sins.

When I miss my period twice in a row, it is Jacob who finds me in the bathroom, sitting on the edge of the bathtub, wrapped in a bath towel, holding the pregnancy test in one hand. He falls to his knees, folds his hands over my thighs. He smiles, pulls my towel open, leaving me naked, and rests his face against my breasts. I run my fingers through his hair, gently massaging his scalp. I imagine the two of us packing a small suitcase, buying a cheap car, driving west on I-80 until we reach something better. I say, "Do you think your brother will be happy?" He says, "I don't give a damn what my brother thinks." For a while, I allow myself to believe him.

I am six months pregnant when Caleb goes to a doctor's appointment with me. He is moody, almost indifferent, there only because Jacob had a meeting he had to attend. These days, I mostly see Caleb late at night, when he steals back to his own home, when he is angry and needs something only I can give. He sits in the chair with the hard plastic arms next to the exam table, arms crossed tightly across his chest. As the doctor glides the sonogram wand across the lower round of my belly, she turns a knob on the machine. "Do you hear that?" she asks. The room is silent but for the identical flutters of two heartbeats.

# Difficult Women

*Loose Women*

### Who a Loose Woman Looks Up To

Never her mother. She is trying to kill her mother or, at least, those parts of her mother lurking beneath her skin. When she spreads her legs she hopes the distance between her and her mother will gape ever wider. She does this because she remembers too much; she has seen too much—her mother pale and frail, cowed by the meat of her father, his fleshy body, his fleshy demands.

### Where a Loose Woman Lives

Her apartment is clean and bright and well appointed though her home doesn't look lived in. There are the suggestions of life, but nothing more. She never stays in one place long. She doesn't need to. When gentlemen visit, their deep voices echo through-out all the clean and bright and empty space. There is a print, black and white, in the hall entrance. Sometimes as he's leaving, a gentleman caller will study the print, try to make sense of it. She will watch him, standing nearby, her body wrapped in a soft robe. He'll say, "This is beautiful, but what does it mean?" She will simply smile.

## How a Loose Woman Longs to Be Touched

There was a boy she once knew. She was twenty-three and he was the same age. He was earnest and she didn't know what to make of that. She had already learned the dangers of sincerity. He told her exactly how he felt. He asked her what she wanted. He touched her with purpose, his hands soft but strong. When she lay beneath him, she arched into his chest willingly, loved the warmth at the places where their bodies met. It was too much. She didn't dare trust it. She broke his heart. When she closes her eyes, she remembers his fingers, tracing the bones of her spine.

## How a Loose Woman Sits at the Bar

Smooth is what they call an ultra lounge—lots of low leather seating, dim lights, overpriced drinks. Electronica blasts through the speakers at uncomfortable volumes and there is a dress code, particularly for men, so they always wear their best jackets, some-times a tie. Their shoes are slick and shiny, just like their hair. They have job titles that often end in the letters -er. Sometimes she goes to the lounge with people who might be considered friends though they know very little about her. She sits where she can be seen while maintaining an indifference about who actually sees her. She crosses her legs and keeps her calves touching. She doesn't blink. She tries not to make it seem like she cares about anything at all.

## What a Loose Woman Sees in the Mirror

Nothing. She doesn't look. She doesn't need to. She knows exactly who she is.

## *Frigid Women*

## How She Got That Way

In second grade, she skinned her knee walking home from school in a plaid skirt and Mary Janes. As she sat on the kitchen counter, watching her mother dab the wound with alcohol, to keep it clean she said, she wanted nothing more than to poke it, to see how much she could make herself hurt.

## With Whom She Surrounds Herself

She has a husband and a child and she loves them in her way though they both like to gang up on her, call her cold. It is her against them. This infuriates her but she says nothing. She smiles coolly. At night, her husband often tries to reach for her but she turns on her side, or digs her fingernails into his wrist as she pushes him away. He misunderstands her motives and when he's golfing with his friends, smoking cigarettes, and drinking beer, the stink of which he will bring home, he likes to say the old ball and chain never puts out. He doesn't cheat, mostly because he's a busy man, and he likes his child well enough but he does frequent strip bars and he brings the stink of those places home with him, too. At night, there is always a burning in her chest as she tries to hold her breath.

## What a Frigid Woman Wears

Every day, she wakes up at 5 a.m. and runs until her body feels like it might fall apart. Everyone tells her she should run marathons but she doesn't see the point. She doesn't need to wear a number on her chest to feel validated. She lives in the country. She can run all she wants. She can go longer than 26.2 miles. She can do anything. She runs because she likes it. She runs because she loves her body, the power of it, how it has always saved her when she most needed saving. She loves to wear formfitting clothing that shows off her musculature—the leanness of her legs, the gentle curves of her calves, the flat of her stomach. When she feels people watching her, she remembers the freedom of running and knows that one day, she will just keep going.

## What Happened When Her Mother Died

She was pregnant with her own child, due any day, her body swollen and unfamiliar. There was a phone call and she stood there, afterward, listening to the dial tone, unable to move. The water ran hot in the kitchen sink and she idly wondered if it would ever stop without human intervention. She drove to the hospital slowly, her belly pressed painfully against the steering wheel. She didn't answer her phone when her husband called. She found her mother's body, stiff and alone, draped in a blue sheet, so still. She ignored the nurse as she slid next to her mother, her belly pulsing against her mother's cooling skin. So many people came and stared, tried to get her to move, but she did not leave her mother alone.

Where a Frigid Woman Goes at Night

There are places for people with secrets and she has secrets, so many of them that sometimes they threaten to choke her. She goes to the places for people with secrets and there she waits.

## Crazy Women

Why a Crazy Woman Is Misunderstood

It started with a phone call after a third date where she followed him home and they had sex, nothing memorable, but overall, adequate. They had breakfast at the diner next door. He ate eggs, scrambled soft. She had pancakes, doused in syrup and butter. "I can't believe you're a woman who eats," he said. "You're a god-damned dream." She smiled at him, the scent of maple heavy in her nose. When they said goodbye, they kissed long and hard, bruising their lips together. It was hours later, in her own apartment, when she remembered she left her briefcase on his couch. She called and he didn't answer and there were important papers, an iPad; she couldn't just let it go. She kept calling and he kept not answering. He called his best friend and said, "This crazy bitch is blowing up my phone." She went to his apartment and when he answered the door he said, "I've got mad skills." She rolled her eyes, said, "It wasn't that good," and pointed to her briefcase, exactly where she left it. His face reddened as she swept past him, grabbed her briefcase, and walked out, head held high.

What a Crazy Woman Talks About in Therapy

The therapist's office is small, so small it could drive a woman crazy. When she and her therapist sit across from each other on small couches, their knees practically touch. This makes her cringe but it can't be helped. She needs someone to talk to. She needs someone to hear her, to understand. She needed help. She has seen many therapists. One told her she was too pretty to have real problems. Another told her to find herself a good man. She knew this therapist wouldn't last long. At the end of her first appointment, after a recitation of all the things that would make anyone crazy, he handed her four pieces of stapled paper—self-care worksheets, and this after she had explicitly told him she didn't believe in affirmation-based therapy. It was the second visit. He asked her if she had completed the worksheets and she said, "I put a one for everything." He leaned forward. She could see a pattern of dryness on his bald scalp. "You mean to say it never occurs to you to eat regularly?" He stared at her, an eyebrow raised. She never looked away.

What a Crazy Woman Thinks About While Walking
Down the Street

She tries to walk not too fast and not too slow. She doesn't want to attract any attention. She pretends she doesn't hear the whistles and catcalls and lewd comments. Sometimes she forgets and leaves her house in a skirt or a tank top because it's a warm day and she wants to feel warm air on her bare skin. Before long, she remembers. She keeps her keys in her hand, three of them held between her fingers, like a dull claw. She makes eye contact only when necessary and if a man should catch her eye, she juts her chin forward, makes sure the line of her jaw is strong. When she leaves work or the bar late, she calls a car service and when the car pulls up to her building, she quickly scans the street to make sure it's safe to walk the short distance from the curb to the door. She once told a boyfriend about these considerations and he said,

"You are completely out of your mind." She told a new friend at work and she said, "Honey, you're not crazy. You're a woman."

## What a Crazy Woman Eats

It is hard to remember the taste of cream, of butter, of salt. In her kitchen, she has a shelf of cookbooks—*Light Eating Right*, *Getting Creative with Kale*, *Thin Eats*, and one very worn copy of *The Art of French Cooking* she opens only when her hunger is so gnawing, the only thing that will sate her is to read of veloutés and bouillabaisse. On Sundays she plans her meals for the week using her cookbooks. It is a dreary process that leaves her tongue dry. Next to the stove there is a small scale she uses to weigh everything. She understands the importance of precise measurements.

## What Happens When a Crazy Woman Snaps

She is sitting at her desk, working late, when her boss hulks his way into her office, sitting too close, on the edge of her desk, taking up space in the way men do. He stares down her blouse and it's the presumption in the way he doesn't hide his interest that makes her hold the sharp letter opener in the cool palm of her hand.

## *Mothers*

## What She Sees in Her Child's Face

From the moment the boy was born, he was the spitting image of his father. "Carved right out of that man's ass," her mom, prone to vulgarity, said in the hospital room as she held her first grandson. When she was finally alone, her husband in the cafeteria looking for something to eat, she held her firstborn child and stared at him, eager to see some mark of herself, eager to feel like the nine months of carrying him, the bed rest, the way he tore her all the way open, was worth it. She never found what she was looking for.

## What She Says to the Other Mothers at Her Child's School

One Wednesday a month, she has to bring a healthy snack to her son's classroom and serve as a helper. Her husband serves on Thursdays. She takes time off from work to do this and makes up the hours at night after she has put her son to sleep. They call this arrangement flextime but really, it's stretch time—she has never worked more hours than after she had her son. It's hard to know what healthy means anymore. That's what she thinks each week. She brought peanut butter and crackers once but one of the other mothers frowned, her lips drawn in a tight line. "Peanut allergies," the other mother muttered. It was all very confusing. For several months she brought only orange wedges until yet another mother pulled her aside and said children need variety to thrive. She said, "Don't they get variety during the other days of the week?" It was soon after that she was told she was no longer needed as a classroom aide and on Wednesday, in her office, when she might have otherwise been in her son's classroom, she felt triumphant.

## What She Thinks About Raising a Boy

Throughout her pregnancy, she was convinced she would be having a girl. She was ready for that. She was ready to love someone who would have something essential in common with her. When the doctor laid her bloody, mewling son on her chest, when she realized he was not a she, it was such a shock she couldn't speak. She warmed to him because he was a fat baby boy. Everywhere on his body, rolls. She loved to trace them and put powder in the folds of his skin to keep him dry and sweet smelling. Even his wrists had rolls and she would kiss them whenever she could. Her husband didn't approve, said too much affection made a boy soft, but she ignored him because she often spied him doing the exact same thing as he changed the boy's diaper or put him down for a nap.

## Where She Went When She Realized She Was Pregnant Again

After work, nauseated and irritable, she went to the bar where she and her colleagues liked to congregate because the martinis were stiff and made with gin the way martinis were supposed to be made. She sat alone, though her friends urged her to join them. She drank one martini after another until she was so drunk she had to call her husband to come get her, which he did. He carried her upstairs and undressed her. He gave her water, two aspirin, and held her close, tried to figure out what was wrong. As she fell asleep, she murmured, "I cannot do it again." He wished, very much, to know what she meant.

## How a Mother Loves

She and her son like to watch documentaries about wild animals. Mothers are often vicious when protecting their cubs, sharp teeth bared and shiny wet. She wishes she could feel that way about her own child, whom she likes well enough. She understands people will never be as true as animals.

## *Dead Girls*

Death makes them more interesting. Death makes them more beautiful. It's something about their bodies on display in final repose—eyes wide open, lips blue, limbs stiff, skin cold. Finally, it might be said, they are at peace.

# FLORIDA

*3333 Palmetto Crest Circle*

The adjustment had been uncomfortable. All her life Marcy had lived in the Midwest with people who ate red meat and starchy foods, who allowed their bodies to spread without shame. And then her husband was transferred to Naples. Marcy's mother said, "Naples, like in Italy?" and Marcy said, "No, Florida," and her mother said, "Oh dear."

The women in Naples all looked the same—lean and darkly tan, their faces narrow with hungered discipline, whittled by the same surgeon. They stared at Marcy's relatively ample physique with disgust or envy or something between the two. At night, Marcy worried about her ass and thighs. Her husband always said, "Baby, you are perfect," and she flushed angrily. His assurances were so reflexive as to be insulting.

In Omaha, they lived in a neighborhood. In Naples, they moved into a gated community, Palmetto Landing, where each estate was blandly unique and sprawling—tall facades, lots of glass and balustrades around the windows, Spanish tiles on the roofs—the streets cobbled with tiny square bricks. The first time they drove up to the gatehouse, manned by a white-haired gentleman in polyester, Marcy leaned forward to study the landscaping, tall cypresses encircled by Peruvian lilies looming over the guardhouse. She sighed, said, "This is a bit much." Her husband said, "Baby, people love the illusion of safety and the spectacle of enclosure." They were given bar-coded stickers for their cars.

Their community had a country club. They joined because the transfer came with a promotion and a raise. Marcy's husband said it was important to live up to their new station. He mostly wanted to play golf with men whose bellies were fatter than his. In Palmetto Landing, the men's bodies expanded in inverse proportion to those of their wives.

Each morning, there was a group fitness class at the club-house—Spinning, Zumba, kickboxing, always something different. The instructor was a young, aggressively fit woman, Caridad. The other wives loved to say her name, trilling their *r*'s to show Caridad *ellas hablan español*. Marcy stood in the back of the studio in sweatpants and an old T-shirt of her husband's while the women around her perspired in their perfectly coordinated outfits fancier than most of Marcy's wardrobe.

Marcy enjoyed the pleasant soreness as she drove the five blocks home after each class. She liked how for an hour, there was a precise set of instructions she was meant to follow, a clear sense of direction.

The other wives were quietly fascinated by Marcy in that she was a rare species in the wealthy enclave—a first wife. Ellen Katz, who lived three doors down, often squeezed Marcy's shoulder with her cool, bony hand. She'd say, "We're rooting for you," and offered words of encouragement as Marcy's figure slimmed. Marcy never knew what to say during these moments, but she smiled politely because she understood these people and how they existed only in relation to those around them.

## 1217 Ridgewood Rd Unit 11

My wife and I watch documentaries about the lives of extraordinarily fat people so we can feel better about ourselves because we work hourly jobs and live in a crappy apartment surrounded by McMansions as part of an "economic diversity initiative" in our gated community. Our GEDs didn't take us as far as we hoped but they got us to Palmetto Landing, and sometimes, we tell ourselves that's enough. We got our GEDs because we wanted to get married. We wanted to get married so we could have sex because back then we believed what our parents told us about going to hell if we fornicated and at that point, we had done everything but have sex and we knew that the disposition of our souls was in grave danger if we didn't do something drastic. Our parents told us we couldn't get married until we had our high school diplomas because we were too young and we needed a good solid education before we could make adult decisions and we thought they were delusional because we actually went to school every day and knew that they weren't teaching us a damn thing. We showed them by going across the state line to get married but then the sex wasn't that great and then we couldn't find jobs that didn't involve customer service and now we've accepted that this is as good as it's going to get. We watch as the extraordinarily fat people tearfully explain how they got to one thousand pounds, how it was a slippery slope, how they tried diets, how now they're stuck in their soiled beds and have to be cut out of their homes and taken to a special fat hospital for emergency surgery with the assistance of special fat SWAT teams with good back strength who wear latex gloves and grave expressions.

The best part of these documentaries is when the medical professionals talk about the fat people like they understand, like they sympathize, like this is all normal, when you know that when those doctors and nurses get home, they sit in bed crying, eating a tub of ice cream asking themselves how tragedies like these happen. The wife and I giggle when the doctors use the word *staggering* or when the fat person says *I let things get out of hand.* For the next week, we'll repeat that phrase as often as we can and then laugh uncontrollably. For example, I'll get home late from work and the wife will be at the kitchen table waiting and she'll be kind of irritated because she took the time to bake a Stouffer's lasagna in the oven and microwave some frozen broccoli so I'll say *I let things get out of hand.* She'll try not to crack a smile and then her cheeks will twitch and she'll start shaking and then we'll both laugh so hard that there's snot coming out of our noses and we're laugh-crying and she's forgotten that I was late and won't spend the next hour interrogating me about why my shirt reeks like cigarette smoke even though we both know that I'm late because I met my best friend, whom she hates mostly because he did finish high school and isn't married, for a couple of beers at the bar he owns.

The sex between the wife and me has improved significantly over the past seven years. I think we're starting to resent getting married at seventeen a lot less. After we watch documentaries about the lives of extraordinarily fat people, my wife fucks me like she's auditioning to become a contract porn star and tells me that she's so fucking glad that we're both thin and that we have families who love us enough not to feed us to death and I tell her *I'm so fucking glad* we're both thin and I lick her nipples and get extra creative and we both moan and pant and I want the moment to last so I think about the poor SOB who needs a team of physical therapists to give him a bath and how he groans in pain as they heave and shift his folds and awkward deposits of fat, all so it will take me a little longer to come. Mornings after Thank God We're Not Fat Sex, the wife and I tend to hate each other a little so we don't speak and make as little eye contact as possible. Instead, we move silently through our morning routines as we try to assess any damage we may have caused. She brushes her teeth and takes a shower and shaves her legs and uses all the hot water and leaves little tiny leg hairs around the drain and curls her hair and puts on her makeup and forgets to cap her mascara and the entire time, I'm sitting on the toilet pretending to read a magazine but really I'm just staring at her naked body because she's hotter than me. She starts the coffee, makes it too strong just the way I hate it, fills her travel thermos, leaves for her job as a receptionist at a beauty salon, and I get to spend an hour or so alone in our apartment watching Home Shopping Network until I have to go to work at a copy shop where I spend my day in front of a Xerox machine pushing buttons, flirting with college girls who need photocopies and *just can't seem to work the machine* while getting high on hot toner fumes.

Invariably, at some point during these documentaries about extraordinarily fat people, there comes a time when a surgeon has to cut away chunks of belly or upper thigh and the fat person is lying on the operating table, vulnerable and spread eagle, unconscious as the surgeon uses special tools to spread and pull and dissect. Then the surgeon triumphantly raises the bloody, excised body parts and shouts out how much they weigh and everyone in the room gasps frenzied-like. It's painfully obvious that they're all really turned on and after they're done sewing their patient back together like they're Dr. Frankenstein, you get the impression that one of those surgeons is going to pull one or more of those nurses into a supply closet so that they too can have Thank God We're Not Fat Sex. The wife doesn't like to watch the operations—she calls it human butchering and blood makes her nauseated. She doesn't even like to change her own tampon so when we're watching the surgical procedures the wife covers her eyes and buries her head against my shoulder, and I narrate in explicit detail how the fat is yellow and serpentine and pulpy and slick and how the excised body parts are dropped into biohazard bags and then we speculate about what happens to the dead fat deposits of extraordinarily fat people and we think it would be nice if they had backyard burial ceremonies for them the way kids do for dead pets.

One night when we're watching one of these documentaries, the wife turns to me and says, "There's no happy endings in these stories," and then she swallows about half of my beer. She looks like she's about to cry and then I feel like I'm about to cry thinking about these large people living such small, impossible lives so I say, "It's a happy ending when they're wheeled out of the hospital and they only weigh five hundred pounds and they go back to their special chair at home where their loved ones will feed them the same way they've always fed them so that in three years, they'll weigh a ton again and we'll have another documentary to watch," and with tears in her eyes, my wife crawls into my lap, straddling me, and she holds my face in her hands and she says, "I love you so fucking much."

## 2945 Palmetto Hollow Cir

Jean-Richard and Elsie Moreau had lived in Palmetto Landing for nearly seven years when they heard the news, by way of Ellen Katz, that another Haitian family was moving into the community—doctors, three children, two still at home, new money and a lot of it. Ellen was giddy as she delivered the news. She saw it as something of a personal responsibility to keep her neighbors abreast of such developments.

They sat on the lanai drinking wine, sweating quietly.

Ellen pointed at Elsie. "I imagine you'll want to invite the new family over, perhaps dinner, something from home."

Elsie took a careful sip of her wine, then twisted the heavy diamond on her finger as she sank into her seat. "Why would you imagine that?" she murmured.

A few weeks later, Elsie was driving her golf cart to the clubhouse for Ladies Golf, slowly bouncing along the cobbled street, when she saw a light-skinned brown woman standing at the edge of her driveway, one hand shielding her eyes from the sun. Elsie immediately knew the woman was one of the new Haitian doctors. Elsie could recognize her people anywhere—it was a point of pride. She stared straight ahead, the electric motor of her golf cart humming softly as she drove past.

Jean-Richard was the more sociable one, willing to do more than his fair share of maintaining their position within the community, always gregarious and outgoing at the various functions, so many functions—barbecues and theme nights and bridge and the like. If he had his way, they would spend every night with their friends at the clubhouse.

Elsie preferred more control over the boundaries of her world. She was in her late forties, she had no need for new friends.

At dinner, Elsie mentioned she had seen the Haitian doctor wife, standing in her driveway.

"We should have them over, welcome them," Jean-Richard said, rubbing his heavy hands together.

Elsie frowned, tried to swallow her sigh. "We left that island for a reason. And you know what the neighbors would think."

Jean-Richard leaned forward, but thought better of saying anything. Instead he smiled, said, "Oui, ma chère."

It had been twenty-five years since Elsie immigrated to the United States. What she remembered of home was the promiscuity—always people, everywhere, hot and clamoring. Elsie did not often think of the towering palm trees or the bright blue water or trips to the country to visit her grandmother or how much she loved her blue school uniform or watching her parents dance in the small courtyard behind their home. Her sharpest memories were of her eight brothers and sisters always crowding any space she tried to make for herself. She remembered small rooms and heavy air and warm concrete walls and slick skin and limbs, stretching desperately for a cooler, dry place.

### 1217 Ridgewood Rd Unit 8

Caridad loved her body, the strength and shape of it. She did not much love how other people loved her body. They misunderstood.

She worked as a fitness instructor at a country club in a gated community in Naples. It was a good job. Mostly she helped old people forget how little time they had left and helped not yet old people keep aging at bay. Vanity was an easy thing to understand. During group fitness classes, Caridad watched the women in the community, wearing their outfits that cost more than her weekly pay, how their makeup shimmered the more they perspired, how their perfume filled the studio, choking the air out of the room. They were always trying to outdo each other, to master the complex moves Caridad modeled for them. She had a soft spot for the women in the back row, often young, the kind with new money and older husbands, who didn't yet know where they fit in the ecosystem of the neighborhood, the kind she might be friends with under different circumstances. Sometimes, after class, Caridad tried to talk to the women in the back row but they were often apprehensive about upsetting the delicate balance demanded of them, the unspoken rules about associating with the *right kind of people*.

It had been a long day. In her morning fitness class, the ladies were unfocused, unable to follow simple moves, complaining each time Caridad tried to increase the intensity. "Por favor, Caridad," they said, "no mas." The ladies in her classes loved to speak to Caridad in broken Spanish, to show her they were comfortable with her ethnicity despite the paleness of their skin and the wealth of their husbands. Each morning before work, Caridad stared at her reflection in the mirror and practiced not rolling her eyes so she could smile politely at the ladies in her classes. One of the community's newest residents lingered in the studio after the Zumba class. She was young and the only one who didn't wear coordinated designer outfits. Caridad couldn't remember her name. The woman was married to an age-appropriate man and would never be accused of being able to follow a beat but she wasn't afraid to sweat or look ugly.

Caridad walked the length of the studio, picking up discarded water bottles. "How are you enjoying the neighborhood?" she asked.

The woman offered a small smile, waving her hands in front of her. "This all takes a little getting used to."

Caridad arched an eyebrow. "I can imagine."

"I'm Marcy," she said, closing the distance between them, holding her hand out. "This isn't who we are, my husband and I. I have no idea what we're doing here."

"I'm guessing he's a golfer."

Marcy laughed. "Mostly in his mind."

It would be nice to go out for a drink after work, Caridad thought. She wouldn't mind someone nice to talk to. Caridad was about to invite Marcy out for a drink when one of the white-hairs who shared the same face as several of her friends popped into the studio.

"Yoohoo, Marcy, we're ready for lunch," she said.

Marcy shrugged apologetically and shuffled out of the studio. Caridad sighed.

Later, after a personal training session, there was an incident with Sal, who didn't understand why Caridad was uninterested in accompanying him on an overnight trip to South Beach. He held her elbow too firmly, his teeth bared, wet. He loved to recline on the weight bench, spreading his legs wide. He always wore loose shorts and no underwear during their sessions, letting his limp cock hang lazily against his left thigh. No matter how much weight he lifted, he grunted extravagantly. Caridad pretended not to notice. He stood too close to her now, a fluffy white towel draped around his neck. Sal pressed a fat finger against the base of her throat, making Caridad feel choked.

"You will be well compensated. We'll dance, maybe more," he said.

Caridad's face burned but she bit her tongue.

The job was good, mostly.

She pushed Sal away, negotiating the complexity of making her point without getting fired. "I'm only here to help make bodies better. My body isn't for sale."

Sal snorted, said, "We'll see about that," as he walked away.

Caridad lived with her boyfriend, Manny, in a loud, stuccoed apartment complex in Bonita Springs. They had been dating for four years and their relationship was mostly unremarkable. She was smart enough to want more but tired enough to accept the way things were.

When Caridad came home, Manny was stretching on the living room floor, bare-chested, wearing soccer shorts, knee-high socks, cleats. He played in a local league and his team, Los Toreadors, practiced every evening. They were the most menacing team in the area—sometimes they even traveled around the state playing teams from other leagues. There were rumors—for example, that scouts from professional teams spied on their practices—but nothing ever came of it. That didn't stop the men on the team from dreaming of wearing a Galaxy jersey or maybe the colors of a European team—Manchester United, Real Madrid. When Caridad complained, Manny shrugged, said, "This is who I am, babe. I'm a footballer."

Caridad knelt between his taut, open thighs and pushed Manny onto his back. She lay on his chest and exhaled loudly. "I've had the worst day," she said. Manny lightly massaged her shoulders and Caridad tensed. "Just let me lie here," she whispered.

Manny gently pushed her to the side, kissed her forehead, said, "I've gotta go."

Caridad stared at a curving pattern of mold on the ceiling as he stood. She stared for a long time.

After practice, Manny looked contrite, his dark hair clinging damply to the edges of his face. His jersey was soaked. He kissed her forehead again, tried to ask Caridad about her day, but she no longer had any interest in telling him anything.

The entrance to their complex was lined with palm trees. At night the trees were illuminated in pink and yellow and blue and green. Caridad loved sitting beneath the lights, found them unspeakably beautiful. Caridad grabbed Manny's hand and led him outside. They sat quietly beneath the trees for a few moments, then Manny leaned into Caridad, pawed at her breasts, tried to work his fingers beneath the waistband of her denim skirt.

She laughed, her lilting voice drifting upward as she swatted his hands away, said, "Not yet, baby. Not yet. Just be with me. Just be nice with me," but Manny didn't hear her or wouldn't hear her.

Caridad was too tired to fight too much. She stretched her arms over her head as Manny lay over her, pushing Caridad's skirt up around her slender hips. He kissed her left thigh, said something unimportant. The pink light was of an exceptional quality. Caridad smiled, relished the quiet thrill.

### 4411 Palmetto Pines Way

At first, news of the brothel was only a rumor. Men would rush into and out of the spa in Palmetto Landing at all hours, often looking harried on the way in and relaxed on the way out, but we had no proof. Then Evelyn Marshall caught her husband getting a blowjob. She was getting a hot stone massage and heard a familiar groan from the adjacent room. News spread through our small community quickly but no one alerted the authorities. We felt important, having such goings-on in our midst.

In the afternoon, the *therapists* often sit on the large lanai behind the spa in negligees and peignoirs and heavy makeup, smoking and drinking bright-colored fruity drinks, waiting for their next clients. My front balcony looks out onto this lanai where the ladies lounge. They are not as beautiful as you might imagine but they are interesting and they talk loudly. They never seem to sweat despite the humidity. Their voices are deep and velvety in the way of women who know things. I sit on my balcony most afternoons wearing a pair of dark sunglasses. I hold a book in my lap. I pretend to read.

One of the women who work at the spa is very tall, the kind of tall in a woman that makes people stare. She has long dark hair she always wears down. She is beautiful and I love looking at her, how she moves, the anger in her eyes. She caught me staring once, stood up, her robe falling open. She lifted a leg and propped it on the railing and pointed between her thighs, then threw her hands in the air. I did not stop staring. She did not close her legs.

I went to see her. The woman at the desk studied me carefully. She said, "Nadia is one of our special therapists; she charges high fees." I said, "I know." The receptionist shrugged. Soon after, I was escorted into the back. I heard interesting sounds. Nadia had a thick Russian accent but spoke English well. "You want massage? Candles? What?" she asked. I said, "I want to fuck." The words felt heavy and strange in my mouth. Nadia cocked her head to the side. "You are different," she said. Later, her tongue was cool and soft between my thighs. I twisted my fingers through her hair, resting my heels on her back. I wanted to explain myself. It took me a long time to come, it always does, but Nadia was patient. I reciprocated her attentions. I wasn't afraid.

As I was leaving, I ran into my next-door neighbor. She pulled her purse closer to her body and looked away. I pressed my hand against my neighbor's shoulder as we passed. She still refused to look at me but she leaned into my touch. Now Nadia stares at me when she's on her lanai and I am up on my balcony. I don't look away.

My husband calls me a wildcat. After we make love, he always whistles under his breath and slaps my thigh, says, "Goddamn, woman. You're going to kill me." On our wedding day, my mother pulled me aside at the chapel. I was only half-dressed, walking around in white pantyhose, a corset, and white patent leather heels. My dress was a monstrosity of satin and chiffon and I wanted to wear it for as little time as possible. We stood in a dark vestibule and my mother began straightening my curls, pulling them out of my face, messing with the pearl headband holding my hair back. She said, "There's no mystery to keeping a man." She dabbed at my lipstick with a tissue she had been holding, folded, in the palm of her hand. She said, "You do whatever sick thing he wants, when he wants, and you'll never have a problem." That was the only advice she has ever given me. She and my father divorced when I was nine.

## 1217 Ridgewood Rd Unit 23

Tricia cleaned houses and she was good at it, knew just how to work her way through someone's home to deal with the messes they didn't want to take responsibility for. Tricia loved to talk with her clients. That's how she judged people. If they ignored her or were clipped in their responses she knew they weren't good people and didn't feel bad about availing herself of some of their possessions—little things they would never miss because they had too much. Tricia wore tank tops and denim cutoff shorts while she worked, leaving her tanned arms and long legs bare. She wore her dirty-blond hair on top of her head, a few loose strands wispy against her neck. Sweat often pooled between her breasts, leaving a damp line down the middle of her shirt. This did not concern Tricia. She was proud to work so hard her effort left a mark. The wives Tricia worked for didn't appreciate Tricia's comfort with her body and her labor, particularly if their husbands were home. They took it as something of an insult. A woman who cleaned their homes had such a naturally fine body while they stretched themselves taut with the finest surgeons in South Florida and didn't look half as good. It wasn't fair. Money was supposed to make things fair. Tricia cleaned very big houses—the kinds with rooms that had special designations like *media room* and *fitness center* and *library*. The floors were often marble and when the women who lived in these houses walked, their heels click-click-clacked. Most of the women who cleaned houses in the area were brown-skinned and spoke Spanish or Creole. Tricia was something of a novelty and her services were in high demand because her clients liked having an English-speaking housekeeper as much as it made them uncomfortable to see a white woman doing the work of *la gente*. Once in a while, the wives asked Tricia where she was from and Tricia explained her people were from the Everglades—generations of her family lived deep in the swamp, so deep you had to take an air boat to get to their land, where their homes were all stucco and mold and wide-open windows. The way Tricia said this, it was like she was saying something more, but the wives were never quite sure what.

# La Negra Blanca

At the club, Sarah goes by Sierra. The manager gave her the name the day she was hired four years earlier. He asked if she had a preference but she shrugged, took a sip of warm soda, told him to knock himself out. He looked her up and down and up again. "Sierra," he said. "So you'll turn your head when your name is called."

Sometimes, when she's opening the refrigerator, or reaching into a drawer for a pair of shorts, Sarah will catch herself swiveling her hips and arching her back. Even when she's not on the pole, she's dancing around it. She takes a lot of Advil because even at home she's always hearing the *thump thump thump* of the bass line.

Candy, her best friend at work, took one look at Sarah on her first day and told Sarah to dance to black girl booty-shaking music because guys love to see white girls with juicy asses shake their stuff. Sarah blushed, and pivoted to get a better look at her ass. She said, "My ass is juicy?"

Candy laughed and grabbed a handful of Sarah's ass, but Sarah already knew she had a juicy ass and where it came from. Her mother is black and her father is white but for years people have assumed she's a white girl because she has green eyes and straight blond hair. She's not ashamed of who she is but in Baltimore it's easier to be a white girl with a black girl's ass than to be a black girl who looks white or any other kind of black girl for that matter.

Her signature move is to grip the pole with both hands, arch her back, and slide lower until her long hair brushes the stage while she frantically rocks her pelvis up and down. She hates the pole, how it is always warm and sticky to the touch, coated in human oils, and also how when she's leaning back or wrapping her leg around the pole or hanging upside down while shaking her tits, she's not doing anything special, not really.

Sarah hates the smell of ones and fives but can live with the stink of bigger bills. She tans three days a week, naked, so there are no lines. She sees an aesthetician for a full body waxing once or twice a month, enhances her hairstyle with blond extensions replaced every two months. She works out for two hours a day, seven days a week, eats fourteen hundred calories a day. It is an exhausting regimen but an occupational hazard. She attends Johns Hopkins during the week, where tuition costs almost forty thousand dollars, and financial aid covers only two-thirds of that cost. Sarah pays for the rest out of her own pocket. She has one year remaining before she graduates with degrees in international studies and Romance languages, plus coursework in Arabic. It is 2004. She plans on working for the CIA because she has become quite efficient at passing.

At first, Sarah was a mess of a stripper. She couldn't dance.
She didn't like being watched. She didn't *want* to be touched. She
hated the pretense of the gowns that quickly hit the floor when
she was onstage or giving a lap dance. She hated the improbable
heels and the G-string panties riding up her ass and the way she
stank of smoke after a long night and how she always had to look
over her shoulder as she walked to her car at the end of a shift.
Still, she didn't relish wearing a polyester uniform and visor
cap, either, and she couldn't live on what those jobs paid. Sarah
took Candy's advice and started watching BET for the necessary
instruction. In the privacy of her apartment in Towson, she tried
to clap her ass and bounce and shake her body like the girls in
the videos and the girls she grew up with in West Baltimore who
moved so fast and with such elegant precision.

William Livingston III mostly lives to watch Sierra dance to Lil
Jon's "Get Low," because the song is still very popular in such
establishments. He's willing to pay for the privilege of watching
Sierra dance. He likes Sierra's routine—how she points to the
window, to the wall, and mimics the sweat dripping down her
proverbial balls. He visits her at the club three times a week,
Wednesdays, Fridays, and Saturdays. He stays for two hours. He
tips her anywhere between one hundred and five hundred dollars. After she dances to "Get Low," Sierra gives him a lap dance,
shimmying out of her skimpy gown, draping it over William's
shoulder. She straddles his lap and sexily removes her bra, wrapping it around his balding head and then looping it around his
neck like a leash. She squeezes her breasts together, flicks her
tongue across her nipples, feels William's cock stiffen between

the spread of her thighs. She leans in to his chest, but pulls away before she gets too close.

The more money he slides beneath the narrow waistband of her G-string, the lower and harder she grinds her hips. If Sierra looks down and sees a crown of bills wrapping her waist, she'll let William hold her ass even though he always leaves little bruises. He propositions Sierra regularly. He wants to fuck her in a restaurant bathroom. He wants to take her to a fine hotel and sip champagne from her body, feed her cold grapes. He wants to tongue her navel and shower her with bling and ride her doggy-style. William hasn't yet figured out her price. He was making progress toward being able to see Sierra outside the club—she didn't scowl as much when she saw him—until one day he said, "I want to fuck you filthy because my wife is a goddamned prude." Sierra pushed William away, said, "I can't believe what you just said."

Her scowl returned, seemed deeper even, so he started coming to the club four nights a week, told his wife he found a new bridge group.

Sierra tries to leave Sarah at home but often fails. She is racked with guilt when she thinks about all the married men who leer from the tip rail and sit in the darkened booths with their legs wide open lamenting all the dirty things their wives won't do. Sarah finds such conversations impolite and having seen so much too much of these men, she bears not a small amount of sympathy for their women.

After her shift, Sarah goes to the diner a few doors down from the club, her face scrubbed clean. She wears a T-shirt and jeans, her hair swept up in a neat ponytail. She sits at an empty table and carefully smooths out the bills she's accumulated, separating them into piles by denomination. Sometimes a waiter named Alvarez will sit with her counting out his own tips. She is desperately in love with Alvarez because he doesn't ask her out, because his hands are gentle and clean, because he doesn't say anything unkind about her profession even though he smells it on her. He keeps her coffee fresh and brings her big salads with dressing on the side, then gives her foil-wrapped Handi Wipes to clean her hands with after she's done calculating her worth for that night.

Alvarez loves Sarah with equal fervor but he's illegal, *sin papeles*, and worries what would happen if one thing led to another. Alvarez is a worrier. When he was a baby in Honduras, his mother would find her beautiful boy in his crib, not crying but fretting, chewing on the slender wisps of his baby fingernails. On nights when he's too tired or foolish to worry, he'll sit on the same side of the booth as Sarah and hold her hand. He'll whisper to her in Spanish. Sometimes he'll sing his favorite song, "Volver" by Estrella Morente. As Alvarez sings, he taps the table in a steady beat and Sarah sways from side to side and sometimes she sings along, too. He loves the song because he loves the name Estrella, which means star. He has named their imaginary daughter Estrella. When he walks Sarah to her car, he'll point up to the night sky and say, "Mira las estrellas," and Sarah will look up and her heart will beat fiercely, tenderly.

William loves black women but he's wealthy and his wealth has history. He doesn't have what it takes to go there. Men like him can't go there. His father, William Livingston II, once told him the Livingstons had long been touched by a spot of jungle fever but that men of their class did not give in to such petty demands. As William and his father watched their black housekeepers in their tight gray-and-white uniforms bending over to dust and arrange the objects in their lives, father and son would ogle and grin. William II would grab William III by the shoulder and say, "You can look, boy, but you cannot touch. The family can't afford the scandal." William sublimates his desires by listening to rap music. When the urge becomes unbearable, when his tongue is wet with the desire to taste a black woman's skin, he drives slowly through West Baltimore openly staring at the young black girls in Apple Bottoms jeans, with their hair gelled to their scalps and their bouncing hoop earrings, their brightly painted lips. He stares until they flash him dirty looks and call him a dirty old man or worse. In those moments when these girls are look-ing right at him with their righteous anger, his cock swells and strains against his fine wool slacks. He whispers, "Look but don't touch," until his mouth is dry and full.

He lives in Guilford with his wife and teenage son, in an old but stately brick mansion left to him by his father along with a sig-nificant trust fund. When William first brought his wife, Estelle, a pale blond sliver of Connecticut, she clutched the pearls around her neck and said, "It's like we're nowhere near Baltimore. Thank goodness for that." She had heard things about Baltimore all the way up in Greenwich. Her friends told her moving to Baltimore would be like moving to the jungle. Estelle is unaware of Wil-liam's penchant for the blacker berry though she finds his taste in music curious. At night, before bed, he stands in his media room between his state-of-the-art speakers, blasting DMX and Method Man and Soulja Boy. He watches rap videos, enjoying the lurid images of televised vixens sliding down poles and crawling across floors and allowing rappers to swipe credit cards between their ample ass cheeks. He indulges in the fantasy of fucking one of these ebony women right there, between the speakers, the bass so heavy it presses down on them like a holy spirit.

Carmen, a young black woman, is William and Estelle's housekeeper. She lives in the maid's quarters over the garage. She has dark mahogany skin, full lips, big breasts, narrow waist, a perfect black ass. When William described the young woman to his friends at the country club, he said, "She has the kind of ass they carry babies on back in Africa," and then laughed and enjoyed a sip of brandy. Carmen speaks softly, with a southern lilt. She smells like cocoa butter. When she showed up at the Livingston manse, she was hired on the spot. William promptly installed a series of surveillance cameras and microphones throughout her apartment that recorded to a hard drive he could access anywhere. He used to think his wealth was a burden but quickly realized what he could get away with.

William rents office space so he has a reason to leave the house. Other than monitoring his investments online, he doesn't work. He watches video of Carmen sleeping and showering, talking to her mother in South Carolina, watching TV, reading.

He almost fucked the maid once. It was late at night and he went to her room, his bathrobe cinched tightly around his waist. When Carmen answered her door, it was clear he had woken her up. She crossed her arms across her chest, shifted nervously.

William gripped her shoulders, breathing heavily through his nose. "I own everything in this house," he said, then laughed the same laugh he laughed at his father's deathbed when he realized just how wealthy he was about to become.

Carmen wore only a thin white nightgown with thin straps and flowers embroidered along the neckline. He reached between her thighs and looked right in her eyes. Carmen didn't look away.

She grabbed hold of his wrist, pushed it away. She said, "I need this job." William smiled, looked to the floor. Carmen never spoke much, but she was a smart girl.

When she slowly sank to her knees, William placed a meaty hand on the top of her head, traced her hairline with his thumb. "Are you familiar with that Twista song, 'Wetter'?" He didn't wait for an answer. "In that song, the girl says she needs a daddy. Do you need a daddy, Carmen?"

Carmen loosened the belt holding his bathrobe closed, sighed, leaned forward. As his housekeeper gave him a blowjob, William Livingston III reassured himself that this wasn't the same as fucking a black girl. He was getting his dick wet, something men of his ilk had been doing for more than a hundred years. He closed his eyes, tightened his grip on Carmen's bobbing head, and imagined fucking her on a beach in Ibiza or over his desk in his office. Just before he came he ordered her to remove her nightgown. She acquiesced. He ejaculated on her breasts, ordered her to rub him into her skin. He left just as quickly as he came, then watched the video of Carmen scrubbing herself clean from the quiet comfort of his study. He never bothered her again. He had gotten what he wanted.

When he's not watching his housekeeper, William listens to his music and repeats the lyrics about skeeting and Beckys and backing that ass up and living the gangsta life. His office has a small closet where he keeps urban clothing he sends his assistant to West Baltimore to purchase—Sean John jeans and Phat Farm hoodies and Timberland boots. His understanding of what the kids are wearing is dated. Sometimes he poses in front of the full-length mirror, grabbing handful of denim-clad crotch, and sets his chin to the side and tries to re-create gang signs with his fingers. After a busy day of woolgathering, William retires to the country club for dinner with his wife and son or attends a charity gala or goes to visit Sierra, the white girl with a black girl's ass.

William is becoming more possessive, getting angry if he sees her laughing with or dancing for other customers. His hands are greedier and grabbier than ever. Sierra doesn't like it, doesn't like how he interrogates her about the lap dance she was giving to two college guys when he entered the club. She tells him his jealousy bores her. He frowns. A Ying Yang Twins song is pounding out of the speakers, "The Whisper Song." It is one of William's favorite songs.

She frowns. "You are only paying for my time when you're in here, William. I thought you knew that."

He licks his lips, tries to grab her breasts before settling on holding her ass, enjoying how the ample flesh peeks into the spaces between his fingers. Sierra allows the affection because there is a wreath of at least three hundred dollars around her waist.

"I'd prefer to buy all your time. Why don't you become my private dancer?"

Sierra laughs. "Like the song?"

William's cock throbs. He loves Tina Turner. Those legs. That voice. Those lips. He grins. "Exactly like the song."

Sierra turns so her ass is facing William. She wiggles coquettishly so her cheeks bounce and jiggle in his face. She turns to look at him over her shoulder, tossing her long hair to the side. She licks her lips slowly. William groans, slides lower in his seat, pulls Sierra against him, so they are touching. He closes his eyes and thinks about West Baltimore girls. He listens to the lyrics. He believes in the lyrics. He wants a bitch to see his dick. He wants to beat that pussy up. He comes in his pants, a damp stain slowly inching toward his inseam. When Sierra tries to stand, he holds her tight. She tries to pry his fingers loose, but he is stronger. She glares at the bouncer watching the scene, throws her hands up. The bouncer shrugs, continues to watch. William always tips generously so the bouncer won't intervene when William breaks club rules, which he does, regularly. Sierra gives the bouncer the finger, her slow angry burn spreading.

After work, Sarah is in a foul mood. She goes to the diner and stands near the entrance, pacing back and forth. Alvarez is refilling salt and pepper shakers. He looks up and smiles, then frowns as he observes her rigid posture, the rage rolling off her in waves. He wipes his hands on his apron, tells his boss he has to leave early. Alvarez drives Sarah home in her car. He asks her what's wrong but she is silent. Neither song nor stars will console her. At her apartment, Alvarez follows her inside and sits nervously on her couch. Sarah takes a picture from a bookshelf against one wall and hands it to Alvarez. She points to a tall, attractive woman with caramel skin and a sad smile. She sits. "That's my mother," she says.

Alvarez's eyes widen but he inches closer to Sarah. He says, "Tu madre es bonita. Eres mi negra blanca." He removes his apron, rolls up his sleeves, and runs a bath for Sarah. She disrobes in front of him but does not worry. She steps into the warmth, one foot at a time, and sighs as she settles into the water. Alvarez reaches for the washcloth, neatly folded on a towel rack, and washes her gently, wiping away the human oils and the fingerprints and the stale cigarette smoke and the inappropriate behaviors. Sarah tells Alvarez about her horrible night at work. She tells him about men who can't take no for an answer and other men who allow that sort of thing to happen. She is tired, so very tired. "Voy a matarlos," he mutters. Sarah places her damp hand against his cheek. She says, "No es necesario. It's an occupational hazard." Alvarez nods, but while Sarah lies in her tub, her skin clean and pink, her eyes closed, humming a strange little tune, he clenches his fists until his knuckles turn white. Then he kisses her forehead.

William Livingston III sits in his BMW sedan outside Sierra's apartment. He is irate. He doesn't understand what the stripper is doing with a spic waiter when she could be with a man like him. He's listening to an angry DMX track, smoking a cheap sweet cigar he stole from his son's room. He stares at himself in the rearview mirror and tries to bark fiercely like the rapper. He calls his wife, Estelle, tells her he's going to be late. He can hear the gin in his wife's voice, knows it doesn't matter when he gets home.

When the waiter leaves, William flicks the cigar butt onto the street, tries to smooth his hair over his bald spot. He's followed Sierra home several times now. He knocks on her door, traces the number seven. Sarah answers, wearing only a towel wrapped around her slender torso. She is laughing, but gasps when she recognizes William from the strip club. She tries to shut the door but he wedges his foot against the doorjamb.

Sarah has often reviewed the worst-case scenarios requisite to her occupational hazards but a customer showing up at her apartment, north of the city, never crossed her mind. She tries to close the door again, but this time William pushes past her and into the apartment.

Sarah swallows the chill winding itself around her spine. She thinks about the poli sci paper she has to finish, the Sartre text she needs to read, the excerpt she has to translate, the appointment with her trainer, all this and more before her next shift at the club. She thinks about Alvarez, who has named their daughter Estrella. She thinks about the food he had gone to pick up and his sweet voice when he serenades her with "Volver." She doesn't have time for this.

She says, "If you don't leave, I'm going to call the police. And if my boyfriend finds you here, he'll kill you."

William is undeterred by her anger. He pulls off his tie and shoves Sarah to the floor. She hits her head against the coffee table as she falls. She finds her voice and screams so loudly the windows shake, but all William hears is a loud ringing.

William's fist connects with Sarah's jaw and a sharp pain sinks through the bone. Hot tears stream down her face but she tries to hold it together. She tries to focus past William's pudgy body looming over her. She tries not to pass out so she might bear witness.

William kneels between Sarah's thighs. He uses a condom. He doesn't know where the stripper has been. He practices some of the lingo he has learned from years of listening to rap music. "I've wanted to get all up in that since the day I first saw you, Sierra. I love your phat ass." Sarah moans and heaves, reaches for her cell phone on the coffee table. It is just beyond her reach. William flips her onto her stomach, and then he's inside her breathing hotly into her ear, telling her that fucking her is just like fucking a black girl without having to fuck a black girl. He smacks her thigh and tells her to do as Lil Jon instructs and bounce, bounce, bounce that ass.

Sarah focuses on her fury. She lets it bind her chest and her heart. She lets it cover her skin. She feels it in her blood. Her fury coats her mouth.

He doesn't take long. With a final thrust, William groans into her ear. He presses his thin lips against her shoulder, a small token of affection. Sarah cringes. He lies on top of her, his sweaty weight pressing her farther into the floor. She tries to crawl away but he is too heavy with liquor and food and fat. Eventually he stands, admires Sarah's perfect ass again. He dresses and sits on her couch. He sets ten crisp hundreds on her coffee table and says, "We could have done this the easy way, Sierra." As he's about to take his leave, he looks down at the picture of Sarah's mother and pauses. "This black woman looks just like you," he remarks.

Sarah reaches for her towel, shields herself. She steadies, inhales deeply. "You should leave now," she says, willing her voice strong.

William holds the picture up, pointing angrily. "Why does this woman look like you?"

At the door, Alvarez hears the tension in Sarah's voice, pushes into the apartment. He eyes William, surveys the disarray, understands. He carefully puts his coat around Sarah's shoulders and stands in front of her. She rests her cheek against his back. She wraps one arm around his waist. She breathes.

William's face is flushed through bright red as the picture falls from his hands. He backs out of Sarah's apartment, shaking his head. Alvarez moves to follow but Sarah tightens her grip around his waist.

"We have to go to the police," he says, but Sarah shakes her head.

"Occupational hazard," she whispers, forcing her lips into a semblance of a smile. "I'm too tired." She is beyond tired, really. She is empty and she wants quiet. She wants quiet.

Alvarez turns to look at her, at the bruises on her face, her arms. He worries about the bruises he can't see. He runs her another bath. She sits in the tub, her arms wrapped around her knees. Sarah is silent as he tries to wash her clean again. Later, they will lie in bed together, breathing softly, perfectly still. They won't touch but Alvarez will keep watch. He will forgo his worries and tell Sarah he loves her. He will remind her of Estrella and in the darkness, she will finally smile. Sarah will want to tell Alvarez she loves him, too, but won't, not with her body still bearing the weight of William Livingston III. Instead, she'll reach across the short distance between them.

Instead, she'll hold his hand and hope it's enough.

William settles into the leather of his BMW and is instantly comforted by German engineering. He speeds away but pulls over as soon as he puts distance between himself and the stripper's apartment. He leans out of his car and vomits, the acids burning his throat and mouth. There is whiskey in the glove compartment. He takes a long draw from the bottle, wipes his lips with the back of his hand. He pours some whiskey down his pants. Tries to clean himself. His skin burns. Penance, he thinks. And absolution.

As he drives, he ignores the sour coating on his lips, teeth, tongue. He is horrified. He is gleeful. He catches his reflection in the rearview mirror, ignores his father's disapproval staring back.

William sits in his driveway, his forehead pressed against the leather-wrapped steering wheel for a long while. He tries to make peace with the fact that he has done something generations of Livingstons have had the discipline to avoid.

He hears footsteps and looks up. William Livingston IV is whistling to himself as he walks back toward the main house from the garage. The older Livingston feels a huge weight being lifted as he watches his carefree boy. He gets out of the car and waves. The younger Livingston stops, smiles, waits for his father. "It's a brave new world," William tells his son, clapping the boy's back with his greedy, grabby hands before wrapping his arm around his son's shoulders and leading him inside.

# Baby Arm

'm dating a guy who works as a merchandiser for a large department store and one of his duties is designing window displays. He tells me this on our third date. We have already slept together, twice. I'm not a hard sell. When he tells me about his job, we are at a sleazy bar, drinking beer from the tap in frosted mugs. I tap my foot against his. I say, "I'm ready to go back to your place whenever you are." I am anxious about all the "getting to know you" conversations we are having. I've never enjoyed sitting through previews at movies. It always seems like such a waste of time. He tells me he dresses windows and has access to a storeroom full of mannequins and mannequin parts. I say, "Like in the movie *Mannequin*," and he doesn't get the reference—disappointing. I explain about Andrew McCarthy and Meshach Taylor and Kim Cattrall frolicking in the middle of the night in a department store thanks to the magic of an ancient Egyptian necklace, all set to a synthesized eighties sound track. On our way to his place, we stop at a Redbox and rent the movie and he loves it and for the first time I think the guy is not a complete tool. A couple of months later, he comes over to my apartment in the middle of the night because we've long abandoned any pretense of a mutual interest in anything but dirty sex and he's holding a fiberglass baby arm, painted the color of flesh. He hands it to me and says, "I thought you might like this," and I take the baby arm and tell him if he's not careful, I will fall in love and he says he would be fine with that.

We take a bottle of wine and the baby arm to my bedroom and I caress it while we kill the cheap red. My mouth tastes fruity yet sour, cheap. I don't mind. I'm quickly becoming enamored by the scraggly beard unevenly covering my lover's face and his thin lips and the sensation of him rubbing my back in lazy circles because he never knows how to make a move, still doesn't understand he only needs to push me on my back and tell me to spread my legs. I set the baby arm on my nightstand and provide him with a little seduction instruction. He follows directions well so I lie beneath him and imagine a little more hair on his chest, a little more muscle wrapped around his bones. He grins and I think about my best friend Tate. Tate and I work together as publicists for a record label and often lament how we are sacrificing our souls. We are not motivated to change our professional circumstances. We have to look pretty and make people believe in false idols and hold our liquor. For that, we are handsomely rewarded. We write off our gym memberships and depilatory regimens. Our offices are right next to each other but we spend most of our time on the phone to each other talking about our all-girl fight club, no boys allowed. Boys don't really know how to hurt girls.

"Hey," he says. "Are you with me?" I open my eyes and look up at him. A thin line of sweat beads along his hairline. I smile. I tell him to hate me more. He does, and a pleasant soreness begins spreading from between my thighs and my head is slamming against the headboard. Now I'm with him.

Later, I am still awake because I'm not very good at sleeping and I'm achy so I'm feeling tender toward him. Instead of nudging him awake, telling him to go home, I watch him sleep. I hold the baby arm and marvel at how small and perfect it is, how each finger is exactly where it is supposed to be, slightly curled toward the wrist. I use the baby arm to trace my sort-of boyfriend's arm. His name is Gus. Now that I'm sure of his name, I no longer call him Hey You, or refer to him as "the dude I'm nailing" when talking to my friends. I hold the baby arm to my chest and eventually I fall asleep. I really underestimated Gus.

The next morning at the office, I call Tate and tell her how well Gus takes direction. She says, "Next time you fuck him call me so I can listen to the two of you and when you come, say my name." I tell her I will. That's what friends are for. We talk about the baby arm, how it almost articulates. I tell her how I lovingly cleaned it with a baby wipe and how I kissed each fingertip. She says, "I want a boy who will bring me a baby arm." She asks me how I got so lucky and I am at a loss until I consider the sequence of events bringing Gus into my life. I explain I got so lucky because of a lifelong dedication to slutty and inappropriate behavior and my ability to drink tequila straight. She murmurs approvingly. I want to tell her it's fate but she's hard-core and would probably laugh. I tell her I will ask Gus if he has any straight friends in merchandising. She says, "This calls for a celebration. We're having a fight club tonight," and she recites an address I don't recognize. "How are we going to make a thirteen-year-old pop singer popular?" I ask, briefly steering the conversation toward work. Tate is silent for a few moments. Finally she says, "Old white ladies who perm their hair." We are very good at our jobs.

When it's time for fight club, I show up at a sketchy strip mall, the kind that includes a depressing house of worship filled with posters of black Jesus and folding chairs; a chicken shack with two tables and a dirty counter promising a soupçon of salmonella; a retail emporium for strippers and their friends; and an urgent care clinic. This strip mall is the most perfect place in the world. Tate told me, before I left work, to go into the stripper emporium, and to ask to be escorted to the basement, making note of a pair of clear Lucite heels that would look spectacular on me. Tate is waiting in the basement, her dirty-blond hair slicked back in a fierce ponytail. She's wearing jeans and a wifebeater and a leather jacket and so am I. So are all the girls we've invited, ten of us who are pretty and fucked up, girls who keep their ugly beneath the skin where it belongs, even though sometimes, it's hard to keep it all in. We all look hot. I say, "This room is a wet dream," and everyone laughs nervously, and Tate says, "Let's rock this shit."

She runs up to a thin redhead, a model who is moderately recognizable and lurking near the edge of the room. Tate punches the model in the gut and I feel tingly all over and then someone's knuckles connect with my face and I can taste blood in the back of my throat. I get so angry I start swinging. I don't care what I hurt. We don't waste any time making any rules or pontificating about the meaning of our fight club. We don't do any of that girl-fighting shit. There's no hair pulling or scratching or screeching helplessly. We're all about closed fists and open-handed face slaps and knees to flat stomachs. We hold throats between our fingers until desperate hands claw at our wrists. We wrestle on the sticky floor and call each other terrible names until the room is sweet with sweat and heavy bruising. We fight until our arms are so heavy and sore we can't lift them and one girl, who is pinned by a large, scary-looking tomboy, suddenly shouts, "Get off me, you fat ass!" Her words are so sharp, we all hear them through the fists falling against flesh and the grunts and the heaving. We all gasp because the tomboy is big-boned but she's not *fat*.

Tate stops slamming the head of a pixie girl with pink hair against the floor and stares at me across the room. She mouths, "I love you," and I smile even though it hurts and another set of knuckles connects with my face, ruining the moment—bitches ruin everything. My jaw feels loose and some hideous bruises are forming along my cheekbones. I'm pretty sure a couple of ribs are broken. I crawl toward a nearby wall and sit with my knees pulled to my chest. Tate slowly lowers herself next to me. She holds my hands in hers, kisses each of my fingertips, the undersides of my wrists. She says, "See? No one can hurt like a girl." We're all slumped in piles of damage. We try to pull ourselves together while contemplating cosmetic strategies for work the next day. I buy the Lucite heels and other necessities on the way out and Tate and I flirt with danger by eating at the chicken shack. We tear greasy fried meat from warm bones with our teeth. Our hands are scraped but shiny and slick. We smile at each other. This is the most I will ever love another person.

When Gus comes over a few nights later, he is holding a chubby baby thigh. He has shaved his beard. I tell him if he keeps this up, I might marry him. He says, "I can live with that." Gus hands me the baby thigh, dimpled around the knee, and kisses my cheek. I turn and crush my lips against his even though there isn't an inch of my body that doesn't hurt. We don't bother with wine. We're all teeth and tongue. We tear each other's clothes off and in my room he throws me onto the bed. I'm impressed. He's such a quick study. Gus traces the bruises along my rib cage and on my face, even presses them until I wince. I say harder. He obeys. I hold up my hand, say, "Hold that thought," and dial Tate. I hand him the phone. I say, "She wants to talk to you." He smiles the sleaziest smile and says, "Two chicks. That's hot," and I tell him not to talk too much so we can still fall in love and get married and he can continue to woo me with fiberglass baby parts. Gus puts Tate on speakerphone and she tells him all the terrible things she wants him to do to me. I marvel at her creativity and her cruelty and how much she loves me. Gus does as he's told. He's a good boy. He fucks me like a bad, bad man and when I come, hard, his fingerprints around my throat are still throbbing. I am barely breathing, I can't find the air. I call out Tate's name until it feels like my throat muscles will unravel. I can taste her in my mouth. The next time I talk to Tate I will tell her she's the man of my dreams.

While Gus sleeps, I hold the baby arm and the baby thigh, so hard and smooth and adorable. I think about how the longer I date Gus, the more baby parts he'll bring me and maybe, eventually, we'll have a little family of fiberglass child parts that will never become anything more than what they are.

# North Country

have moved to the edge of the world for two years. If I am not careful, I will fall. After my first department meeting, my new colleagues encourage me to join them on a scenic cruise to meet more locals. The *Peninsula Star* will travel through the Portage Canal, up to Copper Harbor, and then out onto Lake Superior. I am handed a glossy brochure with bright pictures of blue skies and calm lake waters. "You'll be able to enjoy the foliage," they tell me, shining with enthusiasm for the Upper Peninsula. "Do you know how to swim?" they ask.

I arm myself with a flask, a warm coat, and a book. At the dock, there's a long line of ruddy Michiganders chatting amiably about when they expect the first snow to fall. It is August. I have just moved to the Upper Peninsula to assume a postdoc at the Michigan Institute of Technology. My colleagues, all civil engineers, wave to me. "You came!" they shout. They've already started drinking. I take a nip from my flask. I need to catch up. "You're going to love this cruise," they say. "Are you single?" they ask.

We sit in a cramped booth drinking Rolling Rocks. Every few minutes one of my colleagues offers an interesting piece of Upper Peninsula trivia such as the high number of waterfalls in the area or the three hundred inches of snow the place receives annually. I take a long, hard swallow from my flask. I am flanked by a balding, overweight tunnel expert on my right and a dark-skinned hydrologist from India on my left. The hydrologist is lean and quiet and his knee presses uncomfortably against mine. He tells me he has a wife back in Chennai but that in Michigan, he's leaving his options open. I am the only woman in the department and as such, I am a double novelty. My new colleagues continue to buy me drinks and I continue to accept them until my ears are ringing and my cheeks are flushed. Sweat drips down my back. "I need some fresh air," I mumble, excusing myself. I make my way, slowly, to the upper deck, ignoring the stares and lulls in conversation.

Outside, the air is crisp and thin, the upper deck sparsely populated. Near the bow, a young couple make out enthusiastically, loudly. A few feet away from them a group of teenagers stand in a huddle, snickering. I sit on a red plastic bench and hold my head in my hands. My flask sits comfortably and comfortingly against my rib cage.

"I saw you downstairs," a man with a deep voice says.

The sun is setting, casting that strange quality of light rendering everything white, nearly invisible. I squint and look up slowly at a tall man with shaggy hair hanging over his ears. I nod.

"Are you from Detroit?

I have been asked this question twenty-three times since mov-ing to the area. In a month, I will stop counting, having reached a four-digit number. Shortly after that, I will begin telling people I have recently arrived from Africa. They will nod and exhale excit-edly and ask about my tribe. I don't know that in this moment so there is little to comfort me. I shake my head.

"Do you talk?"

"I do," I say. "Are *you* from Detroit?"

He smiles, slow and lazy. He's handsome in his own way—his skin is tanned and weathered and his eyes are almost as blue-gray as the lake we're cruising on. He sits down. I stare at his fingers, the largest fingers I've ever seen. The sweaty beer bottle in his hand looks miniature. "So where are you from?"

I shove my hands into my pockets and slide away from him. "Nebraska."

"I've never met anyone from Nebraska," he says.

I say, "I get that a lot."

The boat is now out of the portage canal and we're so far out on the lake I can't see land. I feel small. The world feels too big.

"I'd better get back to my colleagues," I say, standing up. As I walk away, he shouts, "My name is Magnus!" I throw a hand in the air but don't look back.

In my lab, things make sense. As a structural engineer, I design concrete mixes, experiment with new aggregates like fly ash and other energy by-products, artificial particulates, kinds of water that might make concrete not just stronger but unbreakable, permanent, perfect. I teach a section of Design of Concrete Struc-tures and a section of Structural Dynamics. I have no female students in either class. The boys stare at me and after class, they linger in the hallway just outside the classroom. They try to flirt. I remind them I will assess their final grades. They make inappropriate comments about extra credit.

At night, I sit in my apartment and watch TV and search for faculty positions and other career opportunities closer to the center of the world. There's a pizza restaurant across the street and above the restaurant, an apartment filled with loud white girls who play loud rap music into the middle of the night and have loud fights with their boyfriends, who play basketball for the university. One of the girls has had an abortion and another isn't speaking to her father and the third roommate has athletic sex with her boyfriend even when the other two are awake; she has a child but the child lives with her father. I do not want to know any of these things.

Several unopened boxes are sitting in my new apartment. To unpack those boxes means I will stay. To stay means I will be trapped in this desolate place for two years, alone. I rented my new home over the phone—it is a former dry cleaner converted into an apartment. There are no windows save for one in the front door. The apartment, I thought, as I walked from room to room when I moved in, was like a jail cell. I had been sentenced. My new landlady, an octogenarian Italian who ran the dry cleaner for more than thirty years, gasped when she met me. "You didn't sound like a colored girl on the phone," she said. "I get that a lot," I replied.

The produce is always rotten at the local grocery store—we're too far north to receive timely food deliveries. I stand before a display of tomatoes, limp, covered in wrinkled skin, some dotted with soft white craters ringed by some kind of black mold. I consider the cost to my dignity if I move in with my parents until I feel a heavy hand on my shoulder. When I spin around, struggling to maintain my balance, I recognize Magnus. I grab his wrist between two fingers and step away. "Do you always touch strangers?"

"We're not strangers."

I make quick work of selecting the least decomposed tomatoes and move on to the lettuce. Magnus follows. I say, "We have different understandings of the word *stranger*. You don't even know my name."

"I like the way you talk," he says.

"What is that supposed to mean?"

Magnus reddens. "Exactly what I said. Unless we have different understandings of the words *I*, *like*, *the*, *way*, *you*, and *talk*."

I bite the inside of my cheek to keep from smiling. I have a weakness for charming men who make witty comebacks.

"Can I buy you a drink?"

I look at the pathetic tomatoes in my basket and maybe it's the overwhelming brightness of the fluorescent lighting or the easy listening being piped through the store speakers but I nod. I say, "My name is Kate." Magnus says, "Meet me at the Thirsty Fish, Kate."

On the drive there, I stare at my reflection in the rearview mirror and smooth my eyebrows. My groceries sit in a canvas bag on the backseat. It's cold outside, I tell myself. They can wait and I cannot. At the bar, Magnus entertains me with the silly things girls like to take seriously. He buys me lots of drinks and I drink them. He flatters me with words about my pretty eyes. He says he can tell I'm smart. I haven't had sex in more than two months. I haven't had a real conversation with anyone in more than two months. I'm not at my best.

In the parking lot, I stand next to my car, holding on to the door, trying to steady myself. Magnus says, "I can't let you drive home like this." I mutter something about the altitude affecting my tolerance. He says, "We're not in the mountains." He stands so close. The warmth from his chest fills the short distance between us. Magnus takes my keys and as I reach for them, I fall into him. He lifts my chin with one of his massive fingers and I say, "Fuck." I kiss him, softly. Our lips barely move but we don't pull apart. His hand is solid in the small of my back as he presses me against my car.

When I wake up, my mouth is thick and sour. I groan and sit up, and hit my head against something unfamiliar. I wince. Everything in my head feels loose, lost.

"Be careful. It's a tight fit in here."

I rub my eyes, trying to swallow the panic bubbling at the base of my throat. I clutch at my chest.

"Relax. I didn't know where you lived so I brought you back to my place."

I take a deep breath, look around. I'm sitting on a narrow bed. I see Magnus through a narrow doorway standing near a two-burner stove. My feet are bare. A cat jumps into my lap. I scream.

Magnus lives in a trailer, and not one of those fancy double-wides on a foundation with a well-kept garden in front, but rather, an old, rusty trailer that can be attached to a truck and driven away. It is the kind of trailer you see in sad, forgotten places that have surrendered to rust and overgrown weeds and cars on cinder blocks and sagging laundry lines. The trailer, on the outside, is in a fair amount of disrepair, but the inside is immaculate. Everything has its proper place. I appreciate that.

"You should eat something," he says.

I extricate myself from the cat and walk into the galley area. Magnus invites me to sit at the table and he sets a plate of dry scrambled eggs and a mug of coffee in front of me. My stomach roils wildly. I wrap my hands around the coffee mug and inhale deeply. I try to make sense of the trajectory between rotten tomatoes and this trailer. Magnus slides into the bench across from me. He explains that he lives in this trailer because it's free. It's free because his trailer sits on the corner of a parcel of land his sister Mira and her husband, Jonathan, farm. The farm is twenty minutes outside town. There's no cell phone reception. I can't check my email, he tells me as I wave my phone in different directions, desperate for a signal. I ask him why he lives this way. He says he has a room in his sister's house he rarely uses. He likes his privacy, he says.

"You took my shoes off."

Magnus nods. "You have nice feet."

"Can you take me to my car?"

Magnus sighs, quickly pours out the rest of his coffee in the small sink. He is a patient man. I like that, too.

On the drive back to town I sit as far away from Magnus as possible. I try to re-create the events between standing in the parking lot and waking up in a trailer with a cat in my lap. I refuse to ask Magnus to fill in the blanks. At my car, he grips his steering wheel tightly. I thank him for the ride and he hands me my keys. He says, "I'd love your phone number."

I force myself to smile. I say, "Thank you for not letting me drive last night." I say, "I don't normally drink much, but I just moved here." He says, "Yes, the altitude," and waits until I drive away before heading back to his trailer. My father would appreciate the gesture. I remember the pressure of Magnus's lips against mine, their texture and the smell of his bedsheets. I am in trouble.

In my lab, things make sense. The first snow falls in late September. It will continue to fall until May. I tell my mother I may not survive. I tell her this so many times she starts to worry. I test cement fitness. I fill molds with cylinders of concrete. I experiment with salt water and bottled water and lake water and tap water. I cure and condition specimens. I take detailed notes. I write an article. I turn down three dates with three separate colleagues. The hydrologist from Chennai reaffirms the openness of his options in the United States. I reaffirm my uninterest in his options or being one of them. I administer an exam that compels my students to call me "Battle-Ax." I attend a campus social for single faculty members. There are seven women in attendance and more than thirty men. The hydrologist is there, too. He doesn't wear a wedding ring. I am asked thirty-four times if I am from Detroit, a new record for a single day. I try to remember where Magnus lives and all I recall is a blurry memory of being drunk, burying my face in his arm as we drove, and him, singing along to the Counting Crows. I love the Counting Crows.

There once was a man. There is always some man. We were together for six years. He was an engineer, too. Some people called him my dissertation advisor, which he was. When we got involved, he told me he would teach me things and mold me into a great scholar. He said I was the brightest girl he had ever known. Then he contradicted himself. He said we would marry and thought I believed him. A couple of years passed and he said we would marry when he was promoted to full professor and then it was when I finished my degree. I got pregnant and he said we would marry when the baby was born. The baby was stillborn and he said we would marry when I recovered from the loss. I told him I was as recovered as I was ever going to be. He had no more excuses and I no longer cared to marry him. While he slept soundly, I spent most of my nights awake, remembering what it felt like to rub my swollen belly and feel my baby kicking. He told me I was cold and distant. He told me I had no reason to mourn a child that never lived. He amused himself with a new lab assistant who consistently wore dressy shoes and short skirts even though we spent our days working with sand and cement and other dirty things. I found them fucking, the lab assistant bent over a stack of concrete bricks squealing like a debutante porn star, the man thrusting vigorously, literally fucking the lab assistant right out of her high heels, his fat face red and shiny. He gasped in short, repulsive bursts. The scene was so common I couldn't even get angry. I had long stopped feeling anything where he was concerned. I returned to my office, accepted the postdoc position, and never looked back. I would have named our daughter Amelia. She would have been beautiful despite her father. She would have been four months old when I left.

Snow has been falling incessantly. The locals are overjoyed. Every night, I hear the high-pitched whine of snowmobiles speeding past my apartment. There are things I will need to survive the winter—salt, a shovel, a new toilet seat, rope. I brave the weather and go to the hardware store. I am wearing boots laced high around my calves, a coat, gloves, hat and scarf, thermal underwear. I never remove these items unless I am home. It takes too much effort. I wonder how these people manage to reproduce.

I see Magnus standing over a display of chain saws. He is more handsome than I remember. I turn to walk away but then I don't. I stand still and hope he notices me. I realize that dressed as I am, my own family wouldn't recognize me. I tap his shoulder. I say, "What do you plan on massacring?"

He looks up slowly, shrugs. "Just looking," he says.

"For a victim?"

"Aren't you feeling neighborly?"

"I thought I would say hello."

Magnus nods again. "You've said hello."

I swallow, hard. My irritation tastes bitter. I quickly tell him my phone number and go to find a stronger kind of rope. As I pull away, I notice Magnus watching me from inside the store. I smile.

In my lab things make sense. I teach my students how to make perfect concrete cylinders, how to perform compression tests. They crush their perfect cylinders and roar with delight each time the concrete shatters and the air is filled with a fine dust. There's a lot to love about breaking things.

Everyone I meet dispenses a bit of wisdom on how to survive the "difficult" winters—embrace the outdoors, drinking, travel, drinking, sun lamps, drinking, sex, drinking. The hydrologist offers to prepare spicy curries to keep me warm, offers to give me a taste of his very special curry. I decline, tell him I have a delicate constitution. Nils, my department chair, stops by my office. He says, "How are you holding up?" I assure him all is well. He says, "The first year is always the hardest." He says, "You might want to take a trip to Detroit to see your family." I thank him for the support.

★ ★ ★

I am walking around the lab watching students work when Magnus calls. I excuse myself and take the call in the hallway, ignoring the students milling about with their aimless expressions.

My heart beats loudly. I can hardly hear Magnus. I say, "You didn't need to take so long to call me."

"Is this a lecture?"

"Would you like it to be?"

"Can I make you dinner?"

I ignore my natural impulse to say no. I am more excited than I would ever admit. He invites me back to his trailer, where he prepares steak and green beans and baked potatoes. We drink beer. We talk, or rather, I talk, filling his trailer with all the words I've kept to myself since moving to the North Country. I complain about the weather. At some point, he holds his hand open and I slide my hand in his. He traces my knuckles with his thumb. He is plainspoken and honest. His voice is strong and clear. He has a kind smile and a kind touch. He talks about his job as a logger and his band—he plays guitar. When we finally stop talking he says, "I like you," and then he stands and pulls me to my feet. A man has never told me he likes me. Like is more interesting than love. I stand on his boots and wrap my arms around him. He is thick and solid. When we kiss, he is gentle, too gentle. I say, "You don't have to be soft with me," and he grunts. He clasps my neck with one of his giant hands and kisses me harder, his lips forcing mine open. The flat softness of his tongue thrills me. He brushes his lips across my chin. He sinks his teeth into my neck and I grab his shirt between my fists. I try to remain standing. I say, "My neck is the secret password." He bites my neck harder and I forget about everything and all the noise in my head quiets.

I slip out of my shirt and step out of my jeans and Magnus lifts me up and sits me on the edge of his kitchen table. He places his large hands between my thighs and pulls them apart. I quickly unbuckle his belt, reach for him, and he grabs my wrist. He says, "You don't get to be the boss of everything." I say a silent prayer. I close my eyes and he drags his hand from my chin, down the center of my chest, over the flat of my stomach. He kisses my shoulders, my breasts, my knees. He makes me tremble and whimper. "You don't have to be soft with me," I repeat. Magnus kisses the insides of my ankles and then my lips, his tongue rough and heavy against mine. I try to pull him into me by wrapping my legs around his waist. He laughs, low and deep. He says, "Say you want this." I bite my lower lip. I measure my pride against my desire. When he fucks me, he is slow, deliberate, rough in a terribly controlled way. I bury my face in his shoulder. When he asks why I'm crying, I say nothing. For a little while, he fills all the emptiness.

In the morning, I want to leave quickly even though I can still feel Magnus in my skin. As I sit on the edge of the bed and pull my pants on he says, "I want to see you again." I say "yes" but explain we have to keep things casual, that we can't become a *thing*, though I don't give him a reason. I don't have one, not one that would make any kind of sense. He traces my naked spine with his fingers and I shiver. He says, "We're already a thing." I stand, shaking my head angrily. "That's not even possible." He says, "Sometimes, when I'm miles deep in the woods, looking for a new cutting site, it feels like I'm the first man who has ever been there. I look up and the trees are so thick I can hardly see the sky. I get so scared but the world somehow makes sense there. Being with you feels like that." I shake my head again, my fingers trembling as I finish getting dressed. I feel nauseated and dizzy. I say, "I'm allergic to cats." I say, "You shouldn't talk like that." I say, "I like you, too." I recite his words over and over for the rest of the day, week, month.

Several weeks later, I'm at Magnus's trailer. We've seen each other almost every night, at his place, where he cooks and we talk and we have sex. We're lying naked in his narrow bed. I say, "If this continues much longer, we're going to have to sleep at my place. I have a real bed and actual rooms with doors." He smiles and nods. He says, "Whatever you want." After Magnus falls asleep, I stare up at the low ceiling, then out the small window at the clear winter sky. I wonder what he would think of Amelia, if he could love her. I try to swallow the emptiness. I hold my stomach as hot tears slide down my face and trickle along my neck.

Just as I'm falling asleep, his alarm goes off. Magnus sits up, rubbing his eyes. Even in the darkness I can see his hair standing on end. He says, "I want to show you something." We dress but he tells me I can leave my coat. Instead, he hands me a quilt. Outside, a fresh blanket of snow has fallen. The moon is still high. Everything is perfect and silent and still. The air hurts but feels clean. He cuts a trail to the barn and I follow in his footsteps. As Magnus walks, he stares up into the sky. I tell myself, *I feel nothing.* It is a lie. When I am with him, I feel everything. Inside the barn, I shiver and dance from foot to foot trying to stay warm. He says, "We have to milk the cows." He nods to a small campstool next to a very large cow. I say, "There is absolutely no way." Magnus leads me to the stool and forces me onto it. He hunches down behind me and he pats the cow on her side. He hasn't shaved yet so the stubble from his beard tickles me. He kisses my neck softly. He places his hands over mine and I learn how to milk a cow. Nothing makes sense here.

Hunting season starts. Magnus shows me his rifle, long, polished, powerful. He refers to his rifle as a "she" and a "her." I tease him about his rifle and call her his mistress. He frowns, says he would never do that to me. I believe him. I tell him my father hunts and he gets excited. He says, "Maybe someday your father and I can hunt together." I explain that my father hunts pheasant and by hunt, I mean he rides around with his friends on a four-wheeler, but doesn't really kill much of anything and often gets injured in embarrassing accidents. I say, "You and he hunt differently." He says, "I still want to meet your father." "I introduce only serious boyfriends to my family," I say. Magnus holds my chin between two fingers and looks at me hard. It makes me shiver. This is the first time I've seen real anger from him. I wonder how far I can push. He says, "You won't see me for a few days but I'm going to kill a buck for you." Five days later, Magnus shows up at my apartment still wearing his camouflage and Carhartt overalls. His beard is long and unkempt. He smells rank. He is dirty. I recognize only his eyes. Magnus steps inside and pulls me into a muscular hug that makes me feel like he is rearranging my insides. I inhale deeply. I am surprised by the sharp twinge between my thighs. When he kisses me, he is possessive, controlling, salty. He moans into my mouth and turns me around, pinning my arms over my head. He fucks me against the front door. I smile. Afterward, we both sink to the floor. He says, "The buck is in the car." He says, "I missed you." I want to say something, the right thing, the

kind thing. I slap his thigh. I push. I say, "Please take a shower."
I don't shower, though, not for hours.

I visit my parents in Florida for Thanksgiving and my mother
asks why I don't call as often. I explain how work has gotten busy.
I explain how snow has fallen every single day for more than a
month and how everyone thinks I'm from Detroit. My mother
says I look thin. She says I'm too quiet. We don't talk about
the dead child or the father of the dead child. There is this life
and that life. We pretend that life never happened. It is a mercy.
Magnus calls every morning before he leaves for work and every
night before he falls asleep. One afternoon he calls and my mother
answers my phone. I hear her laughing as she says, "What an
unusual name." When she hands me my phone, she asks, "Who
is this Magnus? Such a nice young man." I push. I say he's no one
important, because I don't know how to explain him or who I am
when I'm with him. I say it a little too loudly. When I put my
phone to my ear I can hear only a dial tone. Magnus doesn't call
for the rest of my trip. We won't speak until the end of January.

In my lab things make sense but they don't. I can't concentrate.
I want to call Magnus but my repeated bad behavior overwhelms
me. The weather has grown colder, sharper. The world grows
and I shrink. My students work on final projects. I have a paper
accepted at a major conference. The semester ends, I return to
Florida for the holidays. My mother says I look thin. She says
I'm too quiet. When she asks if I want to talk about my child I
shake my head. I say, "Please don't ever mention her again, not
ever." My mother holds the palm of one hand to my cheek and
the palm of the other over my heart. I send Magnus a card and

a letter and gift and another letter and another letter offering apologies, admitting that we very much are a thing, admitting that I long for him. He sends me a text message that says, "I'm still angry." I send more letters. He writes back once and I carry his letter with me everywhere. I try to acquire a taste for venison. The new semester starts. I have another paper accepted at a conference, this one in Europe. A new group of students try to flirt with me while learning about the wonder of concrete. I get a research grant and my department chair offers me a tenure-track faculty position with the department. He tells me to take as much time as I need to consider his offer. He says the department really needs someone like me. He says, "You kill two birds with one stone, Katie." I contemplate placing his head in the compression-testing machine and the sound it would make. I say, "I prefer to be called Kate."

The hydrologist corners me in my lab late at night and makes an inappropriate advance that leaves me unsettled. For weeks I will feel his long, skinny fingers, how they grabbed at things that were not his to hold. Even though it's after midnight, I call Magnus. My voice is shaking. He says, "You hurt my feelings," and the simple honesty of his words hurts. I say, "I'm sorry. I never say what I really feel," and I cry. He asks, "What's wrong?" He knows me better than I care to admit. I tell him about the married hydrologist, a dirty man with a bright pink tongue who tried to lick my ear and who called me Black Beauty and who got aggressive when I tried to push him away and how I'm nervous about walking to my car. Magnus says, "I'm on my way." I wait for him by the main entrance and when I recognize his bulky frame trudging through the snow toward me, everything feels more bearable. Magnus doesn't say a word. He just holds me. After a long while, he punches the brick wall and says, "I'm going to kill that guy." I believe him. He walks me to my lab to get my things.

At my apartment, I hold a bag of frozen corn against Magnus's scraped knuckles. I say, "I shouldn't have called." He says, "Yes, you should have." He says, "You have to be nicer to me." I say, "I do." I straddle his lap and kiss his torn knuckles and pull his hands beneath my shirt and look into his beautiful blue-gray eyes and I don't say it, but I think, *I love you.*

Magnus starts picking me up from work every night and if I have to work late, he sits with me, watching me work. There is an encounter with the hydrologist. Words are exchanged. Magnus clarifies for the hydrologist my disinterest in curries of any kind. He doesn't trouble me again. While I work, Magnus tells me about trees and everything a man could ever know from spending his days among them. He often smells like pine and sawdust.

In March, winter lingers. Magnus builds me an igloo and inside, he lights a small fire. He says, "Sometimes, I feel I don't know a thing about you." I am sitting between his legs, my back to his chest. Even though we're wearing layers of clothing, it feels like we're naked. I say, "You know I'm not very nice." He kisses my cheek. He says, "That's not true." He says, "Tell me something true." I tell him how I hold on to the idea of Amelia even though I shouldn't, how she's all I really think about, how she might be trying to walk now or say her first words. I tell him I think I love him and I love how he likes me. He brings my cold fingers to his warm lips. He fills all the hollow spaces.

# How

*How These Things Come to Pass*

Hanna does her best thinking late at night when all the usurpers living in her house are asleep. If it isn't winter, which is not often, she climbs out onto her roof with a pack of cigarettes and a lighter. She smokes and stares up at the blue-black night sky. She lives in the North Country, where the stars make sense. Hanna shares her home with her unemployed husband, her twin sister, her sister's husband, their son, and her father. She is the only one who works—mornings, she waits tables at the Koivu Café, and nights, she tends bar at Karpela's Supper Club. She leaves most of her tips at her best friend Laura's house. Hanna is plotting her escape.

The most popular dish at the Koivu is the *pannukakku*, a Finnish pancake. If Old Larsen is too hungover, Hanna will heat the iron skillet in the oven and mix the batter—first eggs, beating them lightly, slowly adding the honey, salt, and milk, finally sifting the flour in. She enjoys the ratchet sound as she pulls the sift trigger. She sways from side to side and imagines she is a flamenco dancer. She is in Spain, where it is warm, where there is sun and beauty. Hanna likes making *pannukakku* with extra butter so the edges of the pancakes are golden and crisp. Sometimes she'll carefully remove the edges from a pancake and eat them just like that. She's still in Spain, eating bread from a *panadería*, perhaps enjoying a little wine. Then she'll hear someone shout "Order up!" and she is no longer in Spain. She is in the middle of nowhere, standing over a hot, greasy stove.

Peter, Hanna's husband, comes in for breakfast every morning. Hanna saves him a spot at the counter and she takes his order. He stares down her uniform, ogling her cleavage and waggling his eyebrows. She feigns affection, smacks his head with her order pad, and hands his ticket to Old Larsen, who growls, "We don't do any damn substitutions," but then makes Peter three eggs over easy, hash browns with onions and cheese, four slices of bacon, white toast, and two *pannukakku*, slightly undercooked. When his food is ready, Hanna takes a break, sits next to Peter, watches him eat. His beard is growing long. A man without a job doesn't need a clean face, he tells her. She hates watching Peter eat. She hates that he follows her to work. She hates his face.

Her husband thinks they are trying to have a child. He wears boxers instead of briefs though he prefers the security of the latter. Peter once read in a magazine that wearing boxers increased sperm motility. He and Hanna have sex only when the home ovulation kit he bought at Walmart indicates she is fertile. Peter would prefer to have sex every day. Hanna would prefer to never have sex with Peter again, not because she's frigid but because she finds it difficult to become aroused by a perpetually unemployed man. Two years ago, Hanna said she was going on vacation with Laura downstate and instead drove to Marquette and had her tubes tied. She wasn't going to end up like her mother with too many children in a too-small house with too little to eat. Despite her best efforts, however, she has found herself living in a too-small house with too many people and too little to eat. It is a bitter pill to swallow.

When she gets off work at three in the afternoon, Hanna goes home, washes the grease and salt from her skin, and changes into something cute but a little slutty. She heads to the university the next town over. She's twenty-seven but looks far younger, so she pretends she's a student. Sometimes she attends a class in one of the big lecture halls. She takes notes and plays with her hair and thinks about all the things she could have done. Other days she sits in the library and reads books and learns things so that when she finally escapes she can be more than a waitress with a great rack in a dead Upper Michigan town.

Hanna flirts with boys because at the Michigan Institute of Technology there are lots and lots of boys who want nothing more than to be noticed by a pretty girl. She never pretends she's anything but smart. She's too old for that. Sometimes the boys take her to the dining hall or the Campus Café for a snack. She tells them she's in mechanical engineering because Laura is a secretary in that department. Sometimes the boys invite her to their messy dorm rooms littered with dirty laundry and video game consoles and roommates or their squalid apartments off campus. She gives them blowjobs and lies with them on their narrow twin beds covered in thin sheets and tells them lies they like to hear. After the boys fall asleep, Hanna heads back across the bridge to Karpela's, where she tends bar until two in the morning.

Peter visits Hanna at the supper club, too, but he has to pay for his drinks so he doesn't visit often. Don Karpela, the owner, is always around, grabbing at things with his meaty fingers. He's a greedy man and a friend of her father. Even though he's nearing sixty, Don is always breathing down Hanna's neck, bumping up against her in the cramped space behind the bar, telling her he'd make her damn happy if she'd leave her old man. When he does that, Hanna closes her eyes and breathes easy because she needs her job. If Peter is around when Don is making his moves, he'll laugh and raise his glass. "You can have her," he'll slur, as if he has a say in the matter.

After the bar closes Hanna wipes everything down and washes all the glasses and empties the ashtrays. She and Laura, who also works at the supper club, will sit on the hood of Hanna's car in the back alley and hold hands. Hanna will lean against Laura's shoulder and inhale deeply and marvel that her friend can still smell good after hours in that dark, smoky space where men don't hear the word *no*. If the night is empty enough, they will kiss for a very long time, until their cold lips become warm, until the world falls away, until their bodies feel like they will split at the heart. She and Laura never talk about these moments but when Hanna is plotting her escape, she is not going alone.

Hanna's twin sister, Anna, often waits up for Hanna. She worries. She always has. She's a nervous woman. As a child, she was a nervous girl. Their mother, before she left, liked to say that Hanna got all the *sisu*, the fierce strength that should have been shared by both girls. Hanna and Anna always knew their mother didn't know them at all. They were both strong and fierce. Anna's husband worked at the paper mill in Niagara until some foreign company bought it and closed it and then most people in town lost their homes because all the work that needed doing was already done. When Anna called, nervous as always, to ask if she and her family could stay with Hanna, she had not even posed the question before Hanna said, "Yes."

Hanna and Anna are not openly demonstrative but they love each other wildly. In high school, Anna dated a boy who didn't treat her well. When Hanna found out, she put a good hurting on him. Hanna pretended to be her sister and she took the bad boy up to the trails behind the county fairgrounds. She got down on her knees and started to give him head and she told him *if he ever laid a hand on her sister again* and before she finished that sentence, she bit down on his cock and told herself she wouldn't stop biting down until her teeth met. She smiled when she tasted his blood. He screamed so softly it made the hairs on her arm stand on end. Hanna still sees that boy around town once in a while. He's not a boy anymore but he walks with a hitch and always crosses to the other side of the street when he sees her coming.

On the nights when Hanna and Laura sit on the hood of Laura's car and kiss until their cold lips warm, Anna stands outside on the front porch, shivering, waiting. Her cheeks flush. Her heart flutters around her chest awkwardly. Anna asks Hanna if she's seeing another man and Hanna tells her sister the truth. She says, "No," and Anna frowns. She knows Hanna is telling the truth. She knows Hanna is lying. She cannot quite figure out how she's doing both at the same time. The sisters smoke a cigarette together, and before they go in, Anna will place a gentle hand on Hanna's arm. She'll say, "Be careful." Hanna will kiss her twin's forehead, and she'll think, *I will*, and Anna will hear her.

## How Hanna Ikonen Knows It Is Time to Get the Girl and Get Out of Town

Hanna and Anna's father, Red, lives in the basement. He's not allowed on the second floor, where everyone sleeps. When Peter asks why, Hanna just shakes her head and says, "It's personal." She doesn't share personal things with her husband. Her father used to work in the mines. When the last copper mine closed he didn't bother trying to learn a new trade. He started holding his back when he walked around, said he was injured. He collected disability and when that ran out, he lived with a series of girlfriends who each kicked him out before long. Finally, when there was no woman in town who would give him the time of day, Red showed up on Hanna's doorstep, reeking of whiskey, his beard long and unkempt. He slurred an incoherent apology for being a lousy father. He begged his daughter to have mercy on an old man. Hanna wasn't moved by his plea but she knew he would be her problem one way or the other. She told him he could make himself comfortable in the basement, but if she ever saw him on the second floor, that would be that. It has been fifteen years since the mine closed but Red still calls himself a miner.

The whereabouts of Hanna and Anna's mother, Ilse, are unknown. She left when the girls were eleven. It was a Thursday morning. Ilse got the girls and their brothers ready for school, fed them breakfast—steel-cut oats topped with sliced bananas. She kissed them atop their pale blond heads and told them to be good. She was gone when they returned home from school. For a while, they heard a rumor that Ilse had taken up with a shoe salesman in Marquette. Later, there was news of her from Iron Mountain, a dentist's wife, with a new family. Then there was no news at all.

Hanna and Anna have five brothers scattered throughout the state. They are mostly bitter, lazy, indifferent, and unwilling to have a hand in the care and feeding of their father. When Hanna organized a conference call with her siblings to discuss the disposition of their father, the Boys, as they are collectively known, said it was women's work and if the Twins didn't want to do that work, they could let the old man rot. One of the brothers, Venn, offered to send Hanna or Anna, whoever shouldered the burden of caring for Red, twenty dollars a month. Simultaneously, the Twins told him to stick it up his ass and then they told the Boys to go fuck themselves. After they hung up, Hanna called Anna and Anna offered to take care of Red until he drank himself to death but Hanna worried that death by drink would take too long. Anna had a child to raise, after all.

It is an ordinary Tuesday when Hanna decides to go home after working at the café instead of heading across the bridge to the institute to play make-believe with college boys. She can feel grease oozing out of her pores and what she wants, more than anything, is to soak in a clean bathtub, in an empty house. When she pulls into her driveway and sees Anna pacing back and forth in front of the garage, Hanna knows there will be no bath or empty house today. She parks the car, takes a deep breath, and joins her sister, who informs Hanna that their mother is sitting on the Salvation Army couch in the living room drinking a cup of tea. Hanna thinks, *Of course she is.*

## How Hanna Met and Married Peter Lahti

Anna fell in love when she was seventeen. His name was Logan, and he lived on the reservation in Baraga. She loved his long black hair and his smooth brown skin and the softness of his voice. They met at a football game and the day after graduation, they married and moved. When Anna left, Hanna was happy for her sister, but she also hoped beyond all hopes that her sister and her new husband would take her with them. She could have said something. Years later Hanna realized she should have said something, but she became the one who stayed. She got an apartment of her own and started hanging out at the university sitting in on the classes she couldn't afford. Peter lived in the apartment next door and back then he worked as a truck driver hauling lumber downstate, so dating him was fine because he wasn't around much.

After a long trip when Peter was gone for three weeks, he showed up at Hanna's door, his hair slicked back, beard trimmed, wearing a button-down shirt and freshly pressed jeans. In one hand he held a cheap bouquet of carnations. He had forgotten that Hanna had told him, on their first date, that she hated carnations. He thrust the flowers into Hanna's hands, invited himself into her apartment, and said, "I missed you so much. Let's get married." Hanna, elbow deep into a bottle of wine at that point, shrugged. Peter, an optimist at heart, took the gesture as a response in the affirmative. They married not long after in a ceremony attended by Anna and her husband, Red, and three of the Boys. No one from Peter's family attended. His mother was scandalized her boy would marry any child of Red Ikonen.

### How Red Ikonen got His Reputation

Red Ikonen had mining in his blood. His daddy and his daddy's daddy had been miners up in Calumet when mining was something that mattered up there and the town was rich and every Sunday the churches were full of good folks grateful for the bounties of the hard earth. As a boy, Red loved his father's stories about the world beneath the world. By the time it was Red's turn to head underground, there wasn't much mining left to do and that was a hell of a cross to bear. He was like a soldier without a war. Red started drinking to numb his disappointment. He married a pretty girl, had five handsome boys and two lovely girls, and continued drinking to celebrate his good fortune. The pretty girl left and he drank so he wouldn't feel so lonesome. Finally, drinking was the only thing he knew how to do so that's just what he did.

He was a tall man—six foot seven—and he had a loud voice and no sense of how to act right. That sort of thing just wasn't in him. There wasn't a bar in town where Red hadn't started a fight or done something untoward with his woman or someone else's woman. Things had gotten so bad he needed to drive over to South Range or Chassell to drink with the old guys at the VFW who really were soldiers without a war, because no one in town wanted to serve him a drink. When the Boys were still in town, bartenders would call and have one of them come get their father. By the time Red Ikonen was drinking so he wouldn't feel so lonesome he had become a mean drunk. He never had a kind word for his boys who drove miles into the middle of the night to bring their drunk daddy back home.

One by one the Boys left home, tried to get as far away from their father as possible, until it was only the Twins left, and then he started doing untoward things with them and it was a small town so people talked and it wasn't long before no one at all wanted a thing to do with Red Ikonen.

## How Laura and Hanna Became Best Friends

Laura Kappi grew up next door to the Ikonens. For a while in high school, she dated one of the Boys, but then he moved away, went to college, and didn't bother to take her with him. Laura was, in fact, a friend to both Hanna and Anna throughout high school. When Anna and Logan moved down to Niagara, Laura saw how lost Hanna was without her twin. She decided to do her best to take Anna's place. Hanna was more than happy to let her. They became best friends and then they became more than friends but they never talked about it because there wasn't much to be said on the subject.

## How Hanna Reacts When She Sees Her Mother for the First Time in Sixteen Years

Before they go inside, Anna reaches for Hanna's waiting hand. They both squeeze, hard, their knuckles cracking, and then the Twins go inside. Ilse Ikonen is sitting on the edge of the couch. She is a small woman with sharp features. She has always been beautiful and neither time nor distance has changed that. Her hair is graying around the scalp, her features hang a bit lower, but she doesn't look a day over forty. Red is sitting where he always sits during the day, in the recliner next to the couch, staring at his estranged wife. He has tucked in his shirt, but his hands are shaking because he is trying not to drink. He wants to be clearheaded but his wife is so damned beautiful that with or without the drink he doesn't know up from down. Peter is sitting next to Ilse, also staring, because the resemblance between his wife and her mother is uncanny. They have never met. Anna's husband, Logan, is sitting next to Peter, holding their son, half-asleep, in his lap. He is deliberately avoiding any eye contact with his mother-in-law. He is helping his wife with the burden of her anger.

As soon as Hanna and Anna enter the room, their stomachs churn. Beads of sweat slowly spread across their foreheads. Ilse leans forward, setting her teacup on the coffee table. She smiles at her daughters. Hanna thinks, *Why did you offer her tea?* Anna thinks, *I was being polite.* Hanna bites her lip. "What are you doing here, Ilse?" she asks.

Ilse Ikonen uncrosses her legs and folds her hands in her lap. "It has been a long time," she says.

Hanna looks at all the broken people sitting in her living room on her broken furniture looking to her to fix their broken lives. She turns around and walks right back out the front door. Anna makes her excuses and rushes after her sister. She finds Hanna holding on to the still-warm hood of her car, hunched over, throwing up. Anna's stomach rolls uncomfortably. When Hanna stands up, she wipes her lips with the back of her hand and says, "I mean . . . really?"

## How Laura Finally Convinces Hanna to Run Away with Her

Hanna sits in her car until Ilse Ikonen takes her leave and gets a room at the motel down the street. After her mother leaves, Hanna drives to campus and goes to the dank room of one of her college boys. She lies on his musty, narrow twin bed and stares at the constellation of glow-in-the-dark stars on the ceiling while the boy awkwardly fumbles at her breasts with his bony fingers. She sighs, closes her eyes, thinks of Laura. Afterward, when the boy is fast asleep, his fingers curled in a loose fist near his mouth, Hanna slips out of bed and heads back across the bridge to Laura's house.

Laura smiles when she opens her front door. Hanna shrugs and stands in the doorway, her cheeks numb, still nauseated. She shoves her small hands into her pockets, tries to ignore the cold.

Laura wraps her arms around herself, shifts quickly from one foot to the other. "Why don't you come in?"

Hanna shakes her head. "I can't do this anymore."

Laura arches an eyebrow and even though she is barefoot, she steps onto her snowy front porch. She gasps, steps onto Hanna's boots, slides her arms beneath Hanna's coat and around her waist. Laura lightly brushes her lips against Hanna's. Hanna closes her eyes. She breathes deeply.

## How Hanna Falls Even More in Love with Laura Than She Thought Possible

When Laura can no longer feel her toes, she says, "We'd better get inside before I get frostbite and I am forced to spend the rest of my life hobbling after you."

Hanna nods and follows Laura into her house. It is familiar, has looked mostly the same for the past twenty years, and in that there is comfort. Inside the foyer, amid coats and boots, a shovel, a knitted scarf, a bag of salt, Hanna sinks to the floor and sits cross-legged. Laura sits across from Hanna, extends her legs, resting her cold feet in Hanna's lap.

"Do you want to tell me about it?"

Hanna shakes her head angrily. "My mother's back."

"I mean . . . really?" she says.

Hanna doesn't go home. She calls Anna and assures her sister that she's fine. Anna doesn't ask where she is. She's starting to make sense of things. Hanna lets Laura lead her up the steep staircase lined with books. She lets Laura put her into a hot bath. She lets Laura wash her clean. She follows Laura to bed and for the first time in months, she falls asleep in a mostly empty house. She thinks, *This is everything I want.*

As Hanna sleeps, Laura calculates how much money she has saved, the tread on her tires, how far they will need to travel so that Hanna might begin to forget about the life she's leaving behind. It all makes Laura very tired but then she looks at Hanna's lower lip, how it trembles while she's sleeping.

## How It Has Always Been

The next morning, Laura hears the knocking at her front door. She wraps herself in a thin robe and takes one last look at Hanna, still sleeping, lower lip still trembling. Laura has always loved Hanna, even before she understood why her entire body flushed when she saw Hanna at school or running around her backyard or sitting on the roof outside her bedroom window. Dating one of the Boys was a way to get closer to Hanna. Laura would kiss Hanna's brother and think of his sister, her smile, the way she walked around with her shoulder muscles bunched up. Being with the brother was not what Laura wanted but she told herself it was enough. For the first time Laura feels something unfamiliar in her throat. It makes her a little sick to her stomach. She thinks it might be hope. Downstairs, Anna is standing on the front porch shivering. She has a splitting headache. When Laura opens the door Anna quickly slips into the house. Anna squeezes Laura's hand and heads upstairs into Laura's bedroom. Anna crawls into bed behind her sister, wraps her arms around Hanna's waist. Hanna covers one of Anna's hands with hers. She is not quite awake yet.

"Don't make me go back there," Hanna says, hoarsely.

Anna tightens her arms around her sister, kisses Hanna's shoulder. Anna says, "You have to go back to say goodbye." There is a confidence in Anna's voice that reassures Hanna.

Hanna sighs, slowly opens her eyes. She sees Laura standing in the doorway. Hanna smiles. "You don't have to stand so far away," she says. Laura grins and crawls into bed with the Twins. Laura says, "Remember when we were kids and the three of us would lie on your roof at night during the summer to cool down?" Both Hanna and Anna nod. The three women roll onto their backs and stare at the ceiling—the cracks and water stains, how it sags. "We were miserable even then," Laura says.

## How Hanna Finally Confronts Her Mother

Where Hanna has always been the protector, Anna has always been the voice of reason, able to make the right choices between impossible alternatives. When they were girls and Hanna would plot retribution against anyone who had wronged the Twins, it was Anna who would deter her sister from acting thoughtlessly. When Red Ikonen would stumble into their room drunk and Hanna would try to stab him with a kitchen knife or bite his ear off it was Anna who grabbed her sister's arm and said, "It's him or Superior Home." It was Anna who would sing to her father and stroke his beard and soothe all the meanness out of him. In these moments, Hanna would feel so much anger inside her she thought her heart would rip apart but then she would let the knife fall to the floor or she would unclench her teeth because anything was better than Superior Home, the state facility where motherless children were often discarded until they turned eighteen. They heard stories bad enough to make them believe there were worse things than the stink of Red Ikonen's breath against their cheeks as he forgot how to behave like a proper father.

Anna held Hanna's hand as they walked back to their house, a bracing wind pushing their bodies through the snow. Hanna tried to breathe but found the air thin and cold and it hurt her lungs. As they climbed the porch stairs Hanna stopped, leaned against the railing, her body heavy.

"I don't feel so good," she said.

Anna pressed the cool palm of her hand against Hanna's forehead. "You get to leave soon," she said. "Hold on to that."

Hanna stared at her sister. She said, "Come with us—you and Logan and the baby."

Anna shook her head. "It's my turn to stay."

"Bullshit. We've taken our turns long enough."

The front door opened. Peter glared at the Twins. "Where the hell were you last night?" He grabbed Hanna by the elbow, pulling her into the house, and she let him. She wanted to save what fight she had left.

In the living room the scene closely resembled the tableau Hanna stumbled into the previous day with Ilse Ikonen sitting on the couch, poised regally like she had never left and had no need to offer acts of contrition.

Hanna tried to squirm free from Peter's grasp and he finally relented when calmly, quietly, Anna said, "Let go of my sister." Peter held a natural distrust of twins. It wasn't normal, he thought, for there to be two people who were so identical. He also harbored no small amount of jealousy for the relationship twins shared. While he was not a bright man, Peter was smart enough to know he would never be as close to his wife as he wanted.

The Twins stood before their father, their mother, their husbands. They stood in the house where they had grown up filled with broken people and broken things. Anna thought, *This is the last time we will ever stand in this room*, and Hanna suddenly felt like she could breathe again. She tried to say something but she couldn't find her voice. Her throat was dry and hollow. The Twins looked at their parents and thought about everything they had ever wanted to say to two people so ill-suited for doing right by their children.

"I'm sorry to intrude," Ilse said, her voice tight, her words clipped. She crossed her legs and fidgeted with a big diamond ring on her left hand. "I wanted to see how you girls and the Boys were doing, perhaps explain myself."

Anna shook her head. "Explanations aren't necessary," she said. "Your leaving is a long time gone."

Hanna removed her wedding ring and dropped it on the coffee table. Peter sneered and said, "Whatever," and Hanna rolled her eyes.

The Twins stood before their father, their mother, their husbands. They sucked in a great mass of air, threw their shoulders back. They had rehearsed this moment more than once but then they realized that with all the time and wrongs gone by, there was nothing worth saying.

## How Hanna, Laura, Anna, Logan, and the Baby Got Away

They piled into Laura's truck, their belongings packed tightly into a small trailer hitched to the back. They sat perfectly still, held their breaths, looked straight ahead.

# Requiem for a Glass Heart

The stone thrower lives in a glass house with his glass family. He is a flesh-and-blood man going about the business of living with his glass wife and glass child, their glass furniture and glass lives.

The stone thrower, a good yet flawed man given to overindulgence, met his wife on a beach, after a lightning storm on a night when the sky refused to surrender to darkness and yet there were stars up above. He saw the small fissure her body made in the sand first, moved closer, moved carefully. Then he saw her, her body bathed in moonlight, her eyes shining brightly. He instantly fell in love because he could not believe what lay before him. Her beauty was so mystifying and entrancing that it pierced through his skin and into his blood and wove itself tightly around his heart.

He did not think about what it would mean to love a glass woman. He fell to his knees. He took her hand in his, turned the palm over. He gently placed his lips against the tender spot between her thumb and forefinger. He closed his eyes, and inhaled deeply. He prayed that when he opened his eyes she would still be there. When he did, she was.

The stone thrower's wife instantly fell in love because the stone thrower was everything she was not. He was the first man who did not see through her. He helped her to her feet, and then they walked for hours and miles and miles more. He listened and enjoyed her husky voice as she told him all of her hopes, her dreams, her fears. She tried to keep some secrets for herself, but couldn't. His propensity for indulgence was infectious. She laid herself bare and did not think about what it would mean to love a man of flesh.

The stone thrower and his wife courted for seven months and married on the seventh day of that seventh month. She wore a silver gown and diamonds in her glass hair. The stone thrower stood next to her, in front of his friends, their families. They vowed to love, to honor, to protect, to obey, although he did not yet know how he would keep his word.

When the stone thrower and his glass wife make love, she is always on top, her cool glass hands pressed against his chest. She lies down on top of him, leg to leg, breast to chest, face to face. He kisses her long, slender neck, the hollow spaces above her clavicles. He slides his hands along the length of her glass hair, then holds her face, tracing her lips with his thumbs. The stone thrower's wife warms to his touch, just slightly, and though he can't see it, he can feel her body respond. He enjoys the pressure of her glass thighs trembling against his and the way she breathes into his mouth, shallow and fast.

When the stone thrower's wife comes, her body fogs in a random pattern outward from her heart. As she catches her breath, she can often hear her heart threatening to implode with the high-pitched lamentation of glass succumbing to pressure. When she's certain her heart won't break, she rolls onto her side, and the stone thrower lovingly traces lines in the condensation he has left behind. Sometimes, after they make love, the stone thrower will light a candle, sit against the headboard, holding his wife in his arms, her glass spine arched against his thick, matted chest. He'll look down at his seed slowly sliding out of her. He asks her to lay herself bare further, to share secrets he does not yet know. He has become accustomed to seeing too much and now yearns to know too much. She often acquiesces, speaking softly, exposing herself in complicated ways. The stone thrower smiles. His wife does not.

Every morning, the stone thrower sits across from his glass wife at their glass table, and he watches as orange juice sluices down her glass throat into her glass stomach. She rarely bothers with clothes when the drapes are closed, feels she has nothing to hide. It is a remarkable thing, the stone thrower often thinks, being able to see such intimacies, being able to see the separation of her whole into parts. She'll look at him, then to the distance, her cheeks growing warm while she remembers the night before. As they discuss the coming day, the stone thrower's wife will reach across the table and take his hand in hers. She'll trace the calluses, the fingers that are bent but not broken. He'll squeeze back, gently, ever careful not to break her.

After the stone thrower and his glass wife share breakfast, he takes his glass child to school, holding the boy's cool, translucent hand in his. He listens carefully as the boy tells him about his hopes, his dreams, his fears. With every word his son speaks, the stone thrower feels his heart expanding, nearly breaking the cage of bone protecting it. After he kisses the boy on the forehead, sending him on his way, the stone thrower will sometimes stand just outside the child's classroom, peering inside, holding his breath, hoping that the other children will be gentle and kind, however fragile such hope may be.

During the day, the stone thrower's glass wife busies herself with the work of living in a glass house. Room by room, she uses soft cloths to wipe clean every surface because her husband cannot help the things he leaves behind. As she wipes away the fingerprints and skin and stray hairs she smiles to herself and hums the waltz to which she and the stone thrower danced at their wedding. Sometimes her neighbors will stop in front of the glass house and stare as they catch glimpses of her body's glass contours beneath the clothes she wears more for their benefit than hers. They will whisper to each other and shake their heads. They will condemn that which they cannot understand.

What the stone thrower's wife loves most is when she strips out of her clothes and disappears into the world unseen. It is a sacred time, those hours between when her work is done and when her child and husband return home. She steals these moments for herself because her life is so transparent that she craves having something private, something precious. She crafts from these moments secrets for herself that she has not shared and will not share with her husband, who sees too much and loves too carefully.

Most days, the stone thrower's wife goes to a nearby park with wide-open spaces that cannot contain her. She stretches her long limbs and stares into the sky. She marvels at the clear blue brightness above. She closes her eyes and says a small prayer. Then she runs. She runs because she is intoxicated by the sensation of wind against her bare glass skin. She enjoys the abandon of pushing her

glass body and testing its limits and feeling the rough pavement
and the cold slick grass beneath her bare glass feet. Her husband
loves her but he worries. He wearies. He thinks her delicate. He
fears that the slightest thing will splinter her or return her to the
grains of sand from which she rose. The stone thrower prefers to
keep his wife trapped in the safety of their glass house, where the
dangers are not seen but known. She knows that the glass walls
of their home cannot protect her. She runs.

After her afternoons in the park, the stone thrower's wife finds
herself sweaty and pleasantly sore. She walks home slowly, breathing deeply. She revels. Then she takes a cold shower, emerges,
wraps herself in a soft cotton robe. When her son comes home,
she will pull him into her arms, and listen when he tells her about
his hopes, his dreams, his fears. He chatters away and she traces
her child's diaphanous features with her glass fingertips. The
contact between their glass bodies produces a melodious keen-
ing that makes the boy's smile wider. The stone thrower's wife
falls ever more in love with her child each day. Though it pains
her, she accepts that the boy's life is both a blessing and a curse.
When her heart has had its fill of these precious moments, when
she can literally feel the glass veins binding her heart pulsing and
threatening to shatter, she sends her child out to play with his
friends until dinner. She needs him to be part of the world, to
encounter that which is seen but not known.

The stone thrower's son knows that he is a curiosity but he
does not yet know why. In school, he sits at his desk, his glass
frame shrouded by his school uniform. He is quiet but studious.
He is kind but strong, like his mother. His is tough and stub-
born, like his father. Though some of his classmates tease him,
make faces at each other while looking through him, the stone

thrower's son has several friends who no longer concern themselves with that which makes them different, that which they
cannot understand. To them, he is a boy who makes them laugh
and chases them on the playground and who makes beautiful
castles out of sand.

The stone thrower works hard and plays hard and provides well
for his glass family. For eight hours a day, he works in a quarry,
bare-chested and sweaty, throwing all manner of stone from the
depths of the quarry to waiting trucks above. He is so good at his
job that he often attracts an audience. Onlookers hover nearby,
admiring the elaborate web of muscles enfolding his upper body,
and the way he makes his labor seem so effortless. He does not
mind the onlookers. He has become accustomed to living in a
glass house.

When he finally gets home, the stone thrower sits at the kitchen
table with his glass wife and their glass child. The family eats a
dinner that has been lovingly prepared and the stone thrower tries
not to look away from the intimate moments of his wife and son
that he cannot share. He helps the boy with his homework, then
together, husband and wife put the child to bed. Some nights,
they hire a babysitter, leave a careful set of instructions for the
care and feeding of a glass child, and then they go out for a drink
at a nearby cocktail lounge. His wife dresses in her favorite little
black dress, relaxes against her husband's strong frame, enjoys
the pressure of his hand in the small of her back as he steers her
to a table where they can see without being seen, hear without
being heard.

On very special occasions, they will don their finery and attend
the opera. They'll sit in a private box above the orchestra, admire
the ornate ceilings, the rich texture of the seats upon which they

sit. The stone thrower's wife will lose herself in the music, glass tears cresting her eyelids as she is transported to magical places. The stone thrower will try to enjoy himself, but with every note in every aria, his entire body will tense. He worries that it is a matter of time before a diva with perfect pitch and iron lungs will fill the opera house with a note so flawless that it matches the natural frequency of his wife's body. He worries that in that moment of resonance, she will start to vibrate, then quake and then her glass body will fracture. He will be left, kneeling above shards of glass holding his wife's pulsing glass heart in his callused hands. The stone thrower is always quiet when he and his wife leave the opera, humbled by the tenuous nature of a glass wife. She'll ask him what's wrong and he'll look at her tenderly, and he'll lie, he'll say everything is just fine.

The stone thrower, a good yet flawed man given to overindulgence, has a mistress he visits several times a week. She is a woman who is not made of glass. She is all flesh and bone, with a generous, meaty body like his. She is a different kind of mystery.

What the stone thrower's wife hates most is when she strips out of her clothes and slips into the world unseen. She knows about the mistress. She watches her husband and the other woman sometimes, sneaking into the mistress's apartment, padding softly across the thick carpet of the living room. She'll stand in the doorway and watch as her husband holds the other woman in his large, callused hands, how he will be reckless and rough. Then she will walk home, leaving a trail of glass tears for the stone thrower to follow. The stone thrower doesn't love his mistress but he needs the moments they share, those moments when he does not have to see too much or love too carefully.

# In the Event of My Father's Death

When I was a girl, my father once told me that women weren't good for much. We were parked at the mountain overlook just outside town. I was in the backseat, staring at my shoes, chewing my fingernails. He was in the front seat, drinking Maker's Mark from a bottle wrapped in a brown paper bag. He and my mother had just had another heated argument and he had dragged me out of the house as if I would ever choose his side. He said, "Don't become like your mother. She is a small woman." My father didn't love my mother. I don't even think he loved me but he did love making us miserable by refusing to leave.

My father's opinions didn't keep him from fornicating with any number of women. My mother told me that once, after she found another woman's earrings on her nightstand. "Tacky costume jewelry," she said, as if the quality of the earrings angered her more than their presence in her bedroom.

For years, my father dated a woman named Teresa. She was seven years younger and a waitress at a bar called the Mosquito Inn, which was decorated like an African safari. It didn't make much sense to anyone because we were in Upper Michigan. Teresa had red hair she always wore in a messy pile on top of her head. She smoked skinny cigarettes and wore low-cut shirts and too much makeup. She called me Steph no matter how many times I corrected her and said, "My name is Stephanie." She didn't mind that my father was married and had a kid. She never expected much from him. She was the kind of woman who didn't expect much from life. They were well suited.

Every Saturday, my dad told my mom we were going fishing, no matter what the weather was like. I'm not sure if he was being cruel or kind with that lie. We'd leave the house before dawn and the night before, I'd stuff my backpack with books and a notepad and my Walkman, a set of clean underwear. We'd drive the seventeen miles to Teresa's place. She lived in a trailer on a large plot of land her daddy left her. There was nothing around for miles. I know. I looked. When we pulled up, Teresa would be waiting in the doorway, wearing a silky robe that she let fall open. Underneath, she wore only a pair of lacy panties. My father always grinned when he first saw her, then he ruffled my hair and said, "You can look, my darling dear, but you can't touch." I would shrug away from him, and make a face, but I would look because Teresa was beautiful, in the hardened way women like her are.

As we ducked into her trailer, Teresa would toss me the remote to the small television that sat on the kitchen table and tell me to make myself at home. Then she and my dad would lock themselves in her room for hours. They were neither discreet nor quiet. My dad was a sloppy, vulgar lover, from what I could hear—all heavy breathing and grunting and ass slapping. I vowed to never let a man like him touch me like that. Teresa always giggled, her high-pitched laugh inescapable in that tiny trailer. I sat on the small couch next to the kitchen table and flipped through the three channels Teresa's television received and tried to read or draw, but mostly I daydreamed about a time when I wouldn't have to spend my weekends in a shitty trailer watching shitty television listening to my father fuck his mistress.

Eventually, Teresa and my father would emerge from the bedroom. He never wore a shirt, always letting his pale, saggy stomach hang out like he was proud of it. They would both be all smiles and my father would stretch out next to me on the couch, rubbing his bare belly. Teresa would make us grilled cheese sandwiches or corn dogs and tater tots or some other appropriately white trash meal. Then the three of us would watch more television, sometimes a movie. Around nine, they would turn in for the night and I would lie on the couch, staring out the small window, listening to the laughing and grunting and ass slapping and heavy breathing, hoping my mother was having an affair with the guy from the hardware store or one of the deacons from church. We went home late on Sunday evening and my mother was always waiting with a home-cooked meal. My father handed her flowers we picked up at the grocery store and kissed her on the cheek. She never asked me about our fishing trips or why we never brought any fish home.

When my father died after driving too fast over an icy bridge, Teresa came to his funeral. My mother, who never had been any good about making a fuss about things that just weren't right, didn't say anything. She simply stared forward, her eyes burning a hole in my father's casket as his mistress sat on the other side of the aisle. My mother sat with her spine ramrod straight. She didn't shed a single tear. She was going to mourn my father with a dignity he never possessed in life. Teresa, though, was a mess, sobbing openly, blowing her nose into a handkerchief an usher handed her. After the service, my mother stood in front of the church in her neatly pressed lavender suit, greeting the guests, thanking them for attending, ignoring their whispers. Teresa, she stood next to my father, her perfectly manicured hand on his casket, still making a mess of herself with her crying. I guess she loved him. It was nice that someone did.

I went to visit Teresa the first Saturday after my father died. I was driving then, almost on my way to college. At the crack of dawn, I knocked and waited, shifting from foot to foot. When she opened the door, she was wearing her silk robe, as she always did, and it was open, revealing her body, as lovely as it had always been. Her eyes were red. Once my father died, I don't know that she ever stopped crying. Silently, Teresa stepped aside and I ducked under her arm and into the trailer. She sat at the tiny kitchen table and lit a cigarette, then offered me one. I nodded, and for a while, we just sat there, legs crossed, looking at each other, smoking her cheap, skinny cigarettes.

"He loved spending Saturdays with you," she finally said.

I shook my head. "He loved spending Saturdays with you."

Teresa smiled sadly. "It's not that simple."

I shrugged, slid lower in my seat, lit another cigarette.

She slid her hand across the table, dragging her fingers across my knuckles. I looked at Teresa, saw how hard living had taken up residence in her features. I squeezed her hand gently. I wanted her to feel something soft. She stood, let her silk robe fall to the floor, and started walking to her bedroom. Then she turned to look at me over her shoulder and I stood.

# Break All the Way Down

The mother of my boyfriend's youngest child called in the middle of the night. My boyfriend was asleep, the heat from his body wrapping around us. I stared at the dark shadows of the ceiling fan lazily spinning above us. He sleeps soundly despite many reasons he should not.

"I'm at the front door," she said. Her voice was tight and thin.

I tried to shake my boyfriend awake but he merely shifted, stretching his leg across my side of the bed. He snored lightly. I sighed.

Anna Lisa, the mother of my boyfriend's youngest child, handed me her daughter, still in her carrier, as well as a large duffel bag. She nodded toward the bag. "The baby's things." I looked at the baby, neither cute nor ugly, a blob of indeterminate features. We stood quietly, listened to moths and other insects flying into the bright, buzzing lamp covering us in its light. My shoulders ached. The air was damp and heavy. Anna Lisa is beautiful but she looked tired. She wore a loose pair of sweatpants with fading block letters down the left leg. Her T-shirt was stained. Her breasts were swollen. I could see that. Her hair hung limply in her face. She smelled ripe. There were dark circles beneath her eyes. I don't know that we looked different.

I invited her in, offered to give her a bath. I wanted to help her undress, pulling her shirt over her head. I wanted to run a bath of hot water, to wash her body and scrub her back and her thighs, the still loose skin of her stomach, to wash her clean.

"I cannot take care of my child anymore."

I looked at the baby again. The baby stared back, yawned, and blinked tiredly. "You want to leave your baby with him?"

Anna Lisa shook her head. "I'm leaving my baby with you."

My husband hates my new boyfriend. I do, too. He is the kind of person everyone hates. My husband is the man I love. He likes his eggs scrambled soft with freshly ground paper, sea salt. I woke up early every morning to make him breakfast, enjoyed the rhythm of it, enjoyed feeling useful in that way. My husband calls me daily, says, "Why are you punishing yourself?" He says, "Come home."

My boyfriend isn't really my boyfriend; he and I aren't quite living together. We came to a silent agreement where more often than not, I am around. My things are still at my house—four bedrooms, three baths—with my husband. I visit my things, my husband, often. I run my fingers over the modern statue near the front entrance, the dimple in my husband's chin, the thick, ropy muscles of his shoulders, the mahogany mantel over the fireplace. I belong with these things, they are mine, so I do not stay long.

A mosquito bit my cheek and I winced. I pressed my hand to my stomach, ignored the thin roll of scar, how it pulsed against my palm. The baby whimpered so I set the duffel bag just inside the foyer and picked her up out of her carrier, held her against my shoulder. She smelled sweet and powdery and settled as I patted her back, soft, steady. I said *there, there baby love*. Anna Lisa covered my hand with hers as I comforted her child. Anna Lisa's hand was sweaty.

She did not look at the baby as she walked away.

I sat with the baby in the living room, setting her on a clean blanket. When I tired of watching her, I stretched out, resting my hand on her stomach. I fell asleep with the baby staring at me, her eyes wide open.

In the morning, my boyfriend kicked my foot with his heavy work boot. "What the fuck is this?" I sat up quickly, holding a finger to my lips. I stood and pulled him into the bedroom. "Anna Lisa brought the baby last night. She can't take care of her anymore."

My boyfriend shook his head and reached for his phone, quickly dialing his ex. "This is bullshit," he muttered. When Anna Lisa didn't answer, he threw his phone against the wall. "What the hell am I supposed to do with a baby?"

"Keep it alive."

He shook his head and brushed past me. "I have to go to work. You deal with this."

I have read many baby books. After my boyfriend left, I filled the kitchen sink with warm water and soap and washed the baby, gave her a fresh diaper, and chose the cutest outfit. I prepared a bottle and fed the baby and she fell back asleep. I did a quick inventory—a stack of neatly folded onesies, seven outfits, a

stuffed animal, three bottles and a ziplock bag filled with nipples, two cans of formula, a half-filled package of baby wipes,
six diapers, and a notebook filled with detailed instructions
about the baby's personality, likes and dislikes, daily schedule,
what the baby's different sounds mean, the kind of accounting
made possible only by the reach of a mother's love. We needed
to go shopping but first I needed to share this development
with my husband. Once or twice a week, he works from home.
I found him in his office, bare-chested, wearing a pair of flannel pajama pants. He smiled when he saw me and I wanted to
crawl inside him.

When he noticed me carrying a baby, he stood, frowning. "Why
are you holding a baby?"

"A woman gave it to me."

My husband peered into the carrier. "That's not funny."

"I'm not joking."

A lot of people decided I went crazy after the accident. They
kept waiting for me to strip naked in a shopping mall or eat a
cat or something. When I took up with an asshole, they breathed
a sigh of relief. "Your situation is still fixable," my mother said
when I was still taking her calls.

I am not crazy.

My husband, Ben, crouched down and tapped the baby on her
nose. She smiled and he did it again. He looked up. "You didn't,
like, steal this baby, did you?"

I shook my head. "It's his baby. His ex dropped her off last
night. She said she was leaving the baby for me."

Ben sat, and pulled the baby out of her carrier. He started
clapping her hands together and singing a silly song. I felt the

scar across my stomach stretch tightly. I ran to the bathroom and reached the toilet just in time, heaving until my back ached.

Ben appeared in the doorway. "Are you okay?"

I stared at my breakfast, floating calmly on the surface of the toilet water.

That night when my boyfriend came home from work, he was drunk. I heard him at the door trying to make sense of how his key fit into the lock and what he was supposed to do next. I didn't try to help. The baby was already asleep in a small basket I bought for her at a baby store for people with too much money and no sense. The saleslady, who knew me from a different time, looked down at the baby and said, "He's gotten so big," because all babies look the same and all women with babies look the same. I bit through my tongue and nodded.

I sat on the couch with the baby in her basket and we watched a reality show, one about famous people pretending to suffer from fake addictions.

My boyfriend finally made his way into the apartment. "Woman, where are you? Goddamnit," he said when he realized I was not alone. "That kid is still here?"

He pulled me up from the couch and dragged me into the bedroom. I relaxed, made myself into meat for him. He threw me onto the bed and started unbuckling his belt. "Why are you always so damn quiet? It creeps me out."

I said nothing. He did not need my voice. He crawled onto the bed, spreading my legs, pulling my jeans down. He lay on top of me, his body so heavy I sank deeply into the mattress. He pressed his boozy lips against my neck, squeezing my breasts between his fingers, reshaping them. It hurt. I groaned. "Say something," he said. I closed my eyes and hoped the baby couldn't hear her father. He slapped me and my eyes watered; the bones in my forehead felt like they would splinter. I tuned my head slightly, offering him my face.

"Seriously, say something or I will lose it."

I opened my eyes. "Don't wake the baby. She had a long day."

He clasped my throat and squeezed harder and harder, leaving his mark. I held his gaze. I waited for him to punish me and when he did, it was perfect relief.

My husband called the next day. "If you felt like coming by with that baby, I wouldn't mind."

I looked for a long-sleeved shirt with a high neck but couldn't find one so I covered myself with a hooded jacket and too much makeup. I talked to the baby in the rearview mirror as we drove. Ben was waiting on the front porch and he came out to the car when we pulled up, carefully removed the baby from her car seat, opened my door for me. "Just like old times," he said, softly.

I gritted my teeth as I sat on the couch, one of the first nice things we ever bought.

Ben put the baby in the playpen that had been empty in the corner of our den for months. She began playing with the toys— plastic things that made noise. He sat next to me, pulled the hood of my jacket down. He slammed his fist into the coffee table. One of the books slid onto the floor. "I'm going to kill him."

I leaned into his shoulder, the warmth of it, and then I laid my head in his lap. "I'm really tired."

He pushed out a heavy burst of air, rubbed my arm softly. "You can rest here," he said, and so I did and he watched over me.

A few days later, the baby had a fever. She cried and cried, her face red with tiny, heated rage. I stripped her down to her diaper and stood with her near the open freezer while the air conditioner covered us in frigid air. She wouldn't stop crying. She missed her mother, I decided. My boyfriend came out of the bedroom, his boxers hanging off his narrow hips at an awkward angle. I held the baby closer, whispering sweetly.

He reached into the refrigerator for a beer and nodded toward us as he removed the cap. "What's wrong with her?"

"She has a fever."

He took a long swig of beer, wiped his lips. "Does she need a doctor or something?"

"I don't know yet." I began bouncing around as the baby calmed a bit. "We'll have to wait and see."

My boyfriend hopped onto the counter and sat, swinging his legs. "How do you know so much about babies?"

I rubbed the baby's back slowly. "We don't ask each other those kinds of questions."

He spit into the sink and took another sip of beer. "Suit yourself." When he grew bored, he wandered back to the bedroom. The baby stopped crying, her body trembling every few minutes as she hiccupped. I sat with her on the balcony because it was cool outside and the air was clean. I called Anna Lisa.

She answered after seven rings. "Is everything okay?"

I nodded even though she couldn't see me. "I thought you might want to know how the baby is doing."

She was silent for a moment, coughed. "Yeah, that'd be good."

The baby held on to my T-shirt, her tiny fingers curling around the cotton. I told her mother about the fever and how Ben and I played with her and took a long walk. I told Anna Lisa how the baby enjoyed bathing in the kitchen sink. I told her about the new outfits.

"Does she miss me?"

"Absolutely."

"Why the hell are you with him?"

"I'll call you next week."

I hung up and stared into the night sky, dark and heavy and still.

The baby was still fussy in the morning, wouldn't rest easy in my arms, sweaty and squirming. She barely slept. I barely slept. My boyfriend got mad because she kept making this sound, a high-pitched whimpering, and she wouldn't stop and it got on his nerves. I lay next to him, waiting for him to explode. He would. He did. I went slack and hoped he would beat me until my bones finally softened.

When he was done, he said, "There's something wrong with you."

Later, Ben called as the baby wailed lustily like an old sorrowful woman. I admired her for it. "I want to see your face," he said.

I smiled. "I want to see your face, too."

"That kid has one hell of a mouth on her."

I bounced the baby on my hip. "That she does."

In the bedroom, my boyfriend sprawled across the bed on his stomach wearing only a pair of jeans. I asked if he planned on going to work and he grunted something unintelligible. At Ben's house, I had to force myself to think of it like that, he was once again waiting in the driveway for us. He took the baby and jogged slowly toward the house. I leaned back as I watched him. He paused on the porch, waved. I nodded and closed my eyes.

Seven months ago, we were in a parking lot at a grocery store, the kind where everything is organic and artisanal and over-priced. For the first time in our marriage, we could afford to shop wherever we wanted. We bought lots of olives in those days because there was an olive bar at the fancy grocery store. The absurdity was irresistible. We made a lot of tapenades. We were adults. We had a boy, who shared his father's name. He was fourteen months old, still getting used to how his legs moved him, his chubby thighs rolling around each other with each awkward step. He always held his hands in front of him when he walked. We called him BZ or Baby Zombie and sometimes, a lot of the time, we gelled his hair so it stood on end. We took a hundred thousand pictures, the excesses of parents of only children, capturing how he curled his fingers when he neared us and how his nose wrinkled just before he laughed and his eyelashes, they were so long, you could see each one like some perfect extension of his beauty. Our parents thought the zombie nickname was crude. It was funny.

Ben and I were flirting as we put the groceries in the trunk. There was a bottle of wine, some organic merlot such-and-such, and a promise of what we were going to do after we drank that wine. I said we didn't need to wait and he said something about blindfolding the baby for the drive home and we laughed and leaned into each other over the cart to kiss, wet-tongue sloppy. Ben Jr. started smacking the handle of the grocery cart, shouting *da da da da da*. He wanted out so I lifted him, enjoying the weight of his body against the curves between my thumbs and forefingers. I kissed both of his cheeks and his forehead and his father rubbed the baby's back as I set our boy on the ground. I pulled his hand to my jeans and told him to hold on to me or he'd have to stay in the cart. He nodded and grinned, his dimples deep and winking as he hugged my leg. I looked at that boy and the man who helped me make him as we stood in the center of a perfect life. The heat of that joy could have burned us all.

A young guy walking some shitty little dog passed by. Ben Jr. loved dogs, called them *doshi*. We have no idea where that came from but it was his word so it became our word. *Doshi doshi doshi.* He shouted, "Doshi," and let go of me and when he let go, when I no longer felt that tug, I was so cold and hollow. There was nothing holding me to the ground. Ben Jr. started running and both Ben and I leapt after him but those tiny, chubby legs of his, when they wanted to, they moved real fast and we were still happy so it was hard to make sense of the urgency. Our son chased the *doshi*, his arms in front of him like he intended to make that dog undead. An eighty-four-year-old woman, Helen McGuigan, came barreling through the parking lot. She couldn't see my little boy over the hood of her 1974 Grand Prix, a real tank of a car. Ben and I screamed. Ben Jr. stopped and turned to look at us, was so startled by the pitch of our voices, he cried. The last thing my child did was cry because he was scared. He held his arms higher, the way he does, the way he did, when he wanted to be held. The curves between my thumbs and forefingers throbbed violently. When the car ran him over, I did not look away. I saw what happened to my boy's body. I saw everything, all of him, everywhere.

I don't allow myself to be around dogs anymore. I could kill them all, every last one of those dirty animals with their wagging tails and long hanging tongues. I cannot stand the stink of them.

Ben and I did not go to the funeral. After the viewing, after seeing the impossible size of that coffin, we had nothing left. Our families could not understand. During the funeral we sat on the floor of Ben's nursery, waiting for him to come home. We are still sitting there.

Ben called my name. He stood on the porch, handsome, his hair wild and curly, the baby strapped to his chest. I swallowed hard as I got out of the car. In the corner of the yard, I saw a red plastic bat. Acid burned my throat and before I could stop myself, I puked over the hedges lining the house. We used to trim them together. We'd wake up on Saturday mornings and say, "We are doing yard work today." We'd giggle because our fathers do yard work, raking their yards in sandals and knee-high socks. Ben rushed to me and rubbed my back. He said soft, soothing things. He led me into the house and gave me water. I drank but my lips remained parched.

As I leaned over the kitchen sink, my shirt rode up. My head was splitting so I forgot to pull the shirt down.

My husband rolled it up farther, hissing. My heart sank. I had no energy for pretending he couldn't see what was there. "What the fuck is this? Seriously, babe, what the fuck is this?" He pulled my shirt up around my shoulders and slowly turned me around. I couldn't look him in the eye. He traced an angry, spreading bruise along my rib cage, dark purple, almost black around the edges. I winced. "That's it," Ben said. "That really is it, Natasha." He unstrapped the baby from his chest and handed her to me. "Stay here."

"Don't," I said, grabbing his arm.

He shook his head and ran out of the house. He kicked the car door before he opened it, kept kicking the door until it caved. I've never seen him so angry. He pointed at me. "Don't you dare leave."

I watched as he sped away. I took the baby into our bedroom and lay on my side, holding the baby to my chest, inhaling her warm, milky breath. She finally stopped fussing and we fell asleep. When I woke up, Ben was sitting in the reading chair near the foot of the bed. I sat slowly and pulled my knees to my chest. There was a bruise on his chin and his knuckles were red raw like meat.

"Enough," he said. "You've broken yourself enough. You're coming home."

I pressed my forehead against my knees. My chest was empty. It was nice for someone to tell me what to do. Ben stood and took the baby, still asleep. He disappeared with her and was alone when he returned. He set a baby monitor on the end table and crawled into the bed next to me. It is hard to breathe in a house with no air but I tried. I stretched myself against him and when he started to undress me I let him. My desire for him was unabated. My tongue could not forget the taste of his skin, his mouth. Pale evening light filled the room, enough light for us to see each other plainly. He kissed the bruises along my collarbone, around my navel, the dark spreads of purple on my upper arms, my thighs, in the small of my back. It had been a long time since a man touched me gently—such luxury. I had almost forgotten. Ben held my face in his hands as he kissed me, and then I fell into him and I fell into us, his tongue in my mouth, his mouth on my breasts, his fingers between my thighs. He filled me in a way that let me know he was taking me back. I opened myself to let him. I kissed his red raw meat knuckles and his chin and wrapped my arms around him. I said, "Hold me to the ground."

It was late, crying from another room. I lay on my back, Ben's body half covering mine as he slept. I covered my chest with my hand, rubbed softly like that might move my heart back to its proper place. Still there was crying from another room. I tried to remember when I was. My mouth was dry and sorrow, my lips still parched, my eyes dry. Everything was dry. I ran my fingers through Ben's hair. The crying grew louder so I kissed my husband's head and slipped out of bed, tried to remember the geography of the room I had not slept in for months. My breasts ached, engorged with the milk of sweetly spoiled fruit. Ben's shirt lay on the floor and I pulled it on, then held my hand to the wall as I walked to the nursery. When I turned on the light, the baby rolled over and blinked. The room still smelled like my son. He was there even though he was not there. I could feel him in my fingers. I picked the baby up and cradled her along the length of my arm, the weight of her nearly tearing my heart out of me. We went outside for fresh air, sat on the patio Ben and I built ourselves, all brick, more yard work. I called Anna Lisa. She answered again after seven rings.

"I am leaving him," I said. "You should know that."

"I left my baby with you."

"You can't be serious. I can't be trusted with a child. This isn't legal."

"I know what happened to your son, saw on the news," Anna Lisa said. "It was not your fault."

"This is not the answer to whatever you or I have going on."

"I don't know anyone else who can help me."

"We can't stay here, especially not with her. We are leaving."

"Don't tell me where you're going," Anna Lisa said. She hung up.

The baby shifted in my arms. I traced her little lips with my finger. "What am I going to do with you?" I asked. She cooed and grabbed my finger, wouldn't let go, so we sat like that for a long time, her grip growing tighter and tighter. I thought she might break me, too. Damp circles spread across Ben's shirt. No matter what I did, my milk refused to dry. My body needed something to feed. When I went inside, Ben was holding his phone and car keys. His hair stood on end. He looked so young, like when we first met. We were freshmen in college and he chased me across a quad because he liked the pink streak in my hair. He said he always knew he would love a woman with a three-syllable name. I wasn't sure which Ben I was looking at and then he came to me and pressed his nose in my hair and told me I smelled like the night air.

"I thought you left."

"I thought you said I couldn't."

His face stretched into what has become his smile.

"We can't live in this house."

Ben nodded.

"We can't live in this city, nowhere near."

"I know."

I looked down at the baby. "She's coming with us. For now. Until her mom can take her. The baby won't fix what's wrong. I'm not crazy the way everyone thinks. I know who this baby is and who she isn't."

"You can say his name." Ben's eyes met mine. Our son had his eyes. There was a time when I wondered if I could stand to look at my husband for the rest of my life. "Say his name," Ben said.

I held my hands open and shook my head.

When Ben Jr. was born, we had been married for seven years. We were both only children. We were still young but our parents had resigned themselves to not having grandchildren and then this bright, beautiful boy found his way to all of us. After the accident, I called my mother to tell her what happened. I told her while sitting on the front porch because I couldn't be in the house, where there was no air. Ben sat next to me. We held the phone between our cheeks. My mother moaned when I explained to her that my son was a bloody stretch on the hot pavement of a parking lot, that he was driven out of his shoes, that he was lying somewhere, alone and cold.

I tried to stay in the morgue with Ben Jr. the day he died but it was against regulations. A stranger with cold hands kept saying, *we're so sorry but you have to leave.* Eventually, two police officers escorted us to the parking lot. I made a wild, messy scene. I'm proud of that. One of the officers said, "We don't want to have to take you into custody," and I shouted, "Are you fucking kidding me?" People walking into and out of the police station stared, pointed, shook their heads. The officer grabbed my elbow, pulled me close enough that I could smell coffee on his breath. He leaned closer, said, "I've got four of my own but you have to leave," and again I shouted, "Are you fucking kidding me?" My throat was raw. All of me was raw. I didn't give a damn. I would not leave my child alone. Finally, Ben snapped out of his trance and dragged me away. I fought him hard. When he finally got me in the car, he stood by my door. He pointed and said, "Stay, baby," then ran around to his side of the car. Sweat trickled down his face and neck. There were damp arcs of sweat around my neck and below my armpits. We were rotten, filthy with grief. He turned and looked at me. "You're stronger than I thought." I pressed my hand against the car window as we pulled away. I said, "You have no idea." Later, we drove back to the station, parked a few blocks away, and sat silently near the morgue window in the back until Ben Jr.'s body could be released to us in the morning.

Instead of saying something kind, instead of saying nothing when I told her my son was dead, my mother said, "How could you let this happen?" I started shaking and yelling at her but I made no sense, all *yerga ghala fraty ghuja*, crazy rage words. Ben took the phone. He said, "How dare you?" We stayed in the garage that night and the next night and the next night. The refrigerator where we store deer meat and High Life hummed loudly. We'd listen to it all night, pretending we were asleep, pretending sleep was possible. It was hot in there, smelled like motor oil and dirt and grass clippings. Ben kept his arms wrapped around me, never let me go.

We moved to a tent in the backyard until the neighbors complained. We cooked canned food on a small camp stove and drank wine and smoked, while we sat in lawn chairs until we were too tired to stay awake. Ben would say, "Talk to me," and I'd try but nothing would come out but dry air. I took a leave of absence from work but Ben kept going to the office, said he needed one thing to make sense. While he was gone, I sat in the parking lot of the fancy grocery store where we bought eight different kinds of olives. Sometimes an employee recognized me and brought me coffee, said, *we are so sorry.* I heard that phrase so often it started to sound like one word, *wearesosorry wesorry sosorry sosorry sosorry.*

I lost all the baby weight that lingered and more. Ben grew angry when I said I couldn't eat, said I had no right to ruin myself. One evening, he made my favorite pasta. When I refused to eat, he straddled me as I sat, and force-fed me. I couldn't keep the food down. Ben got so angry he threw the beautiful clay bowl holding his beautiful pasta onto the kitchen floor. He made a terrible mess. His hands clenched into tight fists and I wanted to feel his knuckles against the bone of my jaw. I threw myself into him. I said, "Hit me," but he wouldn't. I hit him and hit him and he didn't stop me. I said, "Hit me or I'm leaving." He refused so I left. I slept in my car near the railroad tracks where we used to take Ben Jr. when he couldn't sleep. My husband found me and told me to come home. I didn't go home.

At a bar I found a man who would hit me. It wasn't hard. I could smell the anger on him by looking at him. I was drinking Maker's, wearing nothing much, all bare tits and leg. He sat next to me and ordered me a drink even though I wasn't halfway through the one I had. He tapped my rings and said, "Where's your husband?" I slammed back what was left of my drink and the one he bought me. "Don't worry about it," I said. He talked and we drank for hours and when he said, "Let's go out back," I let him pull me along. The man pushed me against the wall and covered my mouth with his like he was trying to eat my face. He came up for air, said, "How do you like it, baby?" I grabbed him by his belt. He tried to kiss me again and I turned away. I said, "I want you to hurt me," so he did, over and over and over again. I stopped sleeping at home. Every time that man sank his fists into my body, I could breathe a little. I used one hurt to cover another. I became a fiercely tender bruise as he broke down my skin and muscle and bone and blood until I felt nothing but the way he used my body for a few perfect moments every day, moments I'd worry between my fingers until they were well worn away.

Ben grabbed me by my shoulders and shook me. "Say his name."

"Harder," I said.

The baby giggled. She grabbed his shirt and mine, like she was trying to pull us into each other. Ben stilled and looked down at the baby. He let go of me.

"Please."

I clasped the back of his neck and stood on the tips of my toes. I closed my eyes and saw each letter, the shape of our child's name. I tried to lose myself in my bruising. I put the baby in the playpen and walked to the nursery. Ben followed on my heels. I stood next to the crib, gripping the railing. Our child's favorite teddy bear was still propped up in one corner. The sleeve of a small T-shirt peeked out from beneath the pillow. And then I couldn't stand anymore. I fell to my knees, gasping.

"Hit me," I said. I begged. I grabbed his hand and curled his fingers into a fist and held his fist to my breastbone. I said, "Please, if you love me, hit me." My voice was so ugly and hungered. If Ben would break the broken places in me a little more, if he would break whatever was left of me beneath my skin, I could finally break all the way down.

Ben knelt beside me, uncurling his fingers. "I do love you." He wrapped his arms around me as I reached for air. He was so gentle, so terrible.

"My God, please do it, Ben. Please." A ringing in my ears made it hard to concentrate on anything but the bitter ache in my chest.

He pulled his arm back and I watched his fingers tighten back into a fist and I cried out but then he relaxed. "No," he said. "I will not."

I held on to that crib, shaking it, slamming it into the wall until the bolts loosened, until the crib that held our child broke all the way down, too. The B-E-N hanging on the wall above the crib fell to the floor. My arms grew tired and I let go of the broken railing in my hands. Sweat pooled in the small of my back. I thought about shoving everything in that room into my mouth, thought if I tried hard enough, I could make room. Ben leaned forward, pressing his forehead against the ground.

"I miss him as much as I love you. I love you as much as I miss him," I said. I collapsed against him and somehow, we fell asleep like that, breaking against each other.

The next morning, we took everything from the nursery and put it in the backyard on our brick patio with the uneven edges. We burned all of it until it was nothing. The neighbors stared from behind parted curtains. They weren't going to be our neighbors for much longer. I raised my middle finger high in the air. We stood

and watched everything melt into a black, hardened mass—toys
and sheets and T-shirts and very small shoes and pacifiers, all of it.
When the fire finally died, our skin was coated with a thin layer of
soot. The air reeked of the scorched memory of things that should
not be burned. The baby slept and slept and slept.

We stumbled inside and I tore at Ben's clothes, kissing him
hard with the bone of my face, the whites of my teeth, wanting
to feel something different even as my body ached sharply, everywhere. Ben folded me over the dining room table, his hand pressed
against the back of my head as he entered me. He breathed hotly
onto my neck. What we did, the way we sounded, was untamed.

After, I said, "Please get me away from here," and Ben said,
"Say our child's name." I held his face and wiped away some of
the soot beneath his eyes with my thumbs.

In a few weeks, we would hand the keys to our house to a real-
tor who would eventually sell the house and wire the money to a
bank account. We would tell Anna Lisa she would always know
where we are. She would tell us she would not follow. We would
pack what we needed in our car. We would put the baby in the
backseat, listening to her babble happily. We would look back at
that girl child, her features growing more and more determined
with each passing day, and say *this is crazy, this is wrong, this is right,
this is wrong*. We would drive north and west and north and west
until we reached an ocean and rocky shores and green everywhere
and a big, big sky to hold the baby up to while she laughed.

Before that, though, I kissed Ben, softer, softer. His curls spilled
through my fingers. We tasted like the whitest heat of a fire closest to the ground where most things burn. I said Ben Jr.'s name
into his mouth, memorized the charred taste of it.

# Bad Priest

Father Mickey—Father Michael Patrick Minty, who went by Mickey to distance himself from the expectations of his mother—was having an affair with a girl named Rebekah. Rebekah was a perfume girl in a department store who still lived with her parents. She was not Catholic. Father Mickey's mother, Nora Minty, a devout Catholic, named her son Michael after the archangel Michael because she was convinced, from the moment she laid eyes on her baby boy, that he would be a warrior for the faith. He was named Patrick for his father, may he rest in peace, who left Nora when Mickey was four, and died three months later from an excess of joy, Patrick Minty's friends would later say, because he died in his studio apartment watching a baseball game with a six-pack of beer in his lap.

While his friends were told bedtime stories, Mickey Minty was nurtured with dark stories about the constant battle for salvation and how David beat Goliath and how Sodom and Gomorrah fell. Over and over, Nora would recite the Book of Daniel, Chapter Twelve, Verse One—*"But at that time shall Michael rise up, the great prince, who standeth for the children of thy people."* He heard the verse so often that the words made him sick to his stomach. That is how, he later decided, the lining of his stomach began to give way to acid and ulcers.

No one was more surprised than Michael Patrick Minty when he entered the seminary and then the priesthood. It was a simple life, he told himself. He didn't have to think that much. He would never have to support anyone. Mickey Minty wasn't incapable of handling responsibility, but given his mother's expectations, he simply didn't have the energy for anything more. There were his parishioners, but at the end of the day, he could lock himself in the rectory, alone, without having to worry about anyone but himself. There was comfort in that, and that comfort made the sacrifices of the priesthood something he could endure.

Mickey Minty did not like to listen to strangers. He did not like to listen to anyone at all. The sounds of other voices, high-pitched and flighty or low and timid or any other variation, they all made him edgy and nauseated. There were days when he heard so many words detailing so many sins and sorrows and hopes and wants and needs that hot sprays of acid burned the back of his throat while he sat, hidden in the confessional, shifting his weight uncomfortably during particularly long excavations of human failing. Having to care, to soothe, to dispense was just too much. Worse yet was the way they looked to him for answers, eagerly listened to his counsel, believed, and dutifully carried out penance. What he hated was the way his parishioners had faith—faith that he would show them the way and faith that he would fight for their faith and faith that there was meaning in all this, and faith that there was something greater than themselves. Mickey Minty had very little faith so he lied to his parishioners. He lied so extravagantly that even though he was not a believer, he feared for his mortal soul.

Rebekah had very little interest in church or faith but she did have a great deal of interest in Mickey Minty, whom she met in the crowded waiting room of the county hospital, where she was waiting for a friend getting stitches. The friend, Ava, had put her fist through a glass door in a dramatic gesture meant to prevent her boyfriend from walking out on her. The gesture had failed spectacularly. Rebekah was waiting and Mickey Minty was sitting next to her wearing a light gray tracksuit while he waited to hear news about an elderly parishioner who had been taken gravely ill. Mickey was looking at Rebekah and listening as she told him how she had just broken up with her boyfriend César, who had just gotten out of rehab and was more annoying than ever with his newfound sobriety and the fervor of twelve steps and the belief in a higher power. She was not sure there was a higher power, she added, leaning in close, resting a perfectly manicured hand on Mickey's knee as she crossed her legs. He tapped her knuckles with his fingers. "We have something in common," he said.

Rebekah liked to talk to strangers, liked to pour her heart out, share the intimate and mundane details of her life with anyone who would listen. She was exactly the kind of parishioner who would get his stomach acids going but Father Minty liked studying her lower lip, full and pouty, slick with gloss. Her mouth, he thought, was perfectly designed for things he shouldn't but often did contemplate. Her mouth was wide and her tongue seemed especially long, coming to a perfect point he would enjoy nipping between his teeth. His faith was temporarily renewed. Mickey also didn't mind Rebekah's cleavage, ample and well displayed beneath the tightly stretched silk of a summer dress. He looked up at the fluorescent lights, shaking his head, then returned his attention to Rebekah's mouth. And not for nothing, she smelled sublime. Most of the time, he was around old people who smelled of ointments and cheap eau de toilette so he was particularly appreciative of the effort Rebekah put into smelling so damn good. Despite her incessant chatter, Mickey knew instantly that he would be more than happy to bend his vows on her behalf.

That night in the emergency room, Mickey Minty listened to Rebekah because she was wearing a short, tight dress and bright red lipstick and her bra straps were showing. She was the kind of girl his mother warned him about when he was a teenager. She was the kind of girl who would have never paid him any mind. He now decided that the way she was dressed was irrefutable evidence that she was the kind of girl who needed saving. This is what he told himself, as he told Rebekah that he was a priest. This is what he told himself, when he invited her for a tour of his church—a tour she took the following weekend, on a Saturday after Mickey Minty performed the O'Kelly wedding and wilting daisies were still hanging on the edges of the pews.

The first time they fucked, they were in the church, and it was late—two in the morning. Moonlight shone through the stained glass and Rebekah laughed and laughed because she liked the way her voice echoed beneath the vaulted ceilings. Rebekah wasn't his first indiscretion, but he was greedy with her. The experience was largely unmemorable for Rebekah, though she remembered that his fingers smelled like incense and his breath tasted like mint. And she remembered staring at two larger-than-life crucifixes, the one hanging behind the altar and the one draped around his neck collaring him to his faithful service, and how they moved into and out of her sight with each of Mickey Minty's vigorous thrusts.

A few nights later, Rebekah showed up at the rectory. Two in the morning, again, and she let herself in. She found Mickey Minty on the second floor, sitting on the edge of a narrow bed in a sparsely decorated room. He was holding a rosary and he was whispering. His eyes were open, but he hardly looked up as she entered the room. Rebekah slipped out of her raincoat, and she sat next to Mickey. She rested a cold hand on the back of his neck, sliding her fingers up through his hair, short, neatly kept. "You shouldn't have come here," Mickey said. Rebekah quickly slipped out of her clothes and lay on her back, draping one arm over her head. The sheets were clean but rough, the mattress thin but firm. She pulled one of Mickey's hands between her thighs. He fingered the rosary beads with one hand and Rebekah with the other. Later, when Mickey was sleeping, his rosary beads still clutched in his hand, Rebekah watched him for as long as she dared, then left before the rest of the church staff arrived for their morning duties.

Rebekah thrived on hopeless relationships. Mickey was the most recent in a long line of inappropriate men who always left Rebekah intrigued but vaguely unsatisfied. What she liked about Mickey Minty was just how extremely inappropriate he was. She would never be able to introduce him to anyone she knew. He wouldn't make grand gestures or treat her kindly. He wasn't that kind of man, with or without the collar. And this heady combination of futility compelled Rebekah to fall madly, desperately in love with Mickey Minty. She gave very little thought to his spiritual obligations. They were minor details and if there was guilt to be had on the subject, she left that to Mickey, who did, after all, deal in such things.

Mickey had a flock to tend. Rebekah took to attending Mass—sitting in the front row and smiling, demurely, as he delivered stern sermons on adhering to Catholic doctrine while the world fell apart. He offered her the body, the blood of Christ, letting his fingers touch the moist tip of her tongue after placing the Communion wafer between her slightly parted lips. After Mass, after the cookies and punch in the atrium, after he had done the home visits to the sick and shut in, Mickey would take Rebekah out to dinner several towns over. They would sit in the back of the restaurant, on the same side of the booth. Mickey would remove his collar and Rebekah would rest her head against his shoulder, unzip his pants beneath the table, slide her hand into the crease, lightly stroking him as the waiter took their order.

She always ordered French onion soup and the roasted chicken. Mickey always ordered the porterhouse steak, rare, mushrooms on the side, and a glass of red wine. When they were done eating, they would sneak into the men's bathroom. They would go into the last stall. Mickey would turn Rebekah around so he didn't have to look at her. He would pull her skirt up, slide his pants down, and fuck her, hard. He would grunt. He would pray under his breath. In his mind he would call her filthy names, then he would castigate himself for his indiscretion. Although he had little faith, he did have shame. When he was done, he would kiss Rebekah on her shoulder and inhale deeply, trying to identify the fragrance she had chosen for the day, always something different, a benefit of her job. He would send her back to their table and then try to clean himself with thin paper towels and foamy dollops of industrial soap.

On the nights when Rebekah knew she couldn't risk sneaking into the rectory, she would call Mickey on the phone. She would talk about her job and her family and how César was still hanging around, trying to make amends. She would ask Mickey if that made him jealous and answer the question for herself. She would talk about her friends and the clubs where they partied and how she wished Mickey could meet the people who mattered. Mickey wouldn't say much, though he would wince as his stomach churned, as he listened to Rebekah's sins and sorrows and hopes and wants and needs. He would endure her confessions as his penance. He prided himself on his ability to endure. He would listen and reach into the drawer in his nightstand, fumbling for a bottle of antacid tablets. He would chew four or five and wash the chalky crumbs down with a sip of water. He would endure. Then he would ask her what she was wearing, and he would stare at the small wooden crucifix on the wall while Rebekah nurtured him with the filthy details of what she would do to him the next time they were together.

Mickey visited his mother every Monday for dinner and a few hours of television, contemplation, her complaining, and, inevitably, prayer. After he started seeing Rebekah, Nora Minty became suspicious. She loved her son but she was not blind to his failings, his weakness. "There's something different about you," she said one Monday evening, eight months after Mickey and Rebekah had first consummated their affair. Nora said this as she carefully sliced a rare roast and lifted a dense, bloody piece of meat onto his plate. Mickey recoiled, gritted his teeth. He willed himself to smile kindly at his mother. He gripped his silverware until his fingers ached and carefully focused on the business of eating the slaughtered calf on the sacrificial altar of his plate. He listened as his mother railed against Satan and weakness and his eternal fight for the faith and the danger of temptation. Mickey willed the muscles in his throat to pull each carefully cut piece of meat into his stomach. He paused only to take sips of wine, cheap, red. He paused often. By the end of the meal, his stomach ached. His head was spinning and his cheeks were flushed. His mother was yet another indignity he was forced to endure.

"There's nothing different about me," he finally said, when they were settled in the family room eating pound cake as the television flickered silently.

Nora sucked her teeth, reached for her Bible sitting on the end table. "We should pray," she said.

Mickey shook his head. "All I do is pray. Let's just enjoy the evening."

Nora's Bible was well worn, and opened easily to her favorite passages. She held it open on her lap. "We'll pray. Corinthians, Chapter Ten, Verse Thirteen."

Mickey swallowed a dry lump of pound cake. "You'll have to refresh my memory."

Nora sighed, then cleared her throat. "No temptation has overtaken you that is not common to man. God is faithful, and he will not let you be tempted beyond your ability, but with the temptation he will also provide the way of escape, that you may be able to endure it."

"Endure, indeed. Thank you, Mother."

Nora reached over, gently patting Mickey's hand, then holding her Bible in the air. "This has all the answers."

He slid lower in his chair, rubbed his temples, reached for the remote, and changed the channel. They sat in silence for the rest of the evening. Later, as he made his goodbyes, his mother shook her head, her lips pursed so tightly they had gone white. Then she grabbed hold of her son, held him tight, so tightly that he gasped. "God is faithful, and he will not let you be tempted beyond your ability," she whispered in his ear, her hot breath sending new sprays of acid into his throat.

When he got back to the rectory, Mickey called Rebekah. His hands were sweaty and he could barely grip the receiver. "Get over here," he said, not unkindly. Rebekah was at a bar a few blocks from the rectory when Mickey called. He didn't call often, leaving the responsibility of communication to her. She answered quickly, said nothing in response because she did not need to say anything. She was drinking with her girlfriends Angel and Sarah, who wanted to know, in explicit detail, who had called and where Rebekah was headed at that time of the night. She remained coy, quickly finished her beer, reapplied a fresh coat of lipstick, and hurried to the rectory, her heels echoing against the pavement. She found Mickey kneeling next to his bed and she smiled when he looked up at her. Under different circumstances, in that moment, Rebekah would tell Mickey she loved him terribly.

Instead, Rebekah stood next to her priest, dragging her long fingernails across the back of his neck the way he liked.

"I'm a bad man," Mickey said, holding her gaze.

Rebekah slid between Mickey and the bed. She pulled her skirt up, her panties down. She pulled Mickey's mouth toward her. "I know," she replied.

# Open Marriage

We are having a heated debate about whether or not yogurt can expire when my husband suggests we stay together but see other people. He says open marriage intrigues him, that he couldn't be happier but that he read this article online. I tell him yogurt cannot expire because it is filled with bacteria. I do not know if this is true but I have seen commercials about yogurt that mention things like bacteria and the word *probiotic* so I feel I have a sufficient command of the topic. I give him a look. I say he's welcome to try to find other women to sleep with but that I'm fine and his face falls because he thinks I am playing a trick on him. I'm not. He has no game, none at all. If I hadn't taken matters in hand, we would still be sitting on his couch in his bachelor apartment, his arm snaking around my shoulders after every yawn. I'm not worried. He's the kind of man who gets ideas but is largely unable to follow through on those ideas. He shoves his hands into his jeans. This is something he does often, wearing right through the pockets of most of his pants. He leans against the kitchen counter. He says he wants cultivating an open marriage to be something we do together. I politely decline once more. I say I'm not inclined to open my half of the marriage, which only confuses him further because I'm quick-tempered and what he calls feisty, which only means I talk back to him and give him road head once in a while and I'm the first woman who has ever done that in his limited experience so it is still something of a novelty, still something that requires terminology. I take a bite of the yogurt that started our scientific debate. It expired more than two months ago but appears edible. When I dip my spoon into the plastic container, the yogurt gives way easily. It tastes sour. My husband's face is red and sweat beads on his upper lip. He asks if I would seriously be fine with him having no-strings-attached sex with another woman and I say, yes, baby, of course. He tells me I'm amazing in bed, that it's not about being unsatisfied, and I say, yes, baby, of course. I rock his world on the regular and we both know it. He can barely string three words together after we make love. He just lies there, trying to catch his breath, muttering, *goddamn*, over and over. I say good luck and be safe and don't you break my heart, baby, don't you break my heart. His eyes widen. I eat the entire container of yogurt, even going so far as to scrape the sides of the container until it is clean. I vocalize my appreciation for the expired yogurt and do a lot of elaborate spoon licking. I hold my husband's gaze the entire time. He was a virgin when we married. He looks away first.

# A Pat

saw a man eating alone in one of those hard plastic booths.
He opened the paper wrapping for his burrito and carefully
smoothed it into a perfect square. The whole scene broke my
heart. He squeezed a small dollop of sauce in one corner from an
orange foil packet and before every bite of his burrito he dipped
the open end into the sauce. He ate slowly.

I had to keep him company. When I entered the restaurant, the
air was thick with the stink of cheap meat and steam and hand
sanitizer. Sweat was on my neck, and down my back, and even
between my thighs. I slid into the empty bench across from the
man eating alone. He looked how you might expect, a messy,
graying beard, his head covered by a wool skullcap. His T-shirt was
dirty and his jeans were torn. He was handsome. He looked up. I
introduced myself because my mother once said every conversation
with a stranger should begin with your name. He stared at me, then

wiped his mouth with his hand and stretched his arm across the
table. The palm of his hand was callused and his knuckles were
red with arthritis. He held my hand. He talked with his mouth
full, introduced himself. His name had a lot of vowels, sounded
made up. I asked him if he'd like to come to my house for a proper
meal. He shrugged. We walked the three miles back to my place.
Sometimes cars honked at us. He walked on the outside, had real
nice manners in his own way.

We sat at my small kitchen table, didn't talk much, but we
ate homemade leftovers and drank red wine. Later we retired to
the living room and drank more wine and still didn't talk much.
I held his hands in mine, held them for as long as he let me. He
nodded toward my bathroom, asked if he could shower. I showed
him where clean towels were, soap. He didn't take long and when
he was done, he stood in my hallway. I quickly finished my wine
and went to him. I lay on my back and let him cover me. He said,
"Thank you," and smiled and left.

When I started grade school, my mother walked me on the first
day. We stood, together, at the bottom of the large brick staircase
leading into the school. She held my hand. She said, "Let me have
a look at you," then licked her thumb and used it to tame my
eyebrows. She straightened the hem of my jumper. She told me
to stand still. I smelled her perfume and hoped the smell of her
would stay with me all day. She said, "You make friends with the
ugliest kids in your class and you make friends with the loneliest
kids in your class, the ones off by themselves. They will be the
best friends you've ever had and they'll make you feel better about
yourself." With a pat on the head, she pushed me.

# Best Features

Milly is fat and ugly but she gives good head so she rarely sleeps alone, which is not to say she's not lonely. Milly is not, in fact, ugly, but she might as well be. She has a pretty face, which is the same thing as ugly when a woman is fat. In the complex calculus between men and women, Milly understands that fat is always ugly and that ugly and skinny makes a woman eminently more desirable than fat and any combination such as beautiful, charming, intelligent, or kind. Milly is all those things. She knows it doesn't matter. The truth of things makes Milly angry but she is quiet about it, her anger. She keeps it to herself, knows it sits at the bottom of her chest growing and growing, but there's not much she can do about it. She knows how difficult it is to change the world. She used to try, to change the world, but she learned better.

Jack is a troubled man. He has done time in county lockup, not hard time, but enough time where he has learned things about how to be the best kind of bad man. Jack is lonely and angry. The world is against him and he's smart enough to know it. Jack is very self-aware. On their first date, which involved a very long drive from the country to the city, Jack told Milly about all his troubles. He talked about loneliness and bad friends and being stuck in a small town. He talked about not having any options and not knowing how to do anything with his dreams. Milly listened and listened and then asked, "What do you have to offer a woman?" Jack rolled down the window, lit a cigarette, inhaled deeply, sighed. "Not a damn thing," he said. Milly looked at him, appreciated the awkwardness and sincerity of his honesty. She took in his pretty gray eyes and thin red lips. She thought, *I might love this man more than he deserves.*

Jack can't drive because he doesn't like knowing the damage he could do behind the wheel of a car. He walks everywhere. His thighs are full of muscles that flex with every step. He is proud of his thighs. He knows they are one of his best features. He knows that having best features is the only thing he gets by on. Jack lives nine miles from Milly's apartment. Every day at four in the afternoon, he starts walking to her place so he will arrive just as she is getting home from work. When Milly lets him in, he immediately takes a shower in her guest bathroom. She has told him he is welcome to use her bathroom but he says, "I am a guest in your home," with real formality. He uses a fresh towel each time. This drives Milly crazy. She leaves them hanging on the towel rack. She doesn't care if they reek of mildew and mold. She hates doing a man's laundry. After he showers, Jack likes to walk around her apartment with his towel tied around his waist like he belongs there. Sometimes he'll stop and flex and pose and preen. Milly pretends to find this charming.

She hates the cliché of it but Milly loves to cook and she is very good at it. The first time she cooked for him Jack said it made sense that a girl like her could cook so well. For a moment, Milly couldn't breathe as her anger flew out of her chest and into her mouth. She ran her tongue over it, hard and bitter, then swallowed it again. Milly makes everything from scratch using natural ingredients, and Jack, accustomed to canned goods and frozen meals, takes real pleasure in eating Milly's food. He asks her detailed questions about how she has prepared her lasagna or chicken cacciatore or paella. He enjoys the sound of her voice, the warmth in it. Jack sits at the head of Milly's table as if he belongs there, too. When he is eating he is not a guest. He is a king. He lets her serve him and always salts his food before tasting it. Milly does not pretend to find this charming. When he does this, she rolls her eyes and comforts herself with the knowledge that his blood pressure cannot be good.

They slept together the night they met after several hours sitting feet apart on her couch, pretending to be absorbed in a popular romantic comedy they had both seen several times. Milly tapped her fingers nervously against the arm of the leather couch, the sound echoing softly through the room. Her apartment has wood floors. Sound carries. Jack inched closer and closer as the night progressed, finally stretching his arms out and moving in to pull her toward him. He said, "I don't normally go for girls like you but big girls try harder," and Milly couldn't help letting some of her anger trickle out. She said, "Don't do me any fucking favors," and Jack turned bright red. "I meant that as a compliment," he stammered. Milly decided she hated him and that turned her on so she said, "Let's get on with it then."

In her bedroom, Milly quickly undressed and slid beneath the sheets, waiting. Her stomach hurt. It always did the first time she slept with a man. She hated knowing how he would look at her body and she hated what he would think but she knew that girls like her had little choice but to put out so that's what she did. She put out whether she wanted to or not. She barely remembered what it felt like to truly want a man. She rarely slept alone. Jack took his time undressing as he took in the spare décor. Milly saw little point in spending much time making a room pretty if most of her time in that room was spent with her eyes closed. "I like this," he said. "I don't care," Milly replied. He was a hairy man, his body covered in a thick mat of dark hair. Later, when he fell asleep as he lay on top of her, the whorls of hair on his chest would tickle her uncomfortably and she would say nothing. She would say nothing, but her anger, just a bit of it, would trickle from between her lips, down her neck, resting at the base of her throat. It burned.

Milly had ample breasts and they were soft and always smelled good. She knew they were her best feature and Jack enjoyed them thoroughly. He couldn't stop talking about their dimensions as he squeezed and licked and nibbled and sucked. "I'm going to come all over your tits," he said. Milly lay beneath him, one arm over her head, and patted his shoulder. Men were all the same. She hated knowing that. When he had drawn enough amusement from her décolletage, Jack wasted no more time. Her forced her thighs apart with his and started fucking her. He stared at the spot on the wall just above her headboard and then he stared into her eyes, which made her uncomfortable so Milly put on a good show, bouncing in rhythm enthusiastically, making the appropriate noises, feigning ecstasy. She told Jack how big he felt inside her and took the Lord's name in vain and demonstrated her flexibility by resting her calves against his narrow shoulders. Jack moaned loudly, made comments about how fucking good she felt, how tight. He told her she was a good girl. He said her pussy felt amazing. She didn't care if he was telling the truth. Milly felt nothing but she was very good at making men think otherwise. Sometimes, she nearly convinced herself.

# Bone Density

Winter is more a state of being than a season, in this place. It takes hold for six or seven dark, cruel months. The cold becomes familiar. There is a silence when it snows. Tonight, we sit, together, but alone with our work. We can see outside, to the street where now and again a car creeps through inches of the white stuff, its sounds muffled by a fresh blanket of powder. The fire is waning but we are too lazy, not intrepid enough to brave the elements and gather more wood from the shed in the back. We sit, not speaking to each other, filling the quiet around us. Every hour or so, I slide my feet into wool slippers, pull my sweater around me, and smoke a cigarette by the back patio door, open only an inch or two. Snow has been falling for several hours and the absence of sound as fresh flakes fall to the ground is seductive. I feel slight pangs of guilt as I ash my cigarette, the dark flakes damaging the winter portrait, and I can hear his heavy sighs. He disapproves. He worries because he reads about the hazards of smoking and is particularly concerned that smoking decreases bone density. He likes me the way I am, doesn't want to see me become less of a woman, he says.

Our relationship is like this—David travels three or four days out of every week of every month of every year. He's a professor of mechanical and biomedical engineering at the local university. He is somewhat renowned in his field. This is what I'm told by his adoring colleagues and students at boring cocktail parties where I play the part of devoted wife. They always marvel at what it must be like to be married to the great Dr. David Foster III. They imagine, I think, that our nights are filled with romantic whisperings about fluid dynamics and heat transfer or the power of biomechanical joints. They forget that I am a writer and maintain only a cursory understanding of and interest in David's work—just enough to assure him that my love is true. In exchange he maintains the same level of understanding about my writing and carefully pores over any story I place before him. He is deliberate in how he reads my work. He leans forward, slides his glasses up his nose, and clears his throat as if that might somehow help him clear his mind and gain greater insight into my words.

Our relationship is like this—a terrible cliché. He is that professor who has torrid but discreet affairs with research assistants and students and strangers he meets in hotel bars. He knows I know. I know he knows I know. It's an interesting equation. But we pretend that we're both faithful and true. The lie suits us and I refuse to play the part of the dissatisfied, jealous wife. I'm not dissatisfied. I know who I married. And I have secrets of my own. There's a poet, Bennett, who lives in a cabin on the other side of town. He has no telephone, lives nearly off the grid. He is

completely different from David—dark, unhappy, brooding. He
is enamored with the idea of himself as a tortured poet in search
of his own Walden Pond. Bennett's self-involvement is one of his
most attractive qualities.

Bennett is not romantic and we don't delude ourselves about
the state of our affair. He is, however, intense and always leaves
me sore in uncomfortable places. When David is out of town, and
only when David is out of town, I sneak away to Bennett's place.
The cabin is small, spare, but clean. It is a home. He heats it with
an antique wood-burning stove. He doesn't want any distractions
when he's writing, he tells me, so he doesn't bother with most
modern conveniences, save for a stereo to play music. His focus
can be so singular it frightens me. When he gets an idea in his
head, nothing else matters. I don't matter. That turns me on, too.
Sometimes I watch him, hunched over a small wooden desk, writing furiously with a lead pencil and I know he has forgotten that
I am on his bed, naked, the flat sheet bunched under my armpits.

There is little ceremony between us. Bennett takes me into
his arms or shoves me against the wall, knocking a picture loose,
the instant I open his door and call his name. He's like a teenager, groping at me awkwardly, pulling my clothes off, sliding his
fingers between my thighs. "You're wet," he'll grunt, as if he's
surprised, each time, that he continues to excite me. We fuck on
his narrow twin bed. The coarse sheets make my skin raw. I grip
the headboard with one hand and hold the wall with the other, my
eyes closed. Bennett buries his head in my shoulder. Eye contact
bothers him—he never wants to reveal too much of himself. I
love his body and enjoy marking him with my fingernails, leaving the skin of his back angry and broken. His arms are strong,
deeply tanned even in the dead of winter, and tightly woven with

sinewy muscles from years of chopping wood and climbing rocks. His thighs are thick from snowshoeing and hiking. He has the look of a man who uses his body more than he uses his mind. It is a contradiction. Looks are deceiving.

With my legs wrapped around Bennett's waist, my body filled (my lover is longer than my husband), I think of David, who is almost delicate in comparison. My husband is soft where Bennett is rough, handsome where Bennett is not.

After he comes, in a loud, ugly display that always scares me the way I like, my lover and I lie next to each other smoking. We use a saucer as an ashtray, leaving it balancing precariously between us. Bennett is not remotely concerned with the density of my bones. He never asks me why I don't come. That I return time and again seems to be enough for him, as it is for me. I like the gnawing dissatisfaction I carry home. I will rest my head on Bennett's chest and listen to him talk about his poetry; sometimes he reads to me or we listen to old bluegrass records. I tell him what's going on in the world beyond the walls of his cabin. I allow myself to drown in the way he smells, natural and sweaty, and his contradictions. When he falls asleep, I tuck a quilt around him, wrap myself in the necessary layers to brave the outdoors, and I leave. He never asks when I'll be back. He knows he will see me again or he doesn't care, which also turns me on.

Tonight, David is home and Bennett is wherever he is. After a last cigarette, I return to the family room and smile at David, his face shadowed by the dim glow of his laptop monitor. I snap the computer shut and sit on his lap, tracing his ear with my finger. "It's time for bed," I say. He kisses the left corner of my mouth, then slides his hands, smooth like alabaster, save for a small callus where he holds his pen, beneath my T-shirt. I shiver, pulling his

hands upward to my breasts. I remove his glasses, kiss his forehead, slide my lips along the length of his nose, and then we're
kissing, our breath warm with tobacco, coffee, hot pepper from
dinner. After eleven years, David knows my body well. While
we make love, I think of Bennett. With David, I allow myself to
come, extravagantly.

I spend our days apart imagining what kind of lover David
must be like with his other women. Is he as insatiable with
them as he is with me? I imagine shiny, nubile girls, their bodies shaved elaborately; breasts round, high, perky; calf muscles
taut. They have their parts to play in the cliché. I imagine
them sitting coyly, in his cluttered office, calling him Doctor,
perched on the edge of his desk. I imagine them playing the
part of ingenue, all plaid skirts, white shirts, thighs spread
wide, revealing pristine white panties, moist all the way to the
edges. It turns me on, to think of him and these tarts, tangled
in rough, impersonal hotel sheets, making a mess of themselves,
and a mess of our marriage. I think of these girls when he's
fucking me and telling me that I'm a hot lay and his hair is
damp, clinging to the edges of his face, and in his eyes I can see
that he does love me. I think of them when he's telling me how
special I am to him. I start to wonder if perhaps, for him, the
word has a different definition.

In the morning, we are in bed, David's heavy arm draped across
my body. He is very possessive when he sleeps, likes to keep me
close, he tells me. It is cold, and from our bedroom window I can
see that it is still snowing. Before winter's end, more than 350
inches will fall. I extract myself from his embrace and go to the
kitchen to start coffee. When I return he is sitting up, channel
surfing, looking more like a young man than someone in his late

thirties. His chest, bare, is covered in goose bumps. Our relationship is like this—I need these moments to remember why I love
him even when I hate him. David grins at me, takes the proffered
coffee. He nods toward the window. "We should go for a walk,"
he says. I shrug. I am not one for the outdoors, but I can make
these small sacrifices.

Outside, the trees are bare and skeletal. He holds my hand, and
I follow in the large footsteps he makes with his boots. "I want to
show you something," he says. We head into the thicket of trees
behind our home and after fifteen minutes, come upon a small
creek, the water still inexplicably running over frozen stones.

He wipes a few snowflakes from my scarf, tightens my jacket
around me. "Don't you love this place?"

I lean against a thick tree trunk and bite my lower lip. David
pulls his camera from his coat pocket. "Don't move," he says.

I glare into the camera. He knows I hate having my picture
taken, and yet he persists. This is what our relationship is like,
the not really knowing one another. He makes a silly face and I
finally crack a smile. David furiously presses the shutter release
to capture the moment. His earnestness makes me smile wider,
and soon I am playing it up for the camera. He pauses, looks at me
carefully. Then he closes the distance between us and he is pressing me against the tree, studying my face carefully. I clasp my
hand around his neck, trying to keep a small separation between
us. I look away. We ignore the camera as it drops into a soft pile
of snow. The branches above me are beautiful, encased in snow
and ice.

Later, I am in our bathroom, drying my hair. David stands
behind me, wrapping his arms around my waist. We watch each
other in the mirror. "I have to go out of town tomorrow," he

says. "It's a last-minute thing. I'm taking the place of a guy in my department at a very important conference. Can't be avoided."

I roll my eyes at David in the mirror and throw the hair dryer onto the bathroom counter. It clatters loudly and I bite my lower lip. I don't want David to think he gets under my skin. "Very important?"

David kisses my right shoulder. "You know how it is."

I smile tightly. The day after David leaves, I will pay Bennett a visit. I will bring him a new record I found at the Salvation Army. I will miss my husband.

The winters here are long, but they are even longer when you spend them alone. There's Bennett, but I know where I stand with him. Such clarity is uncomfortable. After a big snowfall, the white flakes turn to gray sludge, then dark with sand and salt. A fresh layer of ice covers the streets and sidewalks. I long to wear shoes instead of the clunky boots necessary to navigate the outdoors. David is gone for eight days on his *very important* business. I fill the days with my work, which takes a darker turn. It is hard to write about happy things when you can never escape the kind of cold that sinks into your bones and stays there. I am in Siberia, I decide. I am comforted by thoughts of exile, cold solace, meditation, and inspiration born of emotional deprivation. It is all very dramatic.

My evenings are filled with dinner with friends, bad television movies, and planning dream vacations in sunnier climes. David dutifully calls me three times a day, as regular as three square meals. Our conversations are brief during the day, longer at night. He loves to hear me come, he tells me. I love to give him a show. I tell him all the dirty things I am doing to myself in excruciating detail. He makes me beg, over the phone, and I can hear his satisfaction when I do. He revels in the knowledge that no matter the distance, he has a hold over me. The specificity of these conversations and the ways I am willing to debase myself are two of the reasons he enjoys being married to a writer. He often tells me I have a knack for details. I wonder if he's alone during these calls, or if his hand is running through a lover's hair as he listens to his wife playing the part of his whore. A part of me hopes he isn't because sometimes, I am not.

When David returns, he is full of stories about drunken engineers in swanky bars in downtown Philadelphia and the inferior intellects of the people in his field. He beats his chest. "I am a god among men," he says, winking. "But more than anything, I missed you."

"Of course you did," I reply. For the next several weeks, I will tease him mercilessly, and remind him that he is a god among men. He will find this endearing, until he doesn't.

When I unpack David's suitcase, I create neat piles of clothes that can be put away, laundered, or sent to the dry cleaner. I organize his toiletries, making sure he has enough toothpaste, lotion, shaving cream for the next occasion when he must conduct *very important* business. The routine relaxes me, reminds me of my part-time role as wife. I search the pockets for matchbooks, coins, receipts, pens, design ideas on cocktail napkins. Once, I found a joint and before bed we smoked in the shed in the backyard, giggling like teenagers until we singed our fingers on the roach.

This time I find a Polaroid image of David posing with a young brunette, attractive in her own way. She is smiling. He is not. She is hugging him from the side, looking at him the way I imagine all his young lovers look at him—adoringly, desperately. They don't know the man I married, how betrayal comes so easily to him, so they can afford to look at him like that. David looks like he's trying to slide out of this girl's embrace. It's a sad little scene. There's a phone number, written across the bottom of the picture in red lipstick. I leave the Polaroid on his side of the bathroom, perched against the toothbrush holder. This isn't the first time I've found an artifact of his infidelity. It won't be the last. I leave the tokens for him to find, because he has left them for me to find. We play games because we can and we like it. Most days these games keep us together, somehow.

Later tonight he will tell me it's time for bed. We'll slide, naked, between our sheets. He'll lie on top of me, and I will relax, enjoy how my chest constricts beneath the weight of his body, like I'm suffocating. I'll drown in the scent of cologne and his hair products and body wash. We'll make love like we haven't shared our bodies with anyone else, like we are still the people we once promised to be.

After I've finished putting his things in order and I've cooked us dinner and we've made the small talk married people who know each other too well make, we sit in our family room, on our couch, in our familiar positions between laptops and secrets and lovers and the silence of the snow that continues to fall. The old radiators creak as they struggle to cough hot air into the room.

"Are you cold?" David asks, with a shy smile.

I nod and he pulls me close, wrapping his arms around me. His body feels narrow, almost frail against mine, as if his bones have lost some of their density. I return his embrace. I realize I am holding less of a man than he once was. I wonder how much stamina we have left for the games we play. And then I stand in the back doorway for a smoke thinking about Bennett, rough and merciless, necessary. I accept that I am, perhaps, less of a woman.

# I Am a Knife

My husband is a hunter. I am a knife. Last deer season, he took me on a hunt with him. At four in the morning, he shook me awake. He made love to me. He always fucks me before the hunt. There is a quality to his efforts that is different, better. He takes me, he uses me, he marks me. I allow him to. When he finished he told me not to shower. As we dressed, I could still feel him inside me, sticking to my thighs. It was cold outside. In the cab of his truck, I leaned against his arm, my eyes closed. He drank coffee from a thermos that used to belong to his father, who is dead from black lung. His beard would smell like coffee for the rest of the day.

We spent hours in the deer blind, doused in deer piss, waiting. I grew bored but stayed silent. I am a knife. Several does passed before us but my husband held one finger to his lips. We were waiting for a buck. "I want to kill something majestic today," my husband said.

He believes killing brings him closer to God. More time passed. Our bodies grew stiff. My stomach felt hollow. I hungered. His shoulders slumped as his hope faded but then a massive buck galloped into our sights. The creature was indeed majestic—its musculature pronounced, body thick, standing tall. My husband raised his rifle, inhaled deeply, held his finger against the trigger. He waited. The buck turned his head and looked at us with his black, glassy eyes. I held my breath, too. We waited. My husband pulled the trigger and exhaled slowly. We waited. The bullet hit the deer in his neck, making a neat black hole. My husband nodded his head once, set his rifle down. I am a knife. He is a gun.

The buck was still alive when we got to him, breathing shallow. I pressed my hand to his matted fur, felt his warmth, the strength of the muscles beneath his coat and the bones beneath the muscle and the blood holding him together. My husband reached for his knife, preparing to slit the buck's throat. I grabbed his arm, shook my head. I am a knife. I placed my hand over the buck's heart, waited for it to stop beating. We waited. We waited for quite some time. My husband prayed, offering acts of contrition into the air around us. When the buck was finally dead, I used one fingernail, cutting the creature open from his neck to his rear. His flesh fell open slowly, warm innards steaming out into the cold air. The air became sharp and humid with the stench of death surrounded by prayer. I am a knife.

My husband reached into the dead animal, then stared at his hand covered in dark red, almost black blood. He ran his thumb across my lower lip, then slid his thumb into my mouth. I sucked slowly, tasting the deer's blood, salty and thick. I moaned. My husband rubbed his bloody hand over my face and as the blood dried, my skin felt thin and taut. I lay back on the ground, now soaked with the deer's blood. My husband undressed me slowly then stood and stared at me naked, shivering next to the animal he killed. I wondered if he could tell us apart. The woods around us were so silent I felt a certain terror rumbling beneath my rib cage. When he lay on top of me, I spread my thighs, sank my teeth into his shoulder. My husband smelled like an animal and took me like an animal. I left my mark on the broad expanse of his back. I am a knife. He is a gun.

Later, we bound the deer's forelegs and hind legs and my husband carried the open, bloody animal across his shoulders. I carried our guns and followed in his footsteps. When we got home, he took his kill to the work shed behind our home and I began to butcher. I am a knife. It is a long, bloody affair, butchering an animal. There are things that need to be done in order for the kill to provide. For the next several months, we would bring our friends all manner of venison wrapped carefully in brown butcher paper, tied with strong twine. He would make jerky and sausage to share with the men he plays poker with, his brother, strangers at the bar. I would eat none of it. I do not care for the taste of venison. It tastes too much like the flesh of an animal.

We live in a large home that is beautiful and empty. We never talk about the emptiness or our failed attempts to fill the void. It is a sorrow we share but do not share. Sometimes I sit in one of our empty rooms, perfectly decorated, frozen in time. I sit on the floor and stare at the pink wallpaper and the wooden letters on the wall spelling a name and the linens my mother made for a perfect, tiny bed. I rock back and forth until I cannot breathe and then I crawl into the hallway and gasp for air.

My husband's family is religious. His relatives believe in God. Their God is angry and unkind because they made him in their image. Every Sunday, my husband and I go to church with his family—brother, mother, stepfather. This is the only time I spend with them. My husband's faith is weak. I have none left. We sit in church on the hard pews pretending we believe, pretending we belong. Sometimes I feel his mother staring at me with her narrow eyes, pursing her lips. When I feel her staring at me, I dig my fingernails into a hymnal or the pew or my husband's thigh. I am a knife. After church, we go to my in-laws' for a meal. They don't trust me because I don't eat venison. His mother resents having to accommodate my culinary peculiarities but each week she prepares me a dry breast of chicken, carelessly broiled, unseasoned, and I eat the rubbery meat and smile while doing so. This makes her even angrier. I help wash the dishes while my husband and his stepfather work in the barn and then, mercifully, we can leave. His mother always stands on the porch and watches as we drive away. I make sure to sit so close to my husband in the cab of his truck, it looks like I'm sitting on his lap. I make him kiss me, and I kiss him back so hard, it's like I'm devouring his face. I want her to know: I am a knife.

My family lives far away in the heavy heat of South Florida. My relatives rarely visit us, don't know how to deal with the cold. They can't understand why my husband and I stay in the North Country. When we visit my family, my husband is overwhelmed by the humidity and by people who look so different from him, few of whom speak English. He always grips my hand tightly when we're in Florida, and he looks so scared, so young. It is only when we leave our home that I realize it's not that he won't live anywhere else but that he can't. My sister, my twin, comes to visit often because she understands why I stay with my man in a place I do not love. She understands he loves me so good I would live anywhere with him. They get along well. She too is a knife.

She never stays with one man too long, says she lives vicariously through me as I do through her, so she doesn't need to get married and I don't miss being single. She's always calling me to tell me about a man she met in a bar or at a bookstore or in line at a coffee shop and how that man ended up in her bed and occasionally in her heart. When she visits, she fools around with my husband's best friend, a guy named Grant, a powder monkey on my husband's logging crew who thinks he and my sister share something so special it keeps her coming back. The four of us like to go bowling. We drink and bowl and drink and bowl and then we go down by the lake with a case of beer and make out on wooden park benches like teenagers with nowhere else to go. When I shiver after my husband slides his big hands beneath my shirt, she moans, and when she spreads her legs and pulls Grant's hand into her pants, I clench my thighs. People ask us if we have some kind of special connection. We lie and tell them we don't.

The wives of loggers tell stories about men broken by falling limbs or treetops or loose chain saws—they call these things widow makers. I listen to these stories and think, if something happened to my man, I would cut down every tree I ever saw for the rest of my life. I am a knife. When my husband is late coming home from work, I start to feel uneasy. I imagine our empty home even emptier than it already is. I make sure the phone is working, that I haven't missed any calls, and when he does get home, I beat his chest with my fists. I damn him for making me worry. Most nights he comes home smelling of sweat and sap, sometimes sawdust if he's been in the mill. He takes his dirty work boots off and undresses in the mudroom. I watch him, leaning in the doorway, holding a cold beer. He always smiles at me, no matter how his day has been. He takes a long sip of his drink, kisses me, his breath warm and yeasty. I tell him how lonely my body has been without him all day. He presses his lips against my neck, pulls at my skin with his teeth. He is a gun. I am a knife.

When she calls, I can hear in my sister's breathing, before she says a word, that something is wrong, I sit down at the kitchen table. My husband is in the family room watching some documentary on helicopter loggers, complaining loudly about how they're doing everything wrong. "What is it?" I ask. I try to sound calm. My skin hurts. My sister says, "I'm pregnant," and I exhale slowly. I say, "It's going to be okay." I swallow something hard and mournful. I dig my fingernails into the palms of my hand. I am a knife. She says, "I understand," and I smile and hold my stomach, running my fingers along the slightly raised scar that refuses to disappear even though it has been some time since I was cut open. I am not a knife. "Can I come stay with you while I figure out what I'm going to do?" she asks even though she doesn't need to ask. We talk awhile longer, then I join my husband. I sit on his lap and burrow my head against his chest. I tell him my sister is coming and why and he holds me so tight that even hours later, when we're in bed and he's asleep, I can feel him holding me together.

My sister and I were once in a car accident while she was visiting. We were sideswiped by a drunk driver on a backcountry road, the only kind of road up here. There were high stalks of corn lining either side of the road and bugs were everywhere, their high-pitched humming making the night thick. My sister was unconscious, her pulse weak. The drunk driver was passed out, an angry cut pulsing along his hairline. He reeked of cheap wine. The stench of him made me throw up. I pulled him toward our car. He was so heavy it felt like my shoulders might separate from my body as I pulled and pulled and pulled. When we reached my sister, I fell to the ground, sweaty and out of breath. I pressed two fingers to my sister's neck. She was born seven minutes after me. She could not die before me. Her pulse was even weaker. Her heart was dying. My heart was dying. I cut the drunk driver's chest open. I am a knife. I reached into his body, wet and warm, and I pulled out the heart he did not deserve. I felt no sadness or mercy for him as the slick organ throbbed in the palm of my hand. I cut my sister's chest open. I am a knife. I put his heart into her chest next to her heart. The two hearts nestled together and began beating as one. I am a knife. I pulled the flaps of skin back over her open chest and said a silent prayer as her skin fell back into place. I held my sister in my arms until help came. I kissed her forehead and whispered acts of contrition into the night air so she would know she was not alone. I kept her warm and safe.

With my sister around, the house feels less empty. She makes a small home for herself in one of our empty rooms. Her stomach swells and her skin glows. I often catch her walking around our property humming to herself, holding her belly. She is changing. I am not. Sometimes I catch my husband staring at her. When he notices me watching him watching her, he blushes, looks away guiltily. One night, we are lying in bed. We have just made love and he is still lying on top of me. He is still inside me. He brushes my hair out of my face and kisses me hard and I kiss him back and we bruise each other with our mouths. He says, "I wish we could take the child growing in her and put it inside you, where it belongs." I hate him for saying this. I love him for saying this.

Grant stops by almost every evening to check on my sister. He is convinced the child is his. He is not wrong. He brings her clothes for the baby, soft blankets, the food she craves, an expensive stroller. When she is in a good mood, she lets him stay the night. She says he is a comfort. She loves his hands and his voice and the thick mat of hair on his chest. She says she doesn't know if that is enough. I tell her it could be. When I hear them laugh, when I see how he looks at her, there is a loud, painful ringing in my ears that does not go away until I punch myself in the stomach. I imagine reaching into my own belly, cutting out the damage because I am a knife.

Her belly grows and grows and grows. Her ankles swell. She walks slower and slower, holding her lower back. Her skin still glows. Toward the end of March, we sit on the porch. It won't be long before she gives birth. She says, "I love this thing inside of me but I want it out." She stretches her legs and groans, then leans against my shoulder. She takes my hand and holds it over her stomach, covering my hand with hers. She says, "You are a knife." She is asking me something. Her belly is firm and warm and I can feel the baby moving around in its amniotic sac. The child is a boy or a girl. The child is strong. Its mother has two hearts. She asks, "What is it like, giving birth?" I say, "It feels like something wild is tearing your body from the inside out." She closes her eyes, squeezes my hand harder. The scar across my belly splits open and blood dampens my shirt but I sit still, I sit with my sister. She needs this from me.

A piercing scream in the loneliest part of the night wakes me up. My husband leaps out of bed, his hair standing on end, his boxers hanging loosely around his waist. He looks around the room, his fingers balled tightly into fists. He is a gun. His eyes are bright white. We hear another scream. I get out of bed. The floor is cold. I go to my sister's room. She is sitting up in bed, sweating heavily, her long hair clinging to her face. She looks at me, her eyes clouded with fear. Grant is holding his phone. He says, "I called for the ambulance but it will be hours before they can come." This is how life is in the North Country. There is never the kind of help you need when you need it. My husband and I know all too well what happens when the only ambulance in four counties is hours away. You end up bleeding in the cab of a pickup while your child dies inside you, while your husband speeds to the hospital, an hour away, over icy, winding backcountry roads, crying because he knows he cannot get you there in time. I place my hand on Grant's arm. I say, "Leave us," and my husband pulls Grant out of the room.

I kneel on the bed next to my sister. I think about how I am holding her life. I say, "Close your eyes," and she does. She trusts she is safe with me. I am a knife. I drag my fingernail across her lower abdomen and her skin parts easily. There is so much blood. I cut through the layers of dermis, the fat, yellow, soft globes that fall away loosely. I am careful. I am sharp. When I reach the uterus, I am gentle and neat, making another horizontal cut. There is still so much blood. I see the dark head of a child covered in thick fluids. I pull the child free, it is a boy, and he is followed by a long cord of slick membrane. I cut the boy free from the cord, hold the dirty little creature against me as my sister lies quietly, cut open, there is so much blood. My sister waits, she still trusts me. Her boy is hot in my arms. When he opens the slits of his eyes, I bite my tongue until I taste blood. I look at this boy, his tiny fingers curled, his limbs narrow and long, and it hurts to think of all the moments he will have. I am angry. I am a knife. I wish I could carve the anger out of my body the way I cut everything else. My sister holds her arms open. She trusts me.

That night, in the cab of his truck, the heat wouldn't work so every breath made my chest ache. I bled all over the seat and held my husband's thigh and shivered and forgot what warmth felt like. He refused to look at me but over and over he said, "I will get you there." The wild thing inside me was trying to get out and the pain was clear and constant and remarkable. I said the last prayer I would ever pray. At the hospital, my husband carried me inside. He explained to the doctor I was due any day. He said, "Everything's going to be okay, right?" The doctor ignored him. The doctor cut me open and hollowed me out and left an ugly scar, country medicine. He pulled from my womb a frail, bloody girl who could not breathe on her own, could not cry. Her head was strangely large, her skin almost translucent, as if we could see right through her. She was a wild thing but did not live long. We gave her a name.

The night after my nephew is born, after I cut my sister open and hold her life in my hands and close the wounds I made to save her child, my husband fucks me in our bed while my sister and a man and a baby boy sleep in her bed. My husband and I are loud and violent with each other. When I bite him, I draw blood. I am a knife. He fucks me like he's trying to fix everything broken inside me, like he's trying to break me even more, like he is trying through will alone to create another life inside what is left of my womb. I believe through him all things are possible. I wrap my arms around his back. I press my knees against his ribs. We do not look away from each other. His every thrust hurts more, hurts everywhere, but I spread my legs wider, open myself more to him. I am a knife.

# The Sacrifice of Darkness

*I.*

When I was a young girl, my husband's father flew an air machine into the sun. Since then, the days have been dark, the nights bright.

That man who needed to reach the sun, Hiram Hightower, worked his whole life underground, mining, digging through the hard earth to make other men wealthy, to fill their homes with fine things, to clothe their wives with fine linen and silk, to feed their mouths with fine food. He worked the unyielding earth until his lungs blackened and his bones swelled from the pressure of the world bearing down on him day after day after day.

As a young man, Hiram did not mind spending most of his waking hours in the world beneath the world. "It was always a mystery," he said when my husband was a young boy, "to sift the earth through my fingers, looking for the glint of precious metals." As the years passed, though, there was less and less mystery. In the morning, he drank coffee from a tall thermos as he drove to the mine. He put on his coveralls and heavy jacket and took the elevator down into the mine. He clawed through clay and granite always searching for something precious. He shivered as the cold sank into his skin. Sometimes he'd find feldspars and hide them in his pockets. He'd take them home and buff them to a perfect shine for his wife, who kept them on the mantel above the fireplace. Those crystal formations were the only beautiful things he gave to his wife, other than their child, so she treasured them in the way of women who love hard men.

The air in the mine was terrible. After too long, a man couldn't breathe down there. By the end of each day, as the miners rode the slow mile back to the surface, back to fresher, thicker air, they clutched their chests with trembling hands. Most nights when he got home, Hiram was silent, had nothing to say, knew his family would never understand that each time he went down below, he was forced to leave a piece of himself behind, knew that someday, there wouldn't be enough of him left to come home. He ate the food his wife set before him—hearty fare, well-seasoned meats, freshly baked bread, vegetables from the garden she tended. His wife, Mara, always had a smile for Hiram, sat with him patiently, sat through his silence, pretended each night that she was not sharing her table and her bed with a lesser man than the one she had known the night before.

Hiram had lovely hands, Mara has told me many times. His hands could fill a woman with fear if she didn't know better. You could see the strength of them in the thick web of skin and muscle and vein and bone. His whole body was a thick rope of muscle and sorrow. When they were alone, Mara liked to lie on his back, the broad, warm expanse of it. When she kneaded his body with her fingers, he groaned loudly, said, "Woman, you make me never want to leave your side." Mara never feared Hiram, wasn't worried about the size of him. He wasn't gentle when he touched her but he was a good man. He touched her the way she wanted to be touched. She loved how he knew there was strength in her, too.

Something changed in Hiram when he turned forty. He had always been a quiet man, but on his birthday, he became silent. All he could think about each night was how, sooner than he could bear, he would have to go back down into the cold, thin air and the cramped tunnels and the dirt falling into his eyes and nose and mouth, choking him, breaking him. At night Mara stretched herself alongside her husband trying to coax a word from his lips but he could not give her the one thing she needed from him. She started to forget the sound of his voice. He still went to work, still clawed through the earth, still filled the rusty carts with the precious, shiny metals greedier men craved. There was no joy in it, though, none at all. It became harder and harder for him to stand tall or take a deep breath.

One morning, he woke up and realized he could not spend another minute, day, or hour in the dark, thin air of the world beneath the world. His wife shook his shoulder when the alarm sounded. The sun rose but Hiram did not get out of bed. He sat up, leaning against the iron headboard. He nodded toward their bedroom window, asked Mara to tear the curtains down. His request was strange but Mara was so grateful to hear her husband's voice, she did as he asked. She grabbed the length of cloth and pulled the curtains to the floor with one fluid movement. Two jagged holes were left in the wood of the wall but neither Hiram nor Mara minded. Hiram patted the empty space next to him and Mara went to her husband. He looked right into the sun with his wife by his side. He didn't look away even when his skin warmed uncomfortably. Later, after their boy went to school, Hiram pressed his lips to Mara's bare shoulder and turned her over and followed the bony knots of her spine from the length of her neck down. He slid his strong, lovely hands along her thighs, smiling as they trembled against his touch. She rolled onto her back and when he pressed her body into hers, she sighed. She gave in to the weight of him. He held her face between his hands like he might crush her skull. The pressure of his hands made her head throb, almost pleasantly. When Hiram kissed Mara that morning, her lips swelled and bruised, threatened to split open and spill. Her lips felt pulpy against his, beautifully misshapen. The whole of her body felt that way by the time he was done, as if every muscle, every part of her skin, had been worked through his hands and his mouth and his eyes until it was broken all the way down.

When Mara climbed out of bed, sore, heavy, drained, Hiram said, "Don't wash," so she didn't. She went to the kitchen and prepared him a sandwich with thick sliced meat and tomato, a glass of cold milk. She smelled him everywhere, felt him everywhere. When he was of a certain mind, the weight of him was inescapable. Mara loved that about her husband. Hiram joined her in the kitchen and ate slowly. He stared at her in a way that made Mara feel like she was sitting across from a stranger. He did not look away. She did not look away. She tried to ignore the soft ache in her chest that bloomed, slowly, into a nervousness she couldn't quite make sense of. When Hiram finished, he stood and took his plate to the sink, washed it clean, dried it carefully, set it on the counter. He looked out the window above the sink, out into Mara's garden, into the thicket of trees beyond. He squinted as he looked up, toward the sun.

"There's something I must do," he said.

Mara shook her head. "Don't you break my heart, Hiram. Don't you dare."

He reached out and Mara slid her hand into his. Hiram led his wife outside and they stood on the slab of stone behind their house. He pointed up at the sun. "I want to touch it, just once. I need it, woman, I just do, and there's nothing that's going to stop me from trying to get there."

That afternoon, Hiram drove to the nearest purveyor of air machines with a good portion of the money he had earned by making money for other men. The coins were heavy in the satchel he carried. The weight of them tired him but he had important business to attend to. He needed to fill the impossible emptiness inside him. Hiram listened as the salesman tried to sell him a fancy air machine with linen seats and slick lines but that's not what he needed. He needed something strong, sturdy, an air machine that would carry him a long, long way. It was an ugly thing, the air machine he bought. There was no grace to it but he loved the color—a bright red that would make the sky pretty. As he walked around the fuselage, Hiram wondered how something so ungainly could take flight but the salesman assured him the air machine would serve him well. The salesman was a man of his word.

*II.*

I grew up in a valley flanked by two hills some called mountains. We weren't much used to the sun anyway. That's what we tell ourselves now that the sun has been gone so long. Our town was small but pretty, or at least, that's how I always saw it. Pretty isn't always about what you see. Sometimes pretty is what you feel. Minus the people, our town is still pretty to me. There were lots of trees towering over every house and building. As a child, I thought those trees reached straight into the heavens. I still do. I don't much change once I set to feeling a certain way. The streets were and still are lined with wooden sidewalks, sturdy and rough-hewn, raised a few feet off the ground because most folks around here don't trust the ground knowing what they know about what lies beneath, what that world beneath the world can take from you, has taken from all of us. The mine owners live near the center of town like they want their grand homes to be seen from everywhere, all steel and glass reaching toward the sky, almost as high as the trees, sprawled across wide stretches of land. In the shadow of those grand homes are where the rest of us live, some of us in the valley, others in the wooded hills, where the air is sweeter and the land is harder but means more. On the edge of the town are the mines, their entrances carved into the slow stone rise of the hills.

When the darkness came the world changed. It had to. Hiram Hightower flew his bright red air machine into the sun and the sun disappeared and the only light left was that of the moon. The only warmth to be found came from a good fire or a heavy sweater or the skin of another body pressed against yours. I was not yet a woman. I was a girl of eleven wearing a yellow dress. My hair was a long, crazy mess, reaching well past my shoulders. I was a crazy mess, too. I ran in our backyard, barefoot, my face streaked with dirt while my mother hung laundry to dry, wooden clothespins tucked between her lips. She hummed, the same song she always hummed, the first song she and my father ever danced to. She shuffled from side to side, her toes curling in the warm earth. It was a good day in a short life of good days.

We heard Hiram Hightower before we looked up and saw the sun grow brighter than we thought possible. It was a joyful noise, long and wide and full. Then that joyful noise disappeared and the sun grew smaller and smaller and smaller as it filled Hiram Hightower up with the light he craved for so many years working in the cold, lonely mines. When the sun disappeared, a bright red crease appeared in the sky. The air chilled and slowly the world grew cold, not unbearably so, but cold enough that we saw our breath more often than we did not. There was no more light of day. There never would be again.

In the early days of darkness, we thought it might end. We thought we might once again see the sun, feel its golden shine holding our skin. The bright red crease in the sky pulsed, and like the sun, that crease grew smaller and smaller until it disappeared. Scientists tried to make sense of what happened to the sun. It was nearly impossible for them to believe a man could be so full of darkness he needed to swallow all the light of the sun. The mines closed after that. The mine owners were not so greedy as to chance what another miner might do, what he might take from the world, to fill himself up. Their money could buy lots of fine things but it couldn't bring back the sun. Only teenagers and scrappers looking for trouble, looking for a little something to line their pockets, go down in the mines now. They sell what they find on the black market, mostly in towns far away. No one in this town will have anything to do with that lucre.

It didn't take long for the mayor to order gas lamps throughout the town, to provide enough light during the day for life to go on, perhaps a little warmth. That's what I remember most from

my childhood—the pale light of those lamps, and how during
the day, the chilled air was thick with the sweet smell of burning gas, how even at night when the air grew colder, that sweet
smell lingered, clung to our clothes and our hair and the skin of
our fingers.

My husband was a year ahead of me in school and after his
father flew his bright red air machine into the sun, no one would
talk to that boy. Joshua Hightower wasn't teased or taunted much.
He was ignored. That was worse. Silence is the cruelest of cruelties. Each afternoon, his mother stood at the foot of the steps
leading into and out of the brick building where we studied and
when he ran to meet her, his hair wild and curly like mine, she
took his hand and she held her head high and she nodded to him
and he held his head high, too. She wrapped her arm around him
like she could shield her boy from the anger and the darkness
and the cold. They walked home alone, always alone. The only
people who ever talked to Mara and Joshua Hightower in those
days were the other miners Hiram worked with because they
knew what could drive a man to swallow all the light in the world
and because when Hiram flew his bright red air machine into the
sun, for a moment they too felt filled up with warmth and light.
They too felt whole. That moment, however brief and impossible
to hold on to, for the men who knew only the world beneath the
world, was enough.

My mother is a kind woman, always has been. My father often
says she holds on to the kindness most people can't or won't be
bothered with. When Hiram Hightower flew his air machine into
the sun my mother said, "Bless his soul, may he always be filled
with light." When I told her about how Joshua Hightower didn't
have anyone to talk to at school, she frowned, her lips falling into

a tight line. She put her hands on her hips and said, "We certainly cannot have that. You invite that boy home to play with you after school. You be a sweet soul to him."

I wasn't much popular, either. I was too smart and that made people uncomfortable—most folks where we've lived our whole lives don't trust too much intelligence in a woman. There is also the problem of my eyes—they don't hide anything. If I don't care for a person, my eyes make it plain. I don't care for most. Folks are generally comfortable with the small lies they tell each other. They don't know what to do with someone like me, who mostly doesn't bother with small lies.

The day after my mother told me to bring Joshua Hightower home, I studied him, in math class, from three rows back. I had always loved his hair and that day I looked at the shades of brown from dark to auburn, marveled at how those colors formed a lovely pattern along each thick curl. The back of his neck was tanned and slender, though not as tan as it once had been. Soon it would not be tan at all. We would all lose any brown in our skin. Joshua had a strong jaw, even then, and kind eyes. I was flushed with shame as I tried to make sense of why I had ignored him. My cheeks were still hot with my weakness when I sat next to him in the schoolyard, later that day. He sat, quietly, staring up into the dark sky, rubbing his hands together to keep them warm. He flinched as I sat down so I rested my hand on his thigh. I looked up, trying to see what it was he was seeing.

"My father is up there somewhere," he said.

"I know."

"He didn't mean to do a bad thing."

I nodded. "I know that, too."

Joshua turned to look at me. "Why are you talking to me?"

For once, I decided to be comfortable with a small lie. "Because you look like someone I can talk to."

The corners of his mouth tensed like he was fighting something. He shrugged.

"Would you like to come to my house after school?"

He bit his lower lip and looked like he was making the most difficult decision he had ever made. His forehead wrinkled. The longer he took, the angrier I got. Finally I shoved him and stalked off, filled with a different, angrier heat.

Joshua wasn't at school the next day or the day after that. When I saw him again, he had a long, narrow box in his hand. He handed the box to me and looked to the ground.

"I've thought about it," he said. "I would like to visit your home."

"What if I don't want you to come over anymore?"

He nodded toward the box. "That's for you."

I carefully lifted the lid. Inside was a long, silky pink ribbon sitting on a bed of red velvet. It was the most beautiful thing. I was afraid to touch that ribbon but I couldn't resist. It was so soft, like nothing I ever felt. It made me feel perfect and beautiful. I closed the box and tucked it in my skirt pocket.

"We can walk home together," I said.

I could feel the stares as we walked home, bundled in our wool coats. The gas lamps weren't the same as the sun, but they did not hide us. We passed by the Hightower house and I noticed a new iron fence, real high, built all the way around the house. Hiram Hightower would hate to have his house closed in like that, I thought.

I pointed at the fence. "Why is your house caged in like that?"

Joshua shrugged. "My ma wanted to make it harder for people to get in our yard, throw things at the house. My dad made a lot of folks angry."

I was quiet for a moment. "It doesn't seem fair that you should have to live in a cage. It does not seem fair at all."

He grabbed my arm at the elbow. I looked at his fingers, wrapped in thin leather gloves. He loosened his grip but didn't let go. "It's not fair," Joshua said. "I hate it."

"There's no cage at my house," I said.

After that, I wouldn't say we were friends but we spent all our time together. We sat next to each other during class and shared our lunches beneath the skeleton of what once was a tree in the schoolyard. Each afternoon, we walked home beneath the flickering light of the gas lamps, tapping our feet against the wooden sidewalks, making music with our bodies. When people stared or whispered unkind things or when other kids at school tried to warn me off Joshua Hightower, I held my head high the way Joshua and his mother always did. We mostly went to my house, though once in a while, we went to his. Joshua's mother was quiet, her hair always combed into a neat bun. She mostly sat in the front room of their house, staring up into the sky like she was waiting for Hiram Hightower to come back to her. Whenever she looked at me, her eyes were pale blue and watery like a slow-dying body of water. She stared right through me. She made me sad. She made everyone who saw her sad because we could see that the hole Hiram Hightower couldn't fill inside himself found a new body in which to grow.

The kids we went to school with hated Joshua because their parents hated Joshua's father and none of those kids knew how to be any better than the people who brought them into the world. When Joshua walked to the front of the classroom, they hissed. The ones who thought they were clever called him a Son of a Sun Stealer. He kept on holding his head high, always, just like his mother, because he came from good people worth minding. Joshua never turned in to himself or tried to make himself smaller. Instead, he grew and grew and grew. He studied hard. He watched over me and smiled every time I wore my beautiful pink ribbon, which was often. He told me he didn't mind the silence of others so long as I was there to fill it. The older I got, the closer we became, the more I wanted to fill everything hollow inside him.

When Joshua was sixteen and I was fifteen, a council was convened to consider ways to bring back the sun. The members called themselves the Corona, mostly wealthy men, the kind who had created the emptiness in Hiram Hightower in the first place. They made it seem like they wanted to bring back the sun for everyone, so we could bathe in it and stare into it until our eyes burned, so we could remember natural warmth, but such was not the case. Most of us guessed the Corona were mostly interested in finding a way to reopen the mines, to make themselves even more wealthy. It was a dark, ugly thing to see such greed cloaked in false good.

Joshua and his mother were brought before the Corona to answer for Hiram Hightower's crime, which was not a crime. I sat in the gallery with my parents. Every so often, leaning against the wooden railing in front of me, Joshua looked up at me. I held my hand open and he held his hand over his heart. The Corona suggested that perhaps someone from the Hightower bloodline should be sacrificed: if not Joshua, then his firstborn child. Mara Hightower, normally serene and composed, paled.

When she spoke, her voice was strong, colored with fury. She said no more Hightower blood would be spilled in service of the sun. She said the spilling of blood could not possibly force the sun to rise. Many people in the gallery started shouting angry slurs. It terrified me to look at them, their faces drawn tightly into hateful masks, their lips shiny with spittle, their hands clawing forward like they wanted to tear Joshua and Mara Hightower apart, pull their skin from their bones, right then and there. The thought of them touching Joshua made my heart seize and twist itself into a bitter knot. That was when I understood love. While the gallery raged, my parents and I sat in a circle of miners who stood, quietly, pointing up as if there were no roof above them.

None of us knew what their gesture meant.

We did know no Hightower blood would be spilled as long as they drew breath.

By the time we matriculated at secondary school, Joshua was tall enough to fill any doorway, just like his father. He was bone and beating blood, organs and sinewy muscle. His hair was as wild and curly as ever. I was not tall but I grew into myself. I became beautiful—this is what I am told. I am not so vain as to claim beauty for myself. Joshua never told me I was beautiful but he didn't need to. I could see what he saw in me by how he looked at me, how he looked into me, how he touched me, how he wanted me, openly, hungrily.

As the years passed we became the closest of friends and then we became something more. Joshua made me laugh and I made him laugh, too. We talked and talked and talked. We ran together, dark mile after dark mile, our legs growing strong and lean, to stay warm, to sweat even though our damp skin quickly chilled into a thin layer of ice when we stopped to catch our breath. We remembered the sun, the shine of it, how on a clear day, especially out on the lake, it was like the gods themselves were breathing into us. In the days of darkness, something different was breathing into us, something less kind.

The Corona continued to try to salvage the sun. They sent fire into the sky using a massive trebuchet but the higher that fire rose into the sky, the faster it burned out. They tried to capture light with lunar panels and then somehow convert that lunar energy into solar energy that could then be flung into the sky. The more ambitious members of the Corona suggested sending air machines to other planets, finding ways to steal the suns or moons or stars from other systems, willing to create a terrible imbalance in another world to set ours right. There were, eventually, sacrifices of Hightowers from other lands, but those slayings never accomplished anything more than filling the earth with more innocent blood. Splinter councils formed—each group more rabid than the next, more hell-bent on bringing back the sun, more obsessed with the cold and the darkness, choosing to see ruin where a different kind of life was possible.

Mara Hightower and her only child chose to live that different kind of life. They did their best to be good citizens. Mara volunteered all her time to those who needed any help at all, tried to find some kind of redemption where, though she was faultless, there could be none. She never knew the touch of another man, no one would have her, not even the miners who felt a certain kindness toward her.

When Mara and Joshua were summoned before the various councils, they appeared willingly. At one such appearance, Joshua, weary from the weight of his father's burden, offered his life to the Corona, held his wrist forward, the blade of a knife piercing the thick green edge of a vein. As the Corona watched, he began to draw his blade along that vein, a thin line of blood beading in the blade's wake. The council chamber was terrible and silent and still. I could not stay silent. I stood. I shouted, "Don't you do this!" The chief councillor glared up at me, said I had no right to speak in the chamber, said I had been warned. I was not speaking to him. "Stop this," I said, quieter now. One by one, the miners in the gallery stood and looked down at the members of the Corona until the chief councillor raised his hand. Joshua stopped, his blood slowly falling to the floor in bright red drops. Few people understood why the Corona spared Joshua, but I was in the gallery that day, surrounded by the silent, standing miners. I saw how the faces of the Corona darkened, how they tried to fold their bodies together to shield themselves from such quiet anger. It was plain to see they were terrified of what else they could lose to another man who was pushed too far, who got a wild need in him to do something that could not be undone.

Many nights, after his mother fell asleep alone, her eyes wet, Joshua would steal over to my house. We sat on the sloping roof and stared at the moon, which, in the absence of the sun, swelled into a fragile beauty from which it was difficult to look away. We often saw people in the houses on either side of us doing the same thing, sitting on their roofs, their faces beaming upward. It was so very nice to see moonlight, and how we could see beneath its glow the memories of who we used to be. Somehow, staring at the moon made the days less dark, less cold.

## III.

My husband asked me to marry him in the observatory where we worked. Night after night, we pored over ancient astronomical texts, hoping that if we studied the stars, if we understood their long, unfathomable history, we might find a way to bring back the sun. We used powerful telescopes and long-abandoned instruments from the past to stare into the sky, to find some slow-burning memory of the sun. Even though our days and nights were dark and cold, I felt bright and warm everywhere. Joshua was my sun. I was his.

The night Joshua made his claim on me, I was staring at the moon, my eye pressed to the telescope. I marveled at how it made the heavens seem so near. The moon cast a blue glow over everything. I smelled Joshua as he neared, clean, so clean. He slid his arm around my waist and I covered his hand with mine, traced his knuckles. My heart pounded and there was a stirring between my thighs. I moaned softly. I wanted him as I always do, hungered for him deep inside me, my desire trying to claw its way out. Joshua pressed his lips against the back of my neck and I shivered, pulled away from the telescope and swiveled around in my seat, spread my thighs and pulled him against me, squeezed my thighs against his as I pulled his hand down my body, lower, lower.

I grabbed his chin, pulling him closer so I could look into his eyes. "Why are your hands shaking? You have certainly put your hands upon me before."

His cheeks reddened and he looked down, to the side. I pressed my lips to his throat. His pulse throbbed against me, the artery thick and hot, the power of his sun. Joshua reached into his pocket and pulled out a dark gray box similar to the one he had given me twelve years earlier, narrower, thicker. His hands trembled harder. I held his wrists and pulled him closer. When he tried to speak, he only stuttered, his words twisting themselves into complicated knots.

I slid out of my seat and rested my cheek against his chest, hard and soft at the same time. The beating of his heart was so fast and loud it terrified me but I knew I could trust his heart. "Shhh," I said. I took the box from him and set it on my chair. I stood on the tips of my toes, brushing my lips against his ear before grabbing the fleshy lobe between my teeth. He tasted like sweet spice. Joshua's hands found the small of my back like they always do, locking against the base of my spine. We stood like that for a long while, his breath falling against the top of my head, my breath falling against his chest. The beating of his heart slowed.

"What do you mean to say to me, Joshua Hightower?"

He inhaled deeply, like he was trying to pull all the air in the domed room into his body. "I mean to marry you."

"Are you going to be good to me?"

His brow furrowed as he nodded. "How could you ask that?"

I traced his lower lip with my thumb. "Promise me you won't do something that would take you away from me or that would change the world as we know it now."

Joshua fell slackly against me. I gasped but held the weight of him. We are both strong. "I am not my father," he finally said. "My father was a good man. I aim to be better."

"I'm glad you knew the question didn't need asking. I mean to marry you, too."

Joshua reached behind me and opened the box. He held my hand as if my bones were the most delicate things. He slid a beautiful ring onto my finger, the platinum of it cool and solid, an anchor, the diamond bright like the moon and what once was the sun. I had no idea where he got it from but I knew not to ask. Men need their secrets.

We fell to our knees. I slid my hands beneath his shirt, heavy cotton, my palms against muscle sharply carved, the bones of his rib cage. I pulled his shirt over his head and he did the same with mine. I stretched out on the floor of the observatory and he pressed a button. The dome slowly creaked open and I stared past the blue shadow of his body over mine, up into the stars, up into that bright, bright light of night. I dug my fingernails into the tightly stretched skin across his back as he filled me and moved over and through me and meshed his lips with mine. We crushed our teeth together. We were loud and wet and sloppy. I held Joshua deep inside but I never stopped looking at the stars. The pleasure took me all the way over. I cried. He licked my tears with the flat of his tongue. I said, "It is always you."

Soon after that night, the councils started to disband. Obsession lasts only if it can feed. Most people, still angry, still cold, still lonely for the sun, stopped caring as much about turning themselves inside out for something impossible. Enough blood had been spilled, and there were few Hightowers left. It is easy to become accustomed to darkness and chill. If you bear it long enough, you can become accustomed to almost anything. Embrace the cold and dark—that's what we did. We learned to love the different kind of light at night, the pale blue of it. In the moonlight, the world felt purer. Making peace with the world and its black days was the only way to find any kind of happiness. What we all wanted even more than the sun was a little peace to hold in our hands and hearts.

My husband and I married on the lawn outside the observatory, in the middle of the night. My parents and his mother and a preacher stood with us. I wore the pink ribbon, mostly worn to a thin shine, braided through my hair and a long white dress, no sleeves, a dress that swirled around my legs when I walked. Joshua wore his best suit, a fine cut with clean lines. We exchanged promises that were long ago made, however unspoken, and have always been kept.

## IV.

There was a new life between us. I felt that tiny, unknowable creature stirring in my womb from the beginning.

I told Joshua while soaking in the bathtub, the morning after a long night of work, the water still scorching hot. Bathing was one of the few things that made my skin remember the sun. I was red and tender and soft. My husband stood in the bathroom doorway, filling the frame from side to side, nearly from floor to ceiling. He smiled, said something that made my cheeks burn, my thighs tense. When he smiles at me, I am all lit up inside, like I am standing in the whitest heat. I remember what it felt like, when I was a girl, to lie out in the sun, feel that holy warmth on my skin. I cocked my head to the side and dragged my hand across the surface of the water. It rippled in light waves. Joshua shivered, stepped out of his worn shoes, and then his clothes, setting them in a neat pile in the hall. As he sank into the water across from me he sighed, smiled again, and I felt hotter still. I tapped my toe against his chin and he pressed his cheek, then his lips, against the wrinkled bottom of my foot. My hair clung to my face as steam rose around us. We stared at each other for a long while. I never tire of looking into his face.

"You are too quiet," he finally said.

I curled my finger, beckoning him closer. Joshua slid through the water, some of it splashing onto the tiled floor. He floated in front of me, his forehead near my chin as he looked up, eagerly. I cupped his

chin, squeezing. I breathed deeply. There was a strange tightness
in my chest, like my body was trying to hold on to my secret a
little longer.

Joshua nuzzled my neck. "Talk to me. What do you mean to
say?"

"We have made us a child," I said, softly.

He knelt, spilling more water out of the tub. He is a quiet man,
but on that night, there was no limit to his expressions of joy. I
felt freer and lighter once I forced the words out of my mouth.
We talked of how we would love our child, how we already loved
our child. We laughed and laughed, our voices rising through
the small room. When we emerged from the cooling water, my
husband wrapped me in a soft towel and carried me to our bed.
We made love. We were not gentle but we were gentle. He fell
asleep inside me. The next morning, I woke feeling his eyes on
me. He tucked his hand beneath my breasts and said, "We must
keep this between us for as long as we can." We grew even closer,
even stronger because we shared this perfect, desperate secret.

My husband and I tried to hide the growing swell of my belly
as long as we could. We kept to ourselves more than ever. The
townspeople would not welcome a single moment of happiness
from anyone sharing the blood of Hiram Hightower. Though the
councils had mostly disbanded, fringe elements lingered. When
a crazy notion gets in a man's head, there's not much that will
disabuse him of it. Joshua's father taught us that. We learned
the lesson well.

When we walked in town, in the dark of day, it was difficult to
contain the sharp line of joy binding us even more tightly together.
No darkness could hide that. Joshua held me close, his fingers
gripping my arm tightly. If a man or woman looked at me too

long, with unkind eyes, Joshua bared his teeth. We held our heads high. We took strong steps. We kept our secret until one afternoon, while we were laughing and practically skipping along the wooden sidewalks the way we did when we were children, a man we did not know, a man sitting in front of Kershbaum Mercantile & Dry Goods, stretched his leg out in front of me. "Son of a sun stealer," he hissed. He ought to have been ashamed of himself, a grown man speaking a child's taunt. I didn't see the petty cruelty coming. I fell hard, could feel where bruises would form on my knees and thighs, elsewhere. As I fell, I stared at Joshua with wide-open eyes, reached for him, but even though we tried our fingers never quite met. I thought, *My baby, my baby, my baby,* but everything happened too fast for me to think clearly beyond the terrible understanding of what we might lose. I hit the ground, slick with frost, and held my arms over my stomach. Everything ached and it hurt to breathe and there was a tight cramping between my thighs. I tried to stand but fell again, this time hitting my head. The world blurred.

Joshua's rage, the rage he carried quietly for so many years, the rage of losing his father and the disappearance of the sun and standing before the Corona as he offered up his blood, the rage of living the whole of his life in a place where everyone blamed him for the darkness, that rage split wide open and spilled into the frost-lined street, and through the cracks in the wooden planks below us. Joshua reached up and grabbed a long, clear icicle hanging from an eave. He lunged at that petty man, holding the tip of the icicle against the man's neck. I called my husband's name and he stopped. He threw the icicle to the ground, where it splintered into a hundred pieces. If there had been sun, there would have been hundreds of tiny prisms of light. His hands shaking, red and probably numb, Joshua grabbed that man from where he sat, that man's lips curling into an ugly smile. Joshua lifted that small, unfortunate man high into the air and shook him like he was trying to make the man into someone better. "She's pregnant!" my husband shouted. "How dare you?" The man paled, looked real sickly as he tried to withstand the forceful heat of Joshua's rage. I tried to focus, stretched my arm, pressing my fingers against Joshua's ankle. "We need you," I said so quietly I worried he wouldn't hear me. Joshua released his grip on the man, who ran away, stumbling from side to side, leaving the sharp stench of urine in his wake.

My husband lifted me into his arms and ran three blocks to the infirmary. I hid my face in his chest, shivering. I said, "I am so cold." I said, "Don't let anything happen to me." Joshua kicked the infirmary door open and placed me gently on an examination table. He covered me with thick blankets. He held my hands. The ache settled deeper into my bones. I went limp as the doctor pulled a bright light over my body. I was so drowsy. I sank into a sleep that wasn't really sleep.

Sometime later, nearly two days, I opened my eyes to a room with white walls and a long window and beyond that a dark afternoon sky. I closed my eyes again, sighed, holding my hands against my belly. I smiled and remembered a lovely walk with my husband before a hard fall to the merciless ground. I thought, *Finally, this is the price we pay.* I sat up, stiffly. The deep bone ache returned. I rolled onto my side, slowly, and saw Joshua, his large body sprawled in a tiny chair or a chair that seemed tiny beneath his bulky frame. I reached for him, brushing my fingertips across his knee. He shot up and stepped closer to me, pushing my hair away from my face. He cupped my cheeks and kissed my forehead and my nose and my forehead and my nose. He smiled and I saw he had locked his rage back inside him and that maybe his rage was taking up less room in his chest now that some of it had been let out. When I tried to speak, he pressed a finger to my lips. "You're fine. Our child is fine," he said. I blinked, was falling asleep again now that I knew our private, joyful world would not end. I slid over a bit and touched the empty space next to me. I listened as Joshua stepped out of his shoes and climbed into the bed with me. He covered my hand with his. We held our baby together.

As we left the infirmary, passersby stared but no one dared approach us or speak an unkind word into the air surrounding us. Their rage made the air colder, thinner. After the sun disappeared, everyone harbored some kind of rage. It couldn't be helped. The truth of it was that Joshua and I felt real sorrow for what everyone lost but after so many years, we no longer had the strength to carry it with us. We left the infirmary and picked up fresh bread, some fruit, and wine and then we went home, to our little piece of the world where we were safe, where our child was safe, where happiness was safe. The sun wasn't ever coming back. There was no sacrifice, no blood to be spilled that would make right what Hiram Hightower had undone. If the price for the rising of the sun was the blood of our child, we would continue to learn to celebrate the darkness.

## V.

Our daughter was born in the brightest space of the night, early in the new year. We named her Dawn. Upon hearing of her birth, for we were watched, the Corona convened, but because she was a girl, they decreed she would be spared.

They had no say in the matter, none at all.

The morning after Dawn was born, we sat with her on the deck Joshua built. In the farthest corner of the sky, we could see a light spread of gray where once there had been nothing but the black memory of the sun. The air was a little warmer. It was strange. Joshua stood and held our child up to this gray glow and even though we doubted she could understand us, we told her about days when the sun burned so bright it darkened our skin and covered the world in light.

We always knew we would not hide our child from the world. Such joy could not be contained. On lazy afternoons, we drove into town and walked beneath the flickering gaslights, inhaling their sweet, sweet smell. We reveled in the darkness covering us, holding on to the carriage handle tightly, smiling easily as Dawn spoke to us in the intimate language we tried so hard to understand.

When Dawn turned nine months old, she and I stood on the edge of what was once a lake but in the absence of the sun became a lesser body of water. The light spread of gray had brightened into a pale white. We could walk outside without coats or sweaters, some days. No one, not anywhere, dared to speak of the black memory of sun that had become something brighter. That day at the lake, Joshua walked along the dusty shore, his arms out at his sides, grinning, doing a silly dance. Dawn and I waved to him and sang to him. Farther along the shore, there were other families, enjoying the cool, clear day. I kissed the baby's forehead and whispered the secret words of mothers into the soft skin of her face.

A woman walked up to me, not much older than I, a woman who had, like me, known the warmth of the sun as a young girl. She was thin and pale and seemed unfamiliar with joy. I held Dawn more tightly. My child cooed and I smiled wider. This woman looked at me and my happy child and my happy husband, who stopped his silly dance and made his way toward us with a careful look in his eye.

The woman looked up into the dark sky that was not as dark as it once was.

She pointed at my daughter with a long, skinny finger. "Was your child's life worth a lifetime of darkness?"

I understood her anger, which was not so much anger as it was sorrow. I wanted to tell her what we did not dare speak, that what was once the sun might once again become the sun. I wanted to tell her the sky lightened the day my perfect child was born and that with time, the world would be bright again. I studied this woman and considered what penance I might offer her as we stood in the cool absence of light. Instead of speaking, I remained silent. Words cannot fill the faithless with faith.

I looked into my daughter's eyes.

There is nothing brighter.

# Noble Things

After the second secession of the South, and the rise in tensions that led to the New Civil War, Parker Coles Johnson VI was a changed man. He was tired. He missed the way things were, when life was more often good than not, and he slept soundly, wrapped in the breath of his wife and child. And he missed fast food, the way he bit into a french fry and a puff of steam filled his mouth, grease coated his tongue, and for hours he could feel the grit of salt in his teeth.

He knew he shouldn't dwell on something so silly, but it was easier to do that than to consider all he, all everyone had lost. All the fast-food restaurants were empty now, mostly boarded up because of the Austerity Articles. There was no place for frivolity, not anymore. It was unseemly buying food at a restaurant that one could prepare at home. So it was written in Article III (Our Union can be strong only if we forgo all that is wasteful), so it was.

Sometimes, driving through town at night, Parker Coles Johnson could see the flicker of a low fire—vagrants or malcontents making their way north, squatting for the night in dark alleys, trying to stay warm. He was kindhearted despite the things he had done so he wondered how those folks survived. He tried not to take his good fortune, or what looked like good fortune in the New South, for granted. He had a sturdy home and a warm bed. His wife, Anna, lay next to him, sleeping soundly or, he suspected, pretending to sleep soundly so he wouldn't paw at her the way he typically did when he couldn't sleep.

Anna wasn't a cold woman, nothing of the sort. When they first met, at a town meeting, she was bold, making eyes at him in such a way there could be no misunderstanding her intentions. Those eyes, dark brown, intense, were the first thing Parker Coles Johnson noticed, and only got bolder after one of the elders told her to quiet down. She was objecting to a motion that only men and married women should be able to hold the floor in town meetings. Such motions were often raised though they rarely went anywhere. Women had sacrificed too much in the war and they weren't going to stand on the sidelines, never again.

During that meeting, Parker stood, and everyone turned to look at him, the General's youngest son, the one who bore the General's name. Parker looked at every member of the town council and said, "A woman has the same right to speak as any man here, no matter how she is attached or not. There are some things we cannot and should not change." With that he nodded, straightened his jacket, and sat back down, his heart beating so fast he could hardly breathe.

Later that night, Anna scratched at Parker's door with those long nails of hers, and when he answered, she slipped past him so softly, so silently, he wasn't quite sure she was really there until he was in bed, on his back, holding her hips in the palms of his hands.

Anna was not so soft in his hands anymore. Turning on his side, Parker studied the gentle slope of her bare shoulder. He slowly moved his hand toward her, but she said, "Don't," her voice clipped and thin. Anna was angry and there wasn't much Parker Coles Johnson was going to be able to do about that anger, which had been finding its current shape for some time now.

The Johnson family, they were Southerners through and through. His great-great-great one or another granddaddy fought in the first Civil War as did lots of other kin. After the South fell, they persevered, prospered in tobacco farming, and would have kept on prospering were it not for the changes no one saw coming. Anna came from a long line of Southerners, too, but she did not hold the same charity toward her ancestry. After the border fence was erected along the Mason-Dixon, most of Anna's family fled north. Too many of them loved people with brown skin and had borne children with brown skin to abide the changes coming, Article II (our Union can be strong only if the provenance of her people can be proved). Anna's family left three months after Anna and Parker met and now, nearly a decade past that, she missed the people whose blood she shared, the roundness of their voices, her mother's hands.

The argument keeping Parker awake ended with Anna saying, "It's not really fair, the price of loving you, and I don't know how much longer I'm willing to pay." Her voice was so quiet it made Parker shiver.

He wasn't opposed to following Anna anywhere and he hated what the South had become. The price of rising again was steep,

steeper than anyone could have imagined. When he was at the
bar with his friends—alcohol, unlike fast food, had been deemed
a necessity—Parker listened to all the angry talk. He gritted his
teeth and wished his friends wouldn't assume he felt the same
way. "You're still here," Anna liked to say. "Why wouldn't people
assume you agree?" And Parker would walk away because he also
hated the sharpness of her tongue when his wife was right.

The real problem was his father, General Parker Coles Johnson
V, who once led the Army of the Federated States of the South,
cobbled together from the military bases below the Mason-Dixon
and not much else. The General, as the family had always called
him, with very little affection, some fear, and grudging respect,
expected the people in *his* bloodline to mind their place, standing tall, albeit behind him. Sometimes, at Sunday dinner, Parker
could feel the General staring, as if his father somehow knew
that love as well as something far more trivial, like french fries,
was pulling Parker's heart north.

In the morning, Parker opened his eyes and shivered, the bed
cold and empty. The house was quiet, the air stale. He rose out
of bed slowly, his body full of familiar aches, and found Anna in
the bathroom, applying eyeliner to her lower eyelid. Women in
the South didn't have much need for makeup anymore, since face
painting was deemed an overly expensive frivolity when money
needed to be directed to rebuilding efforts, but Anna wasn't going
to stop making her face pretty and by the grace of her husband's
name, no one was going to say a word about it.

Parker stood behind his wife, rubbing her shoulders, kissing the
back of her neck through her hair, which smelled clean and sweet.
She studied him in the bathroom mirror. "I'm not thrilled about
dinner at your father's tonight. All this ceremony, and for what?"

He sighed, nodded. Parker gently rubbed at the thick scar on the left side of his chest, an ugly circle of dead tissue. "But you'll come?"

Anna set her eyeliner pencil, contraband from her family in the North, on the lip of the sink. "Have I ever not stood by you?" She scowled, shook her head at his reflection, and stalked out of the bathroom.

There was the boy, Parker Coles Johnson VII, named as such, Anna agreed, grudgingly, because it was his father's name and only after that was it the name of the other men who came before them. He carried both his mother's and his father's looks in him—a smart boy, smarter than most people knew what to do with. Their son often made people uncomfortable when he spoke, so many questions, all incisive, well considered. When the boy was eight, Parker sat with him, studying a map for a geography project. There were the Western Territories, dry land full of people who didn't realize their water came from Michigan and now paid exorbitant prices to quench their thirst, and the Republic of Texas, soon to be annexed by Mexico. The Federated States of the North included pretty much every state that didn't secede, stretched across much of the country, skipping most of the West and including California and Hawaii. And then there was Florida, now a colony of Cuba, where those who could afford it went for sunny vacations and fruity cocktails and spicy food. The boy pointed at the various territories that used to be the United States, his face screwed with concentration. "Why aren't all these states together?" he asked. Parker felt a flush of pride quickly followed by shame.

"They used to be," Parker said, squeezing his son's shoulder. "They ought to be."

Parker explained that once, there was an election and small-minded people couldn't handle the man who won and then there was anger and then there were petitions and then terrible decisions were made—demands for secession, refusals from Washington, rising tensions, a war to bring secession about, the wall erected, everything going to hell on only one side of the wall, dulling whatever victory was to be had. It all happened so fast, it hardly seemed real, until the war began and it was too real and then the war ended and nothing had been saved, which was always the case when foolish men made foolish, prideful decisions.

The boy nodded, tracing along the Colorado border. "The states should be together again. We should ask grandpa to do that," he said with the conviction only children can have for the people they trust most.

Soon after that Parker and Anna sent the boy away. The borders had reopened after the war even though the fences stayed. For a price, anyone could go north or come south, though generally, people went in only one direction. The boy was with Anna's parents, gone now a year because Anna wasn't going to have any child of hers learning the kind of nonsense they were teaching in the South. He was too smart for that, too good, and on this point, she and Parker agreed. They spoke to their son once a week, on the videophone, saw how he was growing into his boy body—long and lanky—but still, very much a boy. Each week, Anna promised their son they would see him soon and Parker nodded silently, looking away because he didn't dare look in his son's eyes.

The only room in their home with pictures of the boy was his bedroom, which was a shrine to the child, all his belongings waiting patiently for his return. Parker found Anna in their son's bed, on her side, holding the boy's pillow to her face. Without looking up she said, "This still smells like him. Leave me alone, please." There was no anger in her voice, only weariness, and that frightened Parker more than Anna's anger ever could.

Parker wanted to say something but couldn't. His mouth was dry and sour. His chest ached. And then he was angry because none of this was his fault and he couldn't do a damn thing about any of it. He slammed his fist against their son's dresser. "I won't live like this, my woman hating me in my own house."

Anna pulled the pillow from her face. "Then don't," she said.

Hers was a mostly empty threat. From the beginning, they had shared something strong, something beyond anything they had previously known. Anna appreciated Parker's quiet nature, the clean calm of what he believed. Parker loved her edge, how she could never be tamed. He had had his fill of seeing what happened when women lowered their necks too much to the men they loved—his mother, the women his brothers married, how each year, they seemed to grow smaller and smaller. He didn't want a small woman, not like that. During those early months, when Anna slipped through the dark to his house every night, when they tore at each other like their bodies were more than flesh and bone, he told her, "Don't ever become small," and she said, "I never could."

Husband and wife avoided each other for the rest of the day. They were both in the house but it felt empty, silent, as if Anna wouldn't even grant Parker the small pleasure of hearing her move and hum through their home. As he considered his wife's mood, Parker thought, with no small amount of pride, that she was bigger than ever—small in stature, but she knew how to take up room.

At church, Parker sat up front with his family—mother, father, brothers, their wives and children. He sat so rigidly his back throbbed by the time the preacher finished his sermon on liberty and faith and the goodness of war. After, when he stood next to his parents, Parker ignored questions about Anna and her where-abouts. There weren't many. People in town didn't understand Anna and largely believed her to be godless, a designation she rather enjoyed because she understood that in their community, to be godless was to have a mind of one's own. Back at the family estate, Parker changed into jeans and a flannel shirt and took his nephews fishing, though they caught nothing. He tried not to think of fishing with his boy, how his son stared intently at the water as if he might will fish toward his line.

At six, sharp, Anna was at his parents' home, wearing a blue dress, her hair piled on top of her head, her lips thickly covered in the bright red lipstick her mother-in-law hated. As he greeted her at the door, Parker held his hand against the small of her back and whispered, "Thank you for coming." She looked at him, held his gaze, but didn't smile.

Dinner was a solemn affair, the General droning on and on about the Austerity Articles and how they weren't austere enough and how people were getting lax, soft really, how if something didn't give the South would be overrun by Northern trash once more because the border fence was falling apart. Parker poked at his food, longed for something with no redeem-ing nutritional value. He recalled the tiny bits of artificial onion in a Big Mac and how they crunched between his teeth. Anna didn't bother to hide her disdain. When she said, "The South needs to be overrun so things can be set right again," Parker stared at his plate, cleared his throat softly, wondered when he became the kind of man who looked down instead of standing up. Everyone stopped eating and stared at Anna and she stared right back. Parker was proud, as he always was. His woman wasn't scared of anything. The General started to respond but then didn't. He took a sip of wine, red, staining his lips and teeth and tongue.

When Parker was back home, in bed alone, his right leg ached. The frag still lurked beneath the skin covering his thigh, embedded just above the muscles. When he walked, he felt the splinters of metal and wished he could cut himself open and tear them out. He had learned to live with the pain but lately, in a cold bed without a warm woman, the pain was too much, too fresh, a burden he was forced to carry because of the decisions of other men.

During the war, Parker was a dutiful son. That was the way of the men in their family, though such duty was nothing he would want for his own boy. On the day he left with his father and brothers, Anna stood on their porch, her hair wild, her eyes wild, her voice wild. She would not be contained. She stared at the General. She addressed him by his full name. She said, "Parker Coles Johnson the Fifth, you bring this man back to me of sound body and mind." The General blinked. No one called him anything but General or Sir, and certainly not a woman. The General was so unnerved he removed his hat, held it to his chest. He said, "Yes, ma'am, I will." As they walked to the waiting Humvee, the General turned to his son and said, "Don't you make a liar out of me, son."

It was a long tour—mostly border protection in Maryland. Parker was never sure if they were supposed to be keeping people in or out or what the point of it all was. Parker bunked with his brothers in the tent next to their father's. He was constantly surrounded by the stink of men, their coarse voices. He could hardly bear to think of the home Anna kept, little soaps that smelled of lavender and linen, and her food—such strange flavors from countries he would likely never visit but now longed to.

Every day the Coles boys, as they were called, went on patrol. They were a general's sons. They did useful work and did that useful work well but their service involved nothing that would get them killed, nothing that would keep them from going home to the women who were waiting. What Parker remembers most from those three long years was the boredom, riding around in rusty jeeps, sitting quiet while his brothers jawed about nothing he gave one damn about. It was rare they ever fired their weapons for anything but target practice and hunting deer. Parker thought about Anna, and the yeasty smell of her neck in the morning. He thought about the lines of her body, how she was so smart it scared him, the letters she wrote—short, almost terse, but letting him know she was waiting, and still loved him. In one Anna said, "Don't make me undone by loving you."

The soldiers slept with their rifles on the ground right next to their cots. When he couldn't sleep, Parker lay on his back, holding his rifle against his chest beneath the thick wool blanket, whispering, "This is my rifle. There are many like it, but this one is mine." He would say those words and he would laugh because the words made no sense, no sense at all. The rifle was just a hunk of metal, a heavy thing, a killing thing.

Parker could shoot true and straight. He wasn't afraid of guns. He had been hunting with his father and brothers since he was knee-high, the General beaming as his boys took down all manner of wildlife, slapping their shoulders with his meaty, callused hands. Parker knew how to hold the butt of the rifle against his shoulder just so, how to exhale slowly when depressing the trigger, how to understand the wind and the crispness of air to better gauge how a bullet might fly through it. He understood how a bullet could tear through a body, and leave a man blown open and bleeding. He had seen it. He had done it and so when it was done to him while he and his brothers were doing a sweep near the Potomac River, he wasn't angry. Terrible things happened to men in war.

He never saw the Northern soldiers as they emerged from the brush. He was too far in his head and then he was all the way in his body, on the ground, clutching at his leg, screaming. He screamed so much he spit blood. There was a bullet somewhere in his shoulder, he could feel it burning him from the inside out, and one somewhere in his chest, and two, maybe, in his thigh. His brothers were hunched over him, frantically trying to stanch the bleeding, stabbing him with a shot of morphine. Thom, the eldest, muttered, "The General is going to kill us." William, the second eldest, kept firing his rifle into the empty distance, the enemy soldiers nowhere to be seen, gone just like that. While the Coles boys waited for help, Parker turned his head to the side. He hurt everywhere but was all screamed out, the morphine finally doing its work, dulling everything. He stared at the water of the Potomac, thick with sludge, trash bobbing gently along the surface. He thought of his wife's words—*don't make me undone.*

The General brought Parker home himself, took a week of leave to do it and see to his own wife, who, after being married to a military man all her life, was just about waited out. As they rode in the ambulance, the General talked about why he gave his youngest son his name. "I looked at you," the General said, "and you were so damn little, I was afraid to touch you but you reached out and grabbed my finger and you held on real strong.

I thought to myself, *This boy will be able to carry the weight of my name*. I was right about that." The General's voice cracked and he held on to Parker's arm. "I was right," he said, again, softly.

As they pulled into the driveway, Anna ran down the stairs of their porch to the ambulance. She clutched her chest. She looked very young. Parker tried to sit up, tried to speak, but he was so tired, his mouth dry and thick with his tongue. Anna was gentle with her husband. She smoothed his sweaty hair from his forehead. She pressed her lips against his even though they were dry and cracked. She whispered, "I love you," in his ear, her breath tickling him everywhere. Anna looked him up and down and when she was satisfied that she could live with the man the General had returned to her, she directed the EMTs to bring Parker inside.

When the General tried to follow, Anna stopped him, her small hand planted against the older man's chest, her fingers curled into claws. "You are not welcome in my home," she said. "You broke your promise." The General didn't protest, just tipped the brim of his hat and stared after Anna, marveling that his quietest boy ended up with such a woman. Anna followed her husband's stretcher into their home and Parker smiled wanly.

Before he was shot up, Parker had not known Anna to have any fragility about her, but that first night home, his wife sitting in bed next to him, Parker thought she might shatter if he touched her. She was solemn. She held her hand against his rib cage, near one of his bandages, and said, "You are done serving your father." Parker covered her hand with his and nodded. The war ended soon after and then Parker and Anna's son was conceived and born and life went on but most men in the South kept walking around feeling like they should be fighting something, without knowing quite what.

In the morning, Anna stood in the doorway of their bedroom. "It's time," she said, and Parker slowly sat up, wiped his eyes, longed for a glass of cold water but knew better than to ask for one. He followed Anna into the study, his limp more pronounced after a bad night's sleep, and they sat side by side. They put on the happy faces they knew their son would want to see. When the video call came through and they saw the boy on the screen, his bright eyes, his hair growing long over his face, Anna bit at her lower lip and grabbed Parker's thigh, the wrong one, and he winced as he felt the frag shift and pierce his muscle anew. Parker gritted his teeth and forced himself to smile wider. They listened as their son chattered about everything he had learned in school, how three of his teachers were quite boring, his new friend he really liked even though she was a girl, an experiment he was doing in the refrigerator, the park his grandparents took him to.

"When will I see you again?" Seven, as they called him, asked.

Parker reached out to touch the video monitor but looked away. "Soon, kid. Soon."

Seven nodded, temporarily satisfied with the answer that wasn't really an answer. When the call ended, Anna and Parker sat where they were; they did not move.

"Our son looks more like you every day," Anna said. "I am glad for it. You are a fine-looking man even though you are an infuriating one."

Parker didn't know what to say though he felt a stirring of vanity and smiled. He stretched his legs and cracked his knuckles.

Anna poked Parker's side. "Remember when Seven was born? He was such a strange little creature, so squirmy and red, absolutely unknowable. I was terrified. I don't know that any child has ever been looked at for so long while doing so little."

Parker laughed. "Our boy fit in my hand when we brought him home. I couldn't believe we made him. I do miss him, too, Anna. I miss him more than I can say."

Anna crossed her legs and turned to look at her husband. "We made him and it's time to be with him. You, me, Seven, we don't make sense without each other. Spending the rest of this life without him . . . that would make me small. You have to choose."

There was a loud ringing from somewhere, he wasn't quite sure where. Parker rubbed his chin, the stubble making a raspy sound beneath his fingers. "I love the way the people talk down in Florida. I miss that. I miss the sun."

Their wedding had been held on his father's land, a big affair, everyone dressed in finery, lots of food, lots of drink. They even danced. For one night there was no austerity. Beneath a canopy of tiny white lights, the world felt like it once was. The General toasted the young couple, even toasted his own wife and their many solid years together, which was as demonstrative as he was ever going to get. Parker's mother blushed beneath her husband's attention and for the rest of the night her laughter filled the air as if it were her own wedding.

The newlyweds went to Florida for their honeymoon, Miami. It was hot, which Anna loved. Lots of people spoke Spanish, which Anna loved because she did, too. Parker felt lost but Anna was always there, showing him how little he knew of the world without making him feel lesser for it. They sat by a glittering ocean of blue water during the day, Anna in a tiny bathing suit revealing a lot of skin, Parker in board shorts and a bare chest. Enjoying the heat was decadent and they were decadent and there was no regretting it. They ran in the sand and dived into the surf. They drank rum, lots of rum, and ate rum-soaked fruit and spicy food.

At night they danced to music Parker could barely remember from before the war. He loved it, how the bass thrummed in his chest, how he and his wife sweated together and moved together. Back in their hotel room, after the third night of dancing, Parker lay with his head against the flat of Anna's stomach as she massaged his scalp. She said, "We could stay here, you know. We could never leave." Years later, Parker realized he should have said yes, but that night, in the middle of so much happiness, he kissed the palm of his wife's hand; he said nothing.

In the study, in the quiet of their nearly empty home and so far from the joy they once shared, Parker reached for his wife and pulled her to the floor. She resisted at first, slapped his hands away, twisting her body beyond his reach, but he said, "Don't refuse me," and she stilled. Anna gently held Parker's face between her hands, rubbing her thumbs along his cheekbones. "I could say the same to you," she said. He undressed her slowly, pulling at each exposed instance of her skin with his teeth, making a claim, leaving a mark. Anna was punishing as she rose to meet her husband, their hip bones crashing together. They wanted to hurt each other as much as they loved each other. That's what they needed and demanded from each other.

Later, they sat on the porch swing, wrapped in blankets, drinking whiskey from canning jars. The night was cold and clear, the moon high, the street empty, their bodies tender.

Parker took a slow sip, the whiskey burning his throat. "I never thought it would come to this. I never thought it would go this long."

Anna leaned into Parker's shoulder and closed her eyes. "Pride does things to time," she said. "And foolish pride is worse yet."

"Am I a foolish proud man?"

Anna pulled away. "We will not fall asleep tonight listening to the breathing of our son. You are not a foolish man but you are proud."

Parker reached for his wife's hand and Anna let him show her this small affection. He traced her knuckles in slow circles. "When I was a boy, my father, I didn't understand that man but he was always there, standing so tall over my brothers and me, putting the fear of God in us. He always told us, 'A man stays close to home, close to his blood because that's where he's at his best.'"

A cold gust swept through the porch, the swing rocking lightly. Anna moved back into Parker's arms. "I'm not saying your father is wrong but I'm not saying he's right and if what your father says is true, we have to consider our blood, our son, my blood, our family."

"When I first saw you—"

"Don't," Anna said, sharply, pressing two fingers against Parker's lips. "Memories aren't going to do us any good. We are here, now."

Parker grunted, took another sip of whiskey. Anna did, too, and they continued sitting, silent.

The next morning, Parker woke up before the sun rose, put on his running clothes, and jogged to his parents' home. He was a sweaty mess as he stood in the foyer, his hair clinging damply to his forehead, his neckline. The General hated it when anyone was unkempt and Parker hated his familiarity with everything the General hated. He found his father in the kitchen, sitting at the table with a cup of weak coffee, staring into the distance. The General looked up as his youngest son entered the room.

"I cannot say much for your attire, but at least you're staying in shape. Military discipline has its benefits, wouldn't you say?"

There was a small pool of coffee in the bottom of the carafe on the counter, and Parker poured it into a mug before sitting across from his father. "We need to talk, Daddy."

The General looked up, his features as hard as they ever were. War does things to a man, they said, and many wars do many things to a man. The General was a man to whom many things had been done during tours in Iraq, Afghanistan, Iran, and even here in this land he called home. It was terrible, having to spill blood in the land that held your roots, but there was no choice when the alternative was spilling no blood and surrendering the land to those who could not respect history and place, legacy. This is what the General told himself now that the war was over and little had changed.

"I'm not interested in any conversation you want to have at this time of the day, skulking over here in the dark."

"I'm not skulking," Parker said, evenly. "Anna—"

The General pounded his fist on the table, sending the lid off the sugar jar followed by a thin trail of sugar Parker began tracing, enjoying the grit beneath his fingers. "Don't you come to me with that woman's name the first thing out of your mouth. Speak for yourself. She can certainly speak for herself."

"We cannot stay. I am a son but I am also a father and a year apart from my boy is a year too long."

"Bring the boy back. He belongs here, with us. This land here, this is his land. His history is in this dirt."

"I won't have my boy spending the rest of his life in this, living a lie I don't believe in."

"Our family has been defending and working this land since before we had a name for it. You do not walk away from that. I did not give you my name so you could run away with it."

Parker ran his fingers through his hair and stood. "I am not running away."

The General shrugged, then turned away. "I'm not sure what you want me to say."

Parker approached his father slowly, squeezed the older man's shoulder. "I don't want you to say anything. I am just telling you where things stand."

The General grunted and the men stood, together, in silence for quite a long time.

As he ran home, Parker kept repeating, "I am not running away." He said it until the inside of his mouth was dry and his teeth were dry and it hurt to say the words.

Each morning when Anna awoke, she remembered the day she and Parker sent their son away. She remembered setting out his clothes—a button-down shirt, white with narrow gray stripes, and a worn pair of jeans she had recently mended. She remembered packing the last of his suitcases, trying to put some necessary part of herself alongside the clothes and books, an old action figure, a map of this new world because the boy loved maps, understanding the geography of things. Seven had not wanted to leave but his sorrow was dignified in the way of a child who understood the complexity of what his parents were deciding for him. They stood on the train platform, Parker gripping Seven's shoulder so firmly the boy winced, but remained quiet.

Anna kept brushing Seven's hair out of his face, adjusting the collar of his shirt. She tucked his passport into his shirt pocket and put his coat around his shoulders. She kissed his forehead and told him, "You be good for your grandparents. Don't you forget us. Don't forget me." And then she went to the car to wait, telling Parker, "I'll leave this to you now." He was never sure if it was a punishment or a blessing because alone with his son as the train tracks hummed with electricity, he cried and hugged his son and inhaled deeply, trying to breathe in the smell of the boy. Parker watched as the train pulled away, Seven staring out the small window at his father, his hand pressed against the glass. Long after the train had departed, Parker stayed on the platform, his legs locked stiffly. He didn't know how to stop crying, didn't want his woman to see how broken down he was. She did, eventually, because she came and found him. She said, "My poor, poor love." She wrapped her arms around him beneath his coat. She said, "This had to be done."

Waiting for Parker to return from his run, Anna stared at the ceiling and said, "I have been apart from my son for three hundred and eighty-nine days." It was the refrain she offered up every morning as she thought of the last moment she had her child near her hands. She was going to leave soon. She did not want to leave Parker but she would. She prayed it would not come to that but she had been planning and she was ready. All she needed to do was make peace with her heart. "That's all I need to do," she whispered into her pillow. Anna rolled onto her side, pulled her knees into her chest. She thought of the suitcases, hidden in the back of her closet, filled with the things she had convinced herself she needed. Anna kept repeating, "I am not running away." She said it until the inside of her mouth was dry and her teeth were dry and it hurt to say the words.

Late at night, when they lay together, as much of their bodies touching as possible, Anna and Parker had the conversations they could have only with each other. They tried to remember the before, when they were children and there was only one place to call home, one country, the flag billowing on windy days in front of homes up and down every street—bands of red and white, fifty stars, one nation, indivisible until it wasn't, how quickly it all came apart.

# Strange Gods

There are things you do not know about me. These things are not inconsequential. We woke up this morning and before we got out of bed, you kissed my bare shoulder. I could still smell you from last night on my skin. You reached from beneath your pillow and set a small velvet box on my stomach, told me I could not say no. I opened the box and saw a bright prism of light, then tucked it under my own pillow, turned away. I smiled into the sheets, tried to control my breathing, lay perfectly still. You huffed and got out of bed and stomped around the house muttering things you wanted me to hear about commitment and patience and pushing limits. After you were dressed, you kissed me on the forehead and left for work but before closing the front door, you shouted, "You really are too fucking much!" That gave me a thrill. I love when you use foul language. This morning was your fifth proposal in four years; I understand your frustration. The first time, I slapped you. I left a mark. I'm sorry. In my defense, I was angry you would commit the rest of your life to me.

My mother holds on to grudges. To this day she can recount every wrong. She once told me to never forget anything. She said there's no such thing as forgiveness. Then she reminded me of the time I was in first grade and got an answer wrong on a homework assignment, how I stuffed the paper with the teacher's corrections into the folds of my bus seat because I knew my parents would be displeased. She told me how sad it made her that a six-year-old could understand deceit.

Our neighborhood was nestled in a vast forest of deciduous trees. I learned the word *deciduous* in the sixth grade. It is one of the few pieces of knowledge I retained because I love the meaning of the word, how the deciduous trees get rid of those things they no longer need, those things that have fulfilled their purpose. We spent a lot of time in those woods. We explored and made maps and created secret places meant for hiding. We grew older and the woods became less a place of discovery. We secreted ourselves between thick tree trunks, beneath the dark canopy of leaves. We smoked cigarettes and drank Mad Dog 20/20 and basked in being the worst kinds of suburban clichés. I also learned the word *dendrochronology*—analyzing the patterns of tree rings to know everything that has ever happened to a tree. This is how I love you. I am peeling back my skin, layer by layer, so you will finally know everything inside me.

My first boyfriend was a beautiful boy named Steven Winthrop. He had an older brother who went to Harvard. Steven loved to wear a Harvard sweatshirt to school over a polo shirt with the collar popped. He had long, dirty-blond hair and let his bangs hang over his eyes. Whenever he looked at me through his hair with his perfect green eyes, I thought maybe I loved him. We lived in a small subdivision of twenty-four colonial homes all less than a decade old. My father, a historian, thought it was an uncomfortable thing, the juxtaposition of new and old. He called our neighborhood a simulacrum, said everything in it was false and constructed. My mother would roll her eyes when he said things like this. She'd say, "And yet here we are," and he would grumble and go to his well-appointed study to grade and bemoan the illiteracy of college students.

The man who came before you once shared his recipe for the perfect date meal. He said it was simple food that tasted amazing. You are nothing like him. He said women were so impressed with the meal they not only slept with him; they also washed the dishes. Take two thick rib-eye steaks, richly marbled with fat. Season them liberally with coarse sea salt and freshly ground pepper. Preheat the oven to 450 degrees. On the stove and using a cast-iron pan, sear the steaks on each side, sealing in the juices. Put the steaks into the oven using the same pan, and allow them to cook for five to seven minutes. Serve with fresh hot bread with butter over very cold lettuce using the meat's juices as dressing.

My mother always told me to cut away the fat from steak because it wasn't good for me. She's a vegetarian and holds a natural distrust of animal flesh and food slaughtered in captivity. I don't cut the fat from meat anymore. I love to eat it, love to feel it hot and salty and gelatinous between my teeth. I love the way it coats my throat and how it upsets my stomach, reminds me I am doing something I should not do.

That boyfriend served me his perfect meal. I slept with him after I washed his dishes but I don't credit the food, which was, as promised, perfect. The wine we drank was red and thick and sweet and it made everything in his hot, cramped kitchen blurry. We were drinking directly from the third bottle, laughing when we blew down the skinny glass neck and awkward sounds echoed back like we were playing recorders. He stood behind me and sank his teeth into my neck. His breath was warm and boozy and as his teeth pressed through my skin, I leaned into him. Later, I couldn't even walk to his bedroom. I was so drunk I crawled and he followed, pressing his bare foot against my ass to shove me forward. I let him do that. I did. He brought another bottle of wine. He threw me onto his bed, undressed me, and rolled me on my stomach.

Cooking is not something I enjoy. My mother often told me a woman should never cook for a man because doing so would give him permission to take her for granted. She resented my father in spite of her love for him. She resented that he got to come and go as he pleased and she resented the commonness of her resentment. She resented being smarter than him. Once I started school, my mother often spent her days in the back of my father's classrooms listening to him lecture. There's something about a man standing at a chalkboard, she would say. At night, she would help him grade and prepare conference presentations and write scholarly articles. She would say, "I should go back to school," and he would pat her hand and chuckle and this made me resent him, too. You have never given me cause to resent you.

As I lay with my face pressed into his coarse sheets he spread my thighs. He planted a sweaty hand against the back of my neck, holding me down, and he fucked me with his wine bottle, the expensive merlot splashing all over the place. He had seen it in a movie once, he said. He was opening me up, he said. I wondered if the wine stained my womb. In that moment I felt wretched and low. It was a moment of such perfect honesty I came and he knew it. He stood above me watching me tremble and whimper and bite my lower lip. He said, "That's right, baby," with wonderment. I let him do much more. I did. The next morning, I had a dry headache and my mouth was a horrible, lonely place. I found my clothes and my keys and when I got home, I dropped my purse in the entryway and went upstairs and walked into the shower without removing my clothes. I stood there beneath the cold water, my jeans and my slutty T-shirt clinging to my body uncomfortably, fresh bruises spreading across my back, down my ass, between my thighs. I thought about how I am fond of repetition.

My best friend is in love with me. You know and you like it. You enjoy having something someone else wants. I like it, too. You worry my attention will wander because I have slept with women but they are too kind and too cruel and you are too true. My best friend is crazy and not in a charming way that inspires interesting stories. She is a middle child, raised by diplomats in the Foreign Service. She became scarred from moving around so much, being forced to blend in across so many cultures. You like to say she is unwell while twirling your finger next to your left ear and whistling loudly. She has an equally crazy girlfriend who lives in Northern California on some kind of hippie commune. They see each other during solstices and spend the rest of their time corresponding with long letters written in tiny, disturbed penmanship. Sometimes, her parents call our place to see if we've heard from her. They're afraid she's going to be one of those sad people who die alone in their home and aren't discovered until it's too late—green and swollen, skin sloughing off. Before I met you, she and I were not different.

I know why you're with me or at least how what is between us began. I'm brown enough to satisfy your desire to be with someone exotic but I'm not so brown as to create insurmountable problems when we spend time with your family. You like to make jokes about how I'm the best of both worlds with my white father and my black mother and my good education—my bland Midwestern accent and caramel skin. You love me most in the summer when we spend our afternoons on the lake, bronzing and drinking and surrendering to mosquitoes and suntan lotion. My skin gets darker beneath the high sun but not dangerously so. It shines and when I'm sweaty, you like to lick my shoulder. You pull at my body with your teeth and moan from somewhere deep and I know you're mine. You are a much better lover in the summer.

Sometimes we venture into the water, curling our toes in the warm silt beneath our feet and you spin us around and around the shallow until we're dizzy. We walk far away from the shore, pressing through the water, talking about silly things. We go just past that shelf where the lake floor drops to unknown depths. You float on your back and I float between your thighs, resting my arms on your legs. You point back at the shore and say, look how far we can go when we're together, and the moment always chokes me. Three summers ago you asked me for the second time to marry you as we floated out there on the wide, blue water. I pulled away from you and let my body submerge completely. I opened my eyes and watched you looking down at me, your arms making wide, gentle waves. I said yes, my words slowly bubbling to the surface.

I love you because you're simple but not in that trite, insulting way to which men are often relegated. No. You are simple because you are an optimist. You believe that those who lead a good life will be blessed with all good gifts. You say we are good people. You say we deserve to be happy. I say I am not good and you say you know better. Your generosity of spirit moves me. I look at you with your beautiful eyes and your smooth face, your open heart and your soft hands. I am a vile thing next to you. I am not beautiful or smooth or soft or simple. We rarely argue, but not for my lack of trying. I lose my temper and you stand there calmly and that makes me even angrier. I make impossible demands and you satisfy them. I say appalling things and you never throw my words back in my face. Only once have you walked out on me. I lied and said I hated you. I said we were just using each other. I said you were suffering from a severe case of jungle fever. Your eyes widened and I could tell I had finally pushed you too far. You wrapped one hand around my throat and pushed me across the room until my back was flat against the wall. As you raised your other hand, my breath caught and I relaxed. My whole body felt loose and free because I finally found who I was looking for inside you. I closed my eyes and waited. I waited for you to hurt me the way I deserved, the way I needed, but you didn't. You loosened your grip and you said nothing. As you walked away, you paused, turned, and pointed one finger at me. Your hand was shaking.

Balloons make me cry, as do marching bands and fireworks. When I was five, I was holding a perfect red balloon in a crowded shopping mall. My mother and I were on the escalator going down. I accidentally let go of my balloon. I started running up the escalator after it, tried to grasp at the escaping string, but I never got anywhere and then I fell against the steel teeth beneath me and broke my collarbone. My mother rushed me to the hospital and stood guard over me. I started to understand how much she loved me and I was terrified to know I mattered that much. There was little the hospital could do for me once they reset the bone. As two doctors held me down and pulled my bones into their proper places, my mother bared her teeth, violently rocking back and forth like something feral. The room went quiet. The doctor put my arm in a sling to keep it immobilized, to allow my body to heal, and quickly left the room. My mother never allowed me to ride an escalator again. That's why I have great calves.

I am my mother's daughter. If something happened to you, I would have to be put down. I would become an animal.

I was a mother once and you were a father and we had a baby or at least the idea of a baby was taking hold in my womb and in our hearts. We bought books and looked for a bigger home and we didn't tell anyone, not because we were worried but because it was wonderful to have this perfect mystery between us. You were the one who woke up with my blood on your thighs and you drove us to the hospital and carried me inside as terrible cramps rolled through me. You cried when the idea of our baby could no longer hold on. Scar tissue and uterine retroversion and plain bad luck, the doctor told us. How could you not know it would be difficult to conceive a child, the doctor asked. When you left the room, the doctor looked at me over the rims of his glasses. He placed his warm and slightly sweaty hand on mine, careful not to press too hard on the IV. He said, "Something happened to cause this kind of damage, the scarring." He said, "I'm sorry. It was a miracle you were pregnant at all." You came back to my room with flowers. You crawled into the bed next to me, and kissed my forehead over and over. For the fourth time you asked me to marry you. I curled into your body. I tried to hold on to you.

Hunting was big where we lived when I was young. Sometimes I'd see men pulling dead deer from the backs of their trucks, the slain animals looking alive save for a neat bullet hole blackened around the edges or a bleeding arrow wound in the neck. Hunters would hang their kill on the scale and gambrel at the general store in town. My mother would always try to cover my eyes but I would elude her protective embrace. I would stare at the fallen deer. I remember their dead bodies and how their eyes were always open during this final indignity.

Steven Winthrop is a real estate agent in Atlanta. He appears quite successful. He looks the same as he always has. His forehead has increased in size and there is a small victory in that, but on the whole, he remains handsome. He specializes in corporate real estate. On his website, he is wearing a gray suit and a pink tie. Beneath his name, a motto: "Experience ex-SELL-ence." I wrote down the address of his office, his email, his phone number. I pressed down so hard the imprint of that information remains on my desk. When I'm working, I rub my fingers over the indentations of the numbers four, six, nine, seven, two. Last Christmas, while we were visiting my parents, I saw him twice. The first time, he was getting out of a late-model German luxury sedan with a tall blond woman and a little boy who looked just like him. He started to wave but stopped, his arm awkwardly hanging in midair. The second time, he was standing on his parents' front porch smoking while I was smoking. When he saw me, he didn't look away and neither did I. He didn't wave and neither did I. After three cigarettes, he stepped off his porch and headed toward me. I ran back into the house. I hid in my bedroom closet, where it was dark and tight. I couldn't breathe. You found me and when I wouldn't move, you sat with me.

A proper deer blind is well camouflaged and has a good gun rest. It should be sturdy, well balanced, and have some kind of floor covering for noise reduction. Steven Winthrop found an abandoned cabin in the woods behind our subdivision. It had two small windows at the right height to serve as gun rests and a dirt floor covered in rocks and sticks, stale cigarette butts, old beer and soda cans, shell casings, and a bright orange hunting vest. A small bench sat along one wall but other than that, the cabin was empty. "Hunters must have used it as a deer blind at some point," Steven said, "but I think they've moved on."

You were gone for three days after I finally pushed you too far, said things that could not be unsaid. Each of those days I went to work. I sat in my office and smiled and pretended to be alive. At night I drove around looking for you. I parked in front of your parents' house and watched their television flicker as they sat in their recliners. I drove by the homes of everyone you've ever known. I called your phone and left messages ordering you home. I logged into your email and bank accounts looking for a clue but you had disappeared completely. By the third night the whole wide world felt unknowable. I left a note in case you came home and I went to the worst part of town. I walked into the loudest bar and looked for the meanest man. He bought me drinks and I drank them until my tongue felt heavy in my mouth and it was impossible to say the word *no*. He was tall and skinny but his body was tightly coiled with muscle. He had olive skin and narrow eyes and a wide nose. His face and neck were covered in stubble. There was a tattoo of an anatomical heart on the inside of his right wrist and when he wrapped his hand through my hair, the heart pulsed. I would have followed him home, and let him do what he pleased with me. I would have let him punish me but as we were standing in front of the bar, in a halo of cigarette smoke, my phone rang. I saw your name on the glowing screen. I fell to my knees.

In college, my best friend was also my roommate. She didn't date much. She was too strange for the gay-until-graduation girls, even at our overpriced, liberal university. Instead she followed me around all the time, earning the nickname Shadow. She thought it was a compliment. That's who she is—she never quite understands how things really are or at least she pretends so people will think she's harmless. I have a soft spot for that sort of thing. I would bring boys and girls back to our room. She would pretend to be asleep. I would pretend to believe she wasn't pretending. I would fuck boys and girls and I wasn't quiet about it and whenever I looked across the room, I saw that strange girl staring at me, the whites of her eyes shining, her breath ragged and matching mine.

The meanest man grabbed me by my hair again and pulled my face toward his crotch. He was already hard, insistent against my cheek. I swallowed hard and told him the whole night had been a misunderstanding. I said I had to excuse myself rather primly and he laughed. He laughed so loudly his voice echoed around us and out onto the street, and after a few seconds, he loosened his grip and pulled me to my feet. He said he hadn't laughed that hard in the longest time. He let me go home to you. You were pacing when I walked through the front door and I was still drunk so I started crying. You yelled at me. Your hands were shaking again. You tried to hug me but I held a hand out in front of me, kept you away. "You don't want to touch me," I said. "I'm all fucked up." You agreed. You said, "Yes, baby. You are," and that was the first time you asked me to marry you. I didn't mean to slap you. It was instinct. As soon as I felt the bone of your cheek beneath my hand, you smiled. You winced and held my hand to your face, then pressed your lips to my palm. You pulled me against you tightly and said you were sorry for leaving. No matter how hard I struggled, you didn't let me go.

Steven Winthrop and I would often ride our bikes single file in the woods because the path was well worn but very narrow. I would linger behind him and admire his lean, athletic body and bask in the wake of him. Sometimes, we would have little picnics in the abandoned deer blind. We pretended we were sophisticated and romantic. We read Judy Blume novels aloud. We kissed for hours and he would lie on top of me, his Harvard sweatshirt soft against my skin. He would slide his hands beneath my shirt and trace my rib cage and tell me I had a beautiful body even though I had none to speak of. His lips always tasted like Red Grape Mad Dog and Swisher Sweets, no matter the time of day.

Your mother does not hate me but she once pulled me aside while you and your father were out chopping wood. She took me into her living room and handed me a glass of wine. She smiled politely, shifted in her seat, rested a hand on my knee, and said what all white mothers say when their precious white sons consort with brown girls. She was worried for our hypothetical children, how difficult it would be for those children, how difficult, really, it would be for her. She did not know about the idea of the baby we once held between us. She said I was different and special but that maybe we should consider the suitability of our union. I thought about the two of us in that hospital bed, how we mourned for so long. I snapped at her, said any child whose parents make six figures would probably not suffer too terribly. I told her my parents had never been a problem for me. Her eyes narrowed and she said money isn't everything, that my parents were the exception. That's why she thinks I'm greedy. I spoke without thinking. I told your mother I couldn't have children, not without serious medical intervention, and her eyes shone brightly. Her whole body hummed. You should know that about your mother.

I believed in Steven Winthrop more than I believed in God. Sometimes we would sneak into his brother's bedroom and look at dirty magazines like *Juggs* and *Gallery* and then he would paw at me and try to understand how my body worked, contorting my limbs like the girls on the glossy pages. I let him do these things even when he made me feel more like meat than girl. My senior year in college, I worked in a porn store during the graveyard shift. The radio station was permanently set on a rock station. I know the words to every classic rock song. That's why I am excellent at karaoke. The store had ten jack shacks where men could rent and watch videos in dark little booths. There was a two-screen movie theater and aisle after aisle of rubber fists and vibrators in the shape of sea animals and red fur-lined handcuffs and high-end glossy Europorn. The best part of the job was selecting movies to air in the theaters. I found the most disturbing pornographic options—obese women being fucked by midgets, geriatric ladies getting hammered by Asian guys, amputees fucking twins with their stumps. It felt like justice.

I'm an only child. My parents had me and realized they had enough love for only one child and I have always appreciated their self-awareness. You have a brother and a sister and you're nothing like them. It's obvious to anyone that your parents love you most and maybe that's why your siblings are always in trouble. Your sister and I have a lot in common. I can tell by the curve of her spine—her body knows things. You worry I'm going to get tired of her late night phone calls asking you for a ride from the bar or to lend her money. You worry I'll get fed up with being trapped in the tense scenes when your family gets together but I won't, not ever. When you go out of town, your sister comes over and spends the night with me because she understands the curve of my spine. We watch Food Network and order pizza. We drink wine and sit on the deck holding sparklers, giggling as the shower of light burns our skin. We fall asleep on the couch and silently count the moments until your return. It's not easy keeping a terrible mess from spilling all over the place. You and I will always do what we can for her until she finds someone to help her hold herself together the way you help me.

Men propositioned me a lot at the porn store. I let them. I did. Most customers were sad, poorly shaven, sagging but harmless. Others were not. A man once slid five crisp twenty-dollar bills and his business card across the counter in the small space hidden from the security cameras. Five minutes later, I followed him into a jack shack and sat next to him on the little bench. It was a dark, tight place, like the confessional, only more honest. I couldn't breathe. I couldn't move. While I listened for the chime of the front door, we watched Steven St. Croix and Chasey Lain go at it. Chasey stood against the shower door with one leg flung over her head. She was very flexible and wore green eye shadow that nicely complemented her blue eyes. I never got that man's name. He grabbed my hand and pulled it to his lap. His cock was dry and hot and small. I wanted the moment to end before it began but there was only one way out of that place. I didn't want to be hurt. He was not the last customer who gave me money in exchange for my mouth or my hand or something more. I still keep some of the business cards in a Rolodex in the back of our closet.

When you're my kind of mess, men can smell it on you. They hunt you down. Your brother is no exception. At your birthday party in July I was in the kitchen opening a fresh bag of ice. Everyone was out in the backyard, laughing and dancing beneath Japanese lanterns and citronella candles. You were drunk and doing the running man and pretending you were dancing ironically when you were really quite serious. You kept shouting for me to join you and you sang one line of your favorite song and I sang the next line back through the window over the kitchen sink. You're a happy drunk so I didn't mind the enthusiastic display even knowing later I would have to drag you to bed and help you get undressed and fall asleep with your heavy arm across my chest, your drunk snoring in my ear. Your brother came up behind me and I was startled. I thought I was alone with you, surrounded by all our friends. Kool & the Gang was playing and I was swaying from side to side as I filled a bucket with fresh ice. My fingers were cold but the cold felt so nice. It was the hottest summer and even late at night, the air was thick and humid and humming.

Your brother grabbed me so hard his fingertips left eight small bruises on my hips. His breath reeked sweetly of fermented hops. He pulled me against his fleshy body, pressing his pointy chin into the top of my head. My stomach rolled uncomfortably and my chest tightened. I thought about my hatred of repetition. I stood perfectly still, slid my hands deeper into the bucket of ice, hoped for some mercy, hoped the ice would make my whole body numb so I wouldn't feel a thing. I didn't want to be hurt. He said, "I like a little coffee in my cream, too," and squeezed my ass, jiggling his hand. You called for me again and sounded so excited, like you hadn't seen me in the longest time. I said I would be right there and hoped I was telling you the truth. You proposed for the third time. You shouted, "Marry me, baby. Marry me now," and our friends laughed and cooed and I grinned and blew you a kiss. I said yes, but my voice got lost in the distance between us. My blood pounded so fiercely, I thought I might come apart. I told your brother, "Don't do this. Don't break his heart. Don't break mine." He trapped me between his body and the counter and the pressure of him took my breath away. Your brother made an ugly sound but he walked away. When he's around, I feel him watching me, waiting. Please don't ever leave me alone with him.

I told my not-so-best-friend, college roommate about my whoring past years after we graduated. We stayed in touch though I am not sure why. I suppose she was all I had. She thought it was the most interesting story. That was the exact phrase she used. We were sitting in her living room drinking gin and tonics and listening to some terrible womyn's music. She sat cross-legged, staring at me, her forehead furrowed deeply. "That is the most interesting story," she said, slightly breathless, overenunciating each word. She asked for an account of each indiscretion, rocking back and forth as I made her my confessor. Her skin flushed darkly and she licked her lips over and over. Imagining me being used turned her on. She's overeducated and has taken too many women's studies classes. She uses words like *empowerment* sincerely. When my accounting was complete, she moved so close our knees were touching and placed her hand in the small of my back. She nuzzled her lips against my neck and I shivered uncomfortably. I leaned away, smiled politely. She slid her other hand beneath my shirt, gently cupped my breast, and then I was on my back, staring at the ceiling as she pressed her warm cheek against the flat of my stomach. She asked, "What would it cost me to be with you?" I hated her. I planted my hands against her shoulders, pushed her away, which only made her angry. She straddled my waist, pinning my arms to my sides. I recognized the look in her eyes, marveled that it was not unique to men. I brought my knee up between her thighs, hard, and she cried out, rolled off me. For the first time in my life, I said, "No." The word felt glorious and strange on my lips.

My mother took me to confession once a week, on Thursdays after school. I waited in the pews while she confessed her sins and I would try to hear what she was saying so I might have a clearer sense of what God expected. I was, for a time, a good girl. I got good grades. I had good manners. I said please and thank you. I wore skirts of an appropriate length. When I sat in the confessional, I couldn't breathe. I hated being in that dark tight place. I sat there and listened to the priest, Father Garibaldi, how he would lick his dry lips and urge me to confess, to confess, to repent. He smelled like garlic. He once gave me a pamphlet, *A Young Person's Guide to the Rosary and Confession.* I learned about the joyful, the sorrowful, the glorious mysteries of the rosary and how to go to confession, how to use the Ten Commandments as my moral guide. I would hear his frustration when I still had nothing to say, when I was unable to account for my misdeeds.

Popular teenage boys travel in packs. Steven Winthrop was the leader of a pack of five. Wherever Steven and his friends went, they moved in disciplined formation, their strides perfectly matched, arms swinging at the same speed. They knew how to fill the space around them. His friends believed in Steven Winthrop more than they believed in God. In *A Young Person's Guide to the Rosary and Confession,* the First Commandment stated, "I am the Lord your God; thou shall have no strange Gods before me." We defied our immortal salvation for Steven Winthrop. We did so with joy in our hearts. You too have always been popular. I have seen the evidence in your childhood bedroom, meticulously preserved by your mother. Even now, you have packs of men following you, willing to make you their strange god. That is the only thing about you that scares me.

You lost your virginity during your sophomore year in college. You think it is almost shameful that you waited when people thought you hadn't. You think it is trite that you loved the first girl you ever made love to, that you planned your first time the way you plan everything—with a great deal of consideration and attention to detail. You cried after your first time because you finally felt complete. You told me this on our first real vacation, ten days in Barcelona when we didn't talk about work or our families or anything ugly. Instead we embarrassed ourselves when we spoke our college Spanish and visited castles and cathedrals and walked up and down Las Ramblas. We talked about how small we felt in the world and all the people who brought us to each other. You think I lost my virginity my junior year in college to a guy named Ethan. You laughed when I told you this fable, said there was no way a man named Ethan could satisfy a woman. You said you loved that I waited, too. You said you wish you had waited for me. I said I wish I had been given the choice and then I changed the subject.

On a perfect Thursday afternoon in June, when I was still so much just a girl, Steven Winthrop took me to our secret place in the woods. As I rode behind him, I kept staring up at the clear shafts of light piercing through the canopy above. I laughed and laughed and I shouted, "I love you!" into the wind. He turned back at me and grinned. When we got to the cabin, Steven Winthrop's pack was waiting for me. They offered me warm cans of beer but I said no. They cracked jokes. I pretended to laugh. I pulled Steven Winthrop aside, said I didn't want to hang out with his friends. I tried to leave but those boys were far bigger than me. They blocked the doorway and they laughed. They said, "This one is going to fight," and they said they had always wanted a little taste of brown sugar. I stood in the middle of the cabin as it became dark and tight. I couldn't breathe.

A therapist once told me that with time and distance memories fade. He lacked imagination or compassion. He also told me I was too pretty to have any real problems. I started seeing him because I was eating everything in sight. From the moment I woke up until I went to sleep I stuffed myself with food. I ate past the point of disgust, until I could see my stomach rolling and misshapen beneath my skin. I was never hungry but I ate and kept eating until the people I knew stopped recognizing me. I ate until I made myself sick, until I made everyone I knew sick to look at me so I would never be trapped in a terrible place again. I won't ever go back to being a grotesquerie of flesh but at the time I needed someone to give me a reason to stop, to feel safe and that therapist, he sat in his expensive Herman Miller chair with his legs crossed effeminately and he helped me catalog my beauty but had nothing else to offer.

Steven Winthrop said, "I'm going first." That's when I understood. He ordered his pack to hold me down. The boys dug their fingers into my wrists and ankles and I screamed so loudly my voice unraveled. Steven Winthrop howled while he fucked me. He pounded his fists against my chest. He shouted, "I am the virgin hunter!" and his friends laughed and shouted in unison, "He is the virgin hunter!" Steven Winthrop's sweat fell into my eyes and then I was blind. I could not see. He smelled so ugly—sour and metallic—and his body was so heavy. He was rabid. He whispered in my ear, called me baby. He told me I liked it. When he came, he groaned loudly in my ear, stayed on me, panting for a long time. His sweat stained me. His pack grew impatient so Steven Winthrop rolled off and pulled his pants up in one motion and then he lay on his side watching. When our eyes met, he didn't look away. He smiled.

The pack took their turns. Their bodies were hard, muscular, demanding, insatiable. They tore me apart. They didn't care that I fought. The smallest of the pack was the cruelest, the most determined to undo me. The more wildly I resisted, the louder they brayed. After an hour or so, Steven Winthrop and his pack took a break, breathless and sweaty. They congratulated each other; they were proud. I sat in the corner of the cabin, my knees pulled to my chest. I stared up through a hole in the ceiling at the perfect sky on a perfect June day. When they started again, I stopped fighting. I just looked into the sun as it set and I looked into the dusky sky and I looked into the early dark of night.

Later, after the rest of the pack went home, Steven Winthrop helped me get dressed. Of all his cruelties, his kindness was the worst. He spit on my torn underwear and used it to wipe my face clean before slipping it into his pocket. He pulled my jeans up over my thighs and gently buttoned them. He kissed my navel and the bruises flowering around it. He pulled my T-shirt over my head and put his letter jacket around my shoulders. He kissed my forehead and told me I was a good girl. We were silent as we walked our bikes home. He escorted me all the way to the edge of my driveway. My parents came running out. They shrieked that they were worried sick and had called the police. They asked Steven where he had found me, their voices pitching even higher.

"I found her wandering in the woods while I was looking for my dog," Steven said. "I wish I could have found her sooner." My parents grew silent, took a hard look at me, said they hardly recognized me. They tried to hug me but I held my hands in front of my body, backed away, begged them to please not touch me, to just let me be. My mother shook her head slowly, holding her hand over her mouth. She cried. My father ran into the house to call an ambulance and when he returned, he thanked Steven for helping me. My father's hands shook as he took Steven's in his, squeezed them tightly. He told Steven to get inside before his parents worried, said there were dangerous people in the world, said the police might want to talk to him. Steven flashed his perfect smile but could no longer look me in the eye as he leaned in, held my wrist, kissed my cheek. I moaned softly and hunched over, vomiting into the bed of yellow daisies surrounding the mailbox.

At the hospital, detectives and social workers and doctors and nurses asked me who had done this terrible thing. They took pictures and plucked and scraped and splayed me open like the deer on the scale and gambrel. They asked more questions, gave me a gray jogging suit, said they needed my clothes. I said nothing. I couldn't breathe. I wished for rain to find me, to fall, to wash everything clean. It was almost three in the morning when we returned home, my father driving, muttering angrily through gritted teeth. I sat in the back with my mother, Steven Winthrop's letter jacket still draped around my shoulders. As we walked into the house, I saw him watching from his bedroom. I let his jacket fall off my shoulders and onto the ground. After I took a shower, my mother sat on the edge of my bed, brushing wet curls away from my face. She twisted her wedding ring back and forth nervously. She said, "You don't ever have to talk about this." She said, "We can pretend this never happened." I didn't and we did.

Venison is peculiar meat—muscular and gamy, tough to digest but popular in many circles. I do not care for venison. I don't trust any meat slaughtered in the wild. You like to hunt, spending ten days in the woods each fall with your father and brother, huddled in tiny deer blinds, doused in deer piss, your fingers numb with cold. Hunting makes you feel like a man, you say. Every season you bring me butchered venison, venison sausage, venison jerky, ground venison. Your mother gave us a deep freezer and we store your spoils in the basement, carefully labeled. The word *venison* comes from the Latin word *venari*, to hunt. I find that cruel, to name something for that end which comes to pass.

You are the joy in my life. I am a mess but I will be the joy in yours. What we have is a perfect thing, like the baby or the idea of a baby we once had, how our unborn child was this sacred secret we held between our hearts. When you touch me, you feel through me, through the ugliness beneath my skin, you make me feel, you hold me together, you push my skin back into its proper place. When you see me next, I will be wearing your ring on my left finger. I will say yes. You will hear me.

Read on for three new stories and an
interview with Roxane Gay

The Q&A first appeared online in
*Electric Literature* on January 3, 2017

# Pilgrims

The long line of cars waiting to enter the fairgrounds begins to move and Garrison edges forward in his seat, his forehead practically pressed against the hot windshield. I cannot believe how many people are here—I whisper the prison-pressed license plate numbers from all over the country. I am wracked with a fresh wave of guilt. The world is overpopulated. The world is suffering. Here we are, with scores of other people who have also chosen to ignore these facts. We are all arrogant assholes.

"Maybe we don't deserve to have kids," I say.

Garrison turns to me. "What makes you say that?"

I can't help but notice that he doesn't disagree. I recite the litany of excuses people like us trot out to condemn our desires. "There are so many children out there who need good homes. Blah blah blah."

He brushes his fingers along my chin but his touch is not gentle. "We've been over this."

After we called the toll-free number, requested the informational DVD and brochure. After we requested the time off from our respective jobs and told our families we were going on a short vacation. After the second-guessing and hand-wringing. Here we are. In our foul, humid Civic with the empty backseat, still infertile. I pictured a neatly paved road leading directly to the hallowed tent of Brother Marcus. He would be waiting for us, just inside the entrance. As we entered, his arms would open wide. He would pull us into an embrace. He would lay a hand on the flat of my stomach, whisper words I couldn't understand. He would grip Garrison's shoulder and counsel my husband on a man's responsibilities. He would hold my hand and counsel me on embracing the joys of motherhood. There would be air-conditioning.

When we finally enter the fairgrounds and park the car, all we see are dusty, foot-worn paths leading to a bright purple tent. I watch the throngs of barren couples around us, all seething with the same desperate urgency to procreate. Garrison and I look at each other. "We should just go home," I say. Garrison gets out of the car, and slaps the roof of the car. "Like hell," he says. "Brother Marcus is gonna make us a baby." As I get out of the car, take Garrison's hand, and head into the tent, I think back to my sixth-grade biology class—the lesson on biomes. My womb is a tundra, unable to provide sustenance.

A wide, circular stage, three feet from the ground, sits in the center of the tent. It is brightly lit, yet sparse. In the center of the stage there is a large tub made of stainless steel, filled with rainwater, large enough for two adults. Brother Marcus believes in a wide variety of religious traditions, the brochure told us, and in that vein, he borrowed from the Jewish concept of *mikvah*, allowing his audience to cleanse themselves, purify the lives that had brought them to this point so they might conceive anew. A few feet to the right of the tub stands a mahogany pulpit with ornate carvings around the edges and above it is a large, flat-screen monitor, suspended from the aluminum tent rafters.

Toward the back of the stage are bleachers, filled with women in varying stages of pregnancy, the mounds of their bellies taunting, teasing, gloating. Their joy is palpable. Behind them, their husbands stand tall, proud, smug. The evidence of their virility is incontrovertible. Surrounding the stage are hundreds of metal folding chairs, arranged in pairs for those of us who have flocked here, two by two. Already, the first few rows are occupied. Garrison and I make our way down a clear aisle and sit near the back where we can feel a slight breeze from an open flap in the tent. The air is tense and thick and filled with the stench of perfumes and deodorants, bodies and, oddly enough, onions. Around us, couples chat nervously but Garrison and I are silent. I hold his hand so tightly my knuckles turn white and he says, "You're going to break my hand, babe."

My husband and I often ask unanswerable questions of each other. Should we give up? Should we find other partners? Why are we putting ourselves through this? But now, we sit here, knowing we're wasting our time, moving forward nonetheless. We hold on to the brittle hope that it will soon be me sitting in those bleachers, caressing my swollen belly, the glow around me incandescent. We hold this bitter hope but ask nothing more of each other. Somewhere along the blanched highways, between rest areas and mile markers, we found the answers to all the questions we are always afraid to ask.

The argument started miles south of Paris, Texas, when the heat finally pushed us to a new breaking point. The air in the car was so thick it hurt to breathe. I said that we needed a new car. He snapped, and pulled onto the shoulder, slammed his hand against the dashboard. He said, "Maybe we could afford a new car if we didn't spend all our money chasing down new ways for you to get pregnant." I said something about his job and future employment prospects. He said *fuck you*. I got out of the car and even though the sun was high and scorching everything around and between us, I started walking, ignoring Garrison as he followed. "Get in the damn car," he said through the passenger window. I gave him the finger. I kept walking. He sped off, leaving an angry trail of rubber. I waited, hands on my waist, ready to resume our argument. He didn't come back.

I walked all the way to Bogata, population 1,401. I found a bench, and fell into it. My mouth was so dry I couldn't swallow. When I felt I could engage Garrison in a conversation without crying, I called him. He sounded panicked, demanded to know where I was, said he had been driving up and down the same stretch of highway for hours. After he picked me up, he apologized through clenched teeth, a lie. We stopped talking after that.

After an hour of waiting and sweating and listening to the couples around us reciting stories we already know, music starts playing. It is not the gospel we expect, but rather, rock and roll, dirty South, stripper-pole rock and roll. I stifle a laugh, and the chatter hushes as a robed figure makes his way through the audience and walks onto the stage, standing before the steel tub. The figure raises his arms, and the hood of the robe falls to his shoulders. The audience instantly breaks into applause. It is Brother Marcus, his face shiny with sweat. His hair is as perfect as it was on the infomercial. He is the Pat Sajak of fertility. *Wheel of Fortune*, indeed. As he shrugs out of his robe, an assistant scurries to his side to grab it and disappears just as quickly. Brother Marcus rubs his hands together, and with a wide sweep of his arm, turns toward his success stories, sitting on the edges of their seats in the bleachers. "My work," Brother Marcus says, "Speaks for itself."

When Garrison chases after his nieces and nephews on Sunday afternoons, he smiles so widely that his features rearrange themselves to accommodate the stretch of his lips. He laughs from somewhere deep and when he finally catches one of them, he throws them over his head, their legs tangling with his arms. When we catch each other's eyes in these moments, there is something bittersweet between us.

For the next few hours, Brother Marcus rambles on about God, fertility, sin and redemption, at a dizzying pace. There seems to be no logical connection between any two words, and yet, the audience is captivated, hanging on to his every word as if there is a mystical meaning to be divined from the incomprehensible babbling. I have grown weary beneath the weight of his words. I press my hands to my womb, imagining a fluttering that is not there. Garrison occasionally kisses my forehead. His lips are warm and moist. I turn to look at him. His long curls cling to the edges of his face and tiny beads of sweat dot his chin. When he puts his arm around me, I wince and pull away. My entire body is tender with sunburn. Even my clothes make my nerve endings ache. He shrugs, then smiles, kisses my forehead again. He is somewhat contrite. I am significantly less so. When it is all over, after Brother Marcus has danced down the aisles and preached himself hoarse, after he has heard testimony from each

wanting couple, after he has taken up a collection because the
work of bringing about conception comes at a price, we walk
back to our car slowly. We are not holding hands. "This was a
mistake," Garrison says. "I'm done with this." I roll my eyes,
open my own door, slouch in my seat as we drive away from a
hope that never was. We won't be returning.

Later, in our motel room, the air-conditioning isn't working.
Our misery, we conclude, is our penance for behaving badly with
one another. Sweat continues to pool between my breasts and
the greasy burgers and fries we brought back to the hotel sit on
a small table lukewarm and covered in congealed cheese. After
rubbing me down with aloe, Garrison props open the door to our
room and sits in the doorway burying his face in a full ice bucket.
I sit on the edge of the bed in a tank top and panties, trying to
remain as still as possible.

"This was a great idea," Garrison says. He lowers his face
deeper into the ice bucket and inhales.

I carefully cross one leg over the other and trace my thigh
muscles with my fingers. I took up distance running three years
ago and my legs have since become my best feature. There was no
real reason for taking up a painful hobby. I simply enjoy things
that make me feel bad and good at the same time. Garrison is like
running for me. I pull my tank top off over my head and lay back
on the bed even though my mother is always telling me that one
should never put their bare skin on a hotel bedspread.

I turn toward the door. "Join me," I say.

Slowly, Garrison stretches himself to his feet and with two
long steps closes the distance between us. He lies next to me,
kissing me, roughly, without preamble. He smells like sweat
and grease and his lips are dry, creating a strange friction. His

body is narrow and slick against mine, and even though every-thing between us is raw and humid and uncomfortable, he is pulling my panties off, working his jeans off, kneeling between my thighs as he traces through the sheen of sweat beneath my breasts. I look up at my husband. He looks completely indiffer-ent. He's looking past me or through me. I'm not sure which. I cover my eyes with my arm and moan softly. As he moves over and inside me, my entire body throbs. His skin abrades against mine. I wrap my arms around him as my body burns. He asks if he should stop. I tell him no, it all hurts. I lick his shoulder, swallow the bitter salt of his skin. He groans loudly. He lies. He says I *love you*. After he comes, he pulls his jeans back on and returns to the doorway and his bucket of water and ice. We are another place to which we will not return.

In the morning, we take the car to a mechanic, and wait for the air-conditioning to be repaired in a small waiting room that smells like motor oil and old coffee. There's a thirteen-inch television on a small table but a clear picture only flickers through once every few minutes. I sit with my arms crossed. I look straight into the blacks of Garrison's eyes, even when it makes me feel sick. He stares right back. We are having a standoff. Neither of us willing to draw first. We are saved from making such a fateful decision when the mechanic interrupts our staring contest, wiping his hands clean. "That should get you back to where you're going," he says. Garrison pays for the repairs with money we don't have and then we're on our way.

As we pull out of Baptiste and feel cool, dry air blowing over us for the first time in days, I burst into tears. The sheen of sweat covering my skin turns into goose bumps. Garrison reaches for my hand, but this time, I wave him away. I lean forward, pressing my forehead against my knees. I lace my fingers behind my head. I cry until I'm cold all over.

In a year, Garrison will have a baby boy who looks just like him. It won't be with me. I'll be having an affair with my boss who is married and already has four children of his own. My husband and I will run into each other while standing in line at the movie theater or at the grocery store. Sometimes, he will be holding his baby boy in his arms. We will pretend we don't know one another. We will be happy.

# We Are All So Happy Now

My father is not an optimist. He was born in Mississippi in 1943 and spent most of his formative years trying to avoid becoming strange fruit, low hanging, easy to split open. When he was a boy he prayed to God that if he had to come back, he wanted to rise again as a white man or rot in hell. When he became a man, he realized there was no God because no God would lay a curse on a people like the one the devil put on the black man. When he says this, my mother will generally add that God doesn't have much love for the black woman either. They'll both laugh until they don't. On those rare occasions when my father allows his picture to be taken, he stands tall, looks directly at the camera, invisible waves of anger around him. His chin is always raised, arms rigidly at his sides. He is ready to fight.

I live in a neighborhood where everything looks exactly the same. The day my wife and I bought our house, my parents cried.

When they tried to buy a house like ours, no bank would give them a mortgage for a home on the right side of the tracks. They also worried. "They don't like our kind in these neighborhoods," they said. "White folks are always worrying about their property values."

"That's exactly why we bought this house," my wife said. My dad laughed. He loves my wife.

I don't mow my lawn so I know which house is mine when I come home at night. My neighbors are intensely concerned about the state of my lawn. They take their suburban agricultural projects very seriously. On Saturday mornings, one of the white guys on either side of me will offer to mow my lawn after they finish theirs. I tell them I am embracing life by refusing to kill my grass with the cruel blades of a lawn mower. Now they think I'm an environmentalist, which confuses them because they don't know any black environmentalists. When my neighbors and I get into our cars every morning and pull out of our driveways, I can feel them glaring at me. It's a great way to start the day.

When you enter the foyer of our home, there's a large portrait of my wife, our son, and me hanging on the wall opposite the front door. The wall is painted with the color Ralph Lauren Soho Loft. I'm wearing a dress shirt, dark slacks, and a tie. My wife is wearing her favorite little black dress, strapless, low cut, highlighting her best assets. She is considerably shorter than me, so she's standing in front of me. My hands rest on her shoulders. Our son is standing next to us, his hand on his mother's shoulder, covering mine. He's wearing cargo pants and an argyle sweater. We're all looking at the camera. They're smiling. I am smirking, eyeing my wife's rack. One eyebrow is arched. Just before the shot was taken, my wife looked up at me and said, "We're all so happy now." I said, "Yes, you are." My wife loves the picture so much she used it for our Christmas card last year and made several smaller prints to send to her parents, my parents, and all the people we've never known. I see this picture every single time I walk through the front door. I am terrified.

I work with this guy Brad who is still active with his fraternity even though he graduated more than a decade ago. He went to Ole Miss. He thinks we're friends. When he talks to me, he likes to pretend he's a gangsta. He'll throw an imaginary gang sign, grab my shoulders and say something like, "*Whazzup homie?*" I'll shirk his grasp and say, "I'm not a rapper." Then I'll stare at the door willing someone to need something from me right away. Brad will laugh like I've said the funniest thing that has ever been said and then he'll say, "*That's why I fucking love you man.*" I smile at Brad a lot.

Every Friday afternoon Brad invites me to join him and his frat buddies for a game of basketball at the Y. Every Friday I remind Brad I don't know how to play basketball. This confuses him. Someday I'm going to become Brad's boss. The very first thing I will do is fire him. My father refused to let me play basketball when I was in high school, even though I wanted to, desperately. I wanted to be like Mike. "No son of mine," my father said, "is going to earn his living playing with some damn ball. I work too hard for that." The only picture of me in my high school yearbook, other than my class picture each year, is me with the debate team, standing in the back row, wearing thick bifocals, a blazer, and khaki pants wishing I were taking a picture with the basketball team. When I would show my mother the yearbook, she would rub my head and say, "Look how happy you are," and I would roll my eyes until they threatened to face the back of my head.

My wife and I met when we were juniors in college, in Atlanta, at a protest march encouraging her university to divest from Coca-Cola. The effort was not successful. I was very invested in authenticity. I wore my hair in a well-picked Afro. I had a number of dashikis I wore over jeans. I threw my fist in the air to punctuate most everything I said even though the revolution had come and gone well before I started college. I never understood why my wife gave me the time of day, particularly because her sorority sisters hated me. I was a Morehouse man, but I wasn't the right kind of Morehouse man. When she informed me of their disapproval, I said, "I'm going to keep it real. I can give you things the sisterhood can't." We married two years later at her parents' home. Our favorite picture from the wedding is one of the two of us on the dance floor beneath a tent in the backyard. I've removed my tuxedo jacket, and my tie is dangling around my neck. She's taken off her heels and is standing on my shoes, her feet bare, her head resting against my chest. We're barely moving. Our eyes are closed. The fingers of her right hand are clasped around my left suspender. Just as the picture was taken, I whispered, "I'm going to make you so happy."

Sometimes, before we fall asleep, my wife likes to reminisce. She'll close her book and straddle my lap, pulling my glasses off and setting them on the nightstand. "You were so different then," she'll say. She'll hold my face in her hands and kiss my forehead and the tip of my nose and my lips. Her mouth will taste like mint because she always brushes her teeth before she comes to bed.

I'll slide my hands beneath her t-shirt, and trace her ribcage with my fingertips sliding my hands lower then lower still. "I'm not different," I'll say. "I'm just more truthful."

My wife will pull my pajama pants down and hover sexily above me until I take control. She'll kiss my neck, inhaling deeply, then behind my ears. "No. You're angrier."

I'll place one finger over her lips. I'll say, "I'm becoming more like my father, I suppose." Then, I'll flip her onto her back, sliding a hand between her thighs, pushing them apart. She doesn't mind my anger.

On my desk at work there is a picture of my wife and son when he was six. We are on vacation at a beach resort in South Carolina. It is a beautiful day. The sun is shining. It's hot and the place is crowded with tourists like us. We are relaxing after spending the morning on the boardwalk, shopping and eating hotdogs and cotton candy and boiled peanuts. I've been ever mindful, as I always am, that I'm doing yet another thing my father never could. I am proud. I am angry. In the picture, my son still doesn't know how to swim so he wears swim trunks and inflatable armbands. He is not embarrassed. My boy does not yet know shame. My wife is wearing a bikini because she has just lost eighteen pounds and wants to show off her new body. Her skin is smooth and brown and slick with sunscreen. They are standing just where the waves crash onto shore. The two of them are smiling; their arms are raised high, fingers splayed widely. Their feet aren't touching the ground because each time a wave rolls in they jump as high as they can like they're trying to grab hold of the sun. As I took the picture, my son shouted, "I am so happy, Daddy." In that moment, my heart pounded so fiercely I thought I might die from the joy of it.

The first time Brad saw this picture he picked it up, and whistled.

"Your wife is hotter than Halle Berry," he said. "You're a lucky motherfucker."

I took the picture from him, returned it to its rightful place. I looked up and for once, I did not smile. I told him, "If you touch that picture again, I will break your arm."

Brad laughed. "You kill me, bro," he said.

Every two weeks, the family and I drive two hours to visit our parents who live only a few miles from each other. We share lunch with her parents and have dinner with mine. We are both only children. These visits are not optional.

Her parents are Old Negro Money. They hate me because I wasn't in Jack and Jill. I didn't escort a debutante to cotillion. I'm the wrong kind of Morehouse man because I relied on scholarships and the *generosity* of people like them for my college education. They have a black maid who wears a uniform and calls them sir or ma'am and probably spits in their food. I'm extra nice to her so she'll leave my food untainted. As we approach their house each fortnight I say, "We're almost at the plantation." We all laugh and my wife smacks my arm then squeezes it affectionately. Her parents serve us lemonade in glasses with lemon slices floating on top and we eat tiny sandwiches that do not satisfy. They interrogate me about how things are going at the firm. They tell my son to sit straight. They tell him to stop listening to his iPod, which is generally blasting a song they would find appalling. They ask when we're going to have more children and when we're going to move to a more appropriate neighborhood. I make up different answers each time. My wife rolls her eyes, pretends to be angry but accepts them for what they are—victims of time and place. Beneath the dining room table, she holds my hand.

At my parents' house, my mother tells us to make ourselves at home and commandeers my wife in the kitchen. My son sits in the living room sulking because my parents don't have cable.

My father consigns me to help him with things that need fixing. While we're working, or rather, while I'm working and my father is supervising, he complains about his neighbors, his arthritic shoulders, nonexistent medical ailments, the white devils at the VA, and that I don't visit often enough. He listens intently as I tell him about work, asking smart questions. My heart cracks a little more each time when I think about what he would have accomplished if he too were not a victim of time and place. At dinner, always fattening and filling, my parents ask when we're going to move closer to home and my mother tells my wife she's letting me get too skinny and that we shouldn't let our son spend all his time with those little plastic things in his ears and that we better get started on another baby because we aren't getting any younger. My wife nods politely and grins when my father winks at her. Beneath the kitchen table, I hold her hand.

I have only had one affair since my wife and I got married but it has been ongoing for several years. My mistress is a bohemian artist who lives in a loft downtown and wears cowrie shells in her dreadlocks and spends a great deal of time barefoot and smoking weed. I hate everything about her. We get together on Tuesdays and Thursdays when my wife thinks I'm playing poker with friends from college who are using that same alibi to spend time with their mistresses. She always smells like coffee grounds because she works as a barista to subsidize her lifestyle. She says our relationship is her muse—she gets off on wanting what she can't have. The sex is incredible. There's nothing she won't let me do.

In my home office hangs one of my mistress's paintings. It is small, abstract, black and white, oil on canvas. It is a painting of what I assume is a man, with asymmetrical features, only one eye, the left one, and a wild mane of kinky hair streaming in every direction. When my mistress gave it to me, I said, "What do you expect me to do with this?" She wrapped it in butcher paper and said, "I don't ask much of you." When my wife first noticed the painting she asked, "What is that hideous thing on the wall?" and I told her that a client's wife gave it to me.

On my cell phone, I have a picture of my mistress. She is lying naked on the floor next to her bed, in a tangle of sheets. On the nightstand above her, there's a half-full wine glass and an empty wine bottle lying on its side. She is holding one hand over her heart and she is looking at me. Her lips are slightly parted. She is not smiling but she refuses to look away. I am not in the picture. I am sitting on the edge of the bed, naked, drinking from my own glass of wine. We've been making love for hours. Just before I took the picture she said, "Even if this is all we ever have, I am so happy."

Once a year, my firm has a corporate retreat. We all bring our wives to a resort in Hawaii, and we spend a few hours each day reinvigorating our team spirit through exercises meant to reinforce our trust in one another. Then we spend the rest of our days on the golf course, deluding ourselves about the state of our game. It is an ordeal. Brad always manages to sit next to me at these retreats. He draws vulgar little pictures on his legal pad and then nudges it toward me until I look down and show some interest in his sad little drawings. He'll look at me for validation then throw in a gang sign for good measure.

Each evening, there's a cocktail hour. Then there's a dinner and the dinner always has a theme meant to unify us as a successful, profit-oriented firm and further contribute to the team building.

The most recent retreat was held in January, just after the new president was inaugurated. The mood was somber. Most of my colleagues could not understand how someone who looked like me was now, essentially, the boss of them and they were frustrated because if I was around, they couldn't really express their feelings. I was always around.

On the flight home, the wife and I drank several little bottles of wine and agreed it was the best retreat we had yet attended.

On the final evening of the retreat, the theme was *Where Do We Go From Here.* The search for answers was sincere.

Each year, the firm takes a group picture that hangs in the lobby of our building until it is replaced with a new picture the following year. In this year's picture, we're all standing beneath an arch of palm trees, surrounded by flickering torches. The men are wearing linen shirts and wrinkled slacks and dismay. Our wives are wearing short dresses, doing their best to prop their men up. Some of us are holding cigars. Others are nursing tumblers of Scotch. Brad and his wife, a gorgeous redhead who is way out of his league and knows it even though Brad doesn't, are standing next to my wife and I. Our arms are around each other. When he took the picture, the photographer said, "Smile like you mean it. Smile like you are all so happy."

# Glass

*What Happened When the Glass Cracked*

My father left. I woke up and could no longer smell him in the closed air of our home. My mother was alone, at the kitchen table. She sat holding a cold cup of tea. She stared out the window above the kitchen sink. She never blinked. Her eyes were dry. When I approached her, touched her shoulder, she turned to look at me. She still did not blink.

My father left but his leaving was slow. Every morning, on his way to work, he'd take some part of himself, neatly packed in a brown leather satchel. Soon, his desk was marked by a cartography of clean spaces surrounded by dust. One by one, he took his suits, socks, shaving kit, shoes. My mother pretended he wasn't leaving, pretended she couldn't see all he refused to leave behind.

My father left but when he did, he said it broke his heart to do it, to leave us kids. He took us to the park, one by one, and then out for ice cream. He explained that he loved us but didn't love our mother anymore, said she was the kind of woman a man could never love for long. We knew our mother and understood what he meant.

My father left and when he did, he said a man wasn't meant to love children enough to stay when a marriage wasn't working. He told my brothers to remember that when they had families of their own. He told them, "Never let children force you to stay with a woman you don't love." He told me, "Marry a better man than me."

My father left and when he did he sat us on the living room couch in a neat row, our knees touching. He stared down at us and said we were the reason for his leaving, said he couldn't stand the smell or sight or sound of us. One of us started to cry and he shook his head. He said, "See what I mean?"

My father left. When he did we were happy. My mother threw a party, left the windows open, and played music real loud. She let us stay up way past our bedtime and we danced with our arms around her as she drank whiskey sours and said in a singsong voice that she was about to have the best years of her life, which she didn't but that night, it felt possible and true.

My father left. When he did we forgot what it meant to be happy. My mother took to her room. The cupboards ran bare. We began running wild, becoming the kind of kids whose father left a big ragged hole in their hearts. My mother took up with another man, a similar version of the man who left her. When we called him Dad, he told us to shut up so we called him Dad a lot.

My father left. When he did, he said it was too painful to see us. He remarried quickly, we heard through my mother's friends, a woman who was much older. Everyone found it strange. I saw them at Safeway and hid behind a tower of canned soup. He held his hand in the small of her back and smiled at everything she said. When he saw me, he shook his head slightly. I understood.

My father left and when he did, he became a better father. Each morning, he would take us to breakfast at his favorite diner and watch us after school. He attended all our games and recitals and helped our mother with us every day, often cooking our dinner and putting us to bed. When he'd go to his apartment, my mother would say how divorce was the one thing that made her love my father.

My father left and when he did, he tried to make us love him even though we could not because his leaving broke our mother in half and we spent the rest of our lives trying to hold her together. No matter what he did—fantastic trips, new toys, new cars when we were older, we couldn't give him the one thing he wanted.

My father left. I was his favorite. I went to see him in his new apartment on Wednesdays and Sundays. We'd watch TV together, his arm around me. He smelled like menthol cigarettes and gin. He always held my hand in his lap and before I went back home, he'd say, "This is just for us," and he'd press his calloused finger to my lips.

My father left. I was not his favorite. When I went to see him in his new apartment, he was stiff, would always sit an awkward distance from me. He'd ask, "Why are you here?" I'd say, "I wanted to see you Daddy." He'd shake his head. He'd say, "I cannot imagine why but the sentiment is not mutual." I persisted, nonetheless.

My father left and when he did, I wrote him hundreds of angry letters. I always chose my words carefully, wrote these letters on small index cards and pretended they were postcards. When I mailed them, I didn't put them in envelopes. I wanted everyone to see what I really thought of him.

My father left and when he did, I became the kind of girl with daddy issues. I learned that boys love girls with daddy issues.

My father left and when he did, my brothers became the kind of boys with daddy issues. They took up too much space in our house, always slamming doors and making a mess and saying coarse things to me and my mother, who loved them as best she could even though they were exactly like my father.

My father left but never for long. He'd stand on the porch with his suitcase and tell us he'd be at the Ramada downtown. He'd even tell us the room number so we could call him and sometimes we did. After a few weeks of room service and instant coffee, he always returned, said, "Let's give this another go." My mother always let him come back and this made us hate her more than him.

My father left but as he drove away from our house, his car was struck by a garbage truck. He died and it was terrible. The accident was craziest thing, witnesses said. He had the top down, singing loud, smiling like the happiest man in the world and then he flew out of his car and landed next to someone's mailbox, his limbs akimbo, but the smile still on his face.

My father left and lost his mind, quit his job selling lumber and became a bartender, sleeping all day, serving drinks all night. He started smoking, learned how to twirl a bottle of booze in the palm of his hand, a trick he taught us to impress our friends, which it did. He did embarrassing things like piercing his left ear and using hair product. He'd often say, "I am living the life."

My father left and moved in with his parents, who he hated. When we visited him at our grandparents, he always said how he wished he could move back home but he never did so we decided our father was probably a liar and our mother agreed.

My father left because he could no longer stand to live in a house. The walls, he said, were weighing him down. He started living on the street, sleeping in the park about a mile away. Sometimes, my mother let him use the shower. She said, "I suppose the vows extended to loving him in cleanliness and filth."

My father left and took two of my brothers with him, the younger set of twins. They missed us at first and we missed them but then they moved three states away. There were letters, written in their terrible handwriting, and then the letters stopped. It was strange, then, to realize, that once there were five of us kids and then there were three.

My father left and took me with him, said I was his best girl. We moved into a gorgeous loft apartment downtown. When women spent the night, they'd say, "You're so lucky to live in a place like this." I could tell they wanted to live with us too but my father said I was the only girl he wanted to live with for the rest of his life.

My father left and took me with him, said he needed someone to take care of him whom he didn't have to love. I wasn't very good at taking care of him and he never let me forget it. He told me I wasn't going to make a good wife for any kind of man. I was just like my mother, he said. I considered that a compliment.

My father left and took all of us with him, said his children were going to see the world, not sit around in a split-level playing by the rules. We got passports and every month we'd be in a new country, learning to eat strange foods and speak strange languages. My mother remarried and had a new child, a girl. She called that baby her clean slate.

My father left and my mother fell apart. Every day, we came home from school and found her sitting in the front room, staring out the window. In a monotone voice, she'd tell us about everything she had seen, the mailman, three dogs, a crying baby, seventeen cars. "I didn't see your father, though," she'd say. She never looked up when she spoke. She often slept in that chair.

My father left and my mother blamed us. Every morning she woke us up by standing at the foot of our beds, screaming all the reasons she hated us. We should have been upset about the depths of her hatred but her face when she screamed, all stretched, eyes wide, skin red, it always made us laugh and laugh and laugh. We started to look forward to our mornings.

My mother left because she wanted to star in pictures. That had always been her dream ever since she saw *Some Like It Hot* and she meant to pursue it. She moved out to Los Angeles and lived in a cheap apartment in Echo Park and she never did star in pictures but she was in the City of Angels and that seemed to be enough for her.

My mother left and joined the army. She wanted to put her strength to good use. She wanted to be told what to do. Every day during basic training, she sent us a postcard with little notes that said things like, "Destroyed a target today," or, "My arms are really ripped," or, "Sometimes, greasepaint gets in your eyes."

My mother left and became someone else's mother, took up with a man who had eight daughters, each one year apart in age. Their real mother died when the eighth child was born. The youngest was three when she left us. My mother saw them walking down the street, each child holding the shoulder of the girl in front of her. That's what made her leave us and seek them out. She loves orderly children.

My mother left and became a dancer. That's what our father told us. Our classmates told us she became a stripper, said, "Your mama is working the pole." We weren't quite sure what that meant but we knew it wasn't good. When the older twins turned eighteen they went to the club where she worked. She was a bit older then. They said she held the pole like it mattered. They said she was beautiful.

My mother left and went to an ashram in upstate New York. She stayed there for three years, shaved her head, lived in complete silence. When she came home, her hair was short and soft. She smiled a lot but said little. At dinner, that first night after her return, my father asked, "Well, did you learn anything?" She smiled, held her hand to her lips. We waited for her answer.

My mother left and moved into the house next door. She said she wasn't leaving us, she was just making a little more room in the world for herself. She hired a contractor and knocked down most of the walls so everything was wide open. We'd visit her during the day and run around the great big room that was her house. "Isn't it so much better this way?" she'd say.

My mother left and for a little while, took my father with her. We were old enough, they said, to look after ourselves. After a month, my father returned. He looked thin, tired. He never told us about what happened or where our mother went even though we asked and asked and asked.

My mother left and took up with another woman. One afternoon while we had coffee, even though I was too young to be drinking coffee, she leaned across the table, winked at me, and said, "I've lived too much of my life feeling dead and dry." She looked from side to side and leaned closer still. "I'm not dry anymore." I had no idea what she meant and then later, I did.

My mother left and went to the end of the driveway where she stood for a very long time. My father came home from work, said, "What's she doing out there?" We didn't know. The sun set. The sun rose. The sun set. The sun rose. She stood at the end of the driveway. She never moved. I don't even think she blinked. I guess she went as far as she needed to go.

My mother left and took up running. Every evening around five she'd run by our house and my brothers and I would sit on the porch and wave to her. She'd turn and stare at us as she ran by but she never waved or stopped. She simply stared until she was out of sight and then she looked ahead and kept on running and running and running.

My mother left but she didn't. She pitched a tent in the back-yard, the fancy kind with rooms. She had a nice air mattress, raised off the ground. She used the house for bathing and cooking for the family but each night after we watched TV, she'd return to her tent, humming happily. Even after my father started dating again, she stayed out in her tent with us, away from us.

My mother left and became the town whore. That's what my father said even though there was little evidence to support his claim. She still went to church, got a job at a camera store selling lenses and tripods and other accessories. Even though she was mostly alone, my father always imagined her with men who were not him. He never understood that was why she left in the first place.

My mother left and became the town whore. My father said people were just talking but she was often seen at the bars in town wearing next to nothing, draping herself across men of inappropriate ages. When I visited her, a man was often leaving, tucking his pants as he stumbled out the door, muttering, "God-damn." My mother would pull her robe closed and smile at me. She'd say, "I love freedom."

My mother left, went to school, and wrote us letters about what she learned. She said she was going to spend the rest of her life trying to understand the world. My mother spent most of her time in the library. She called it travel. We'd ask to see her and she'd say, "I'm on the road right now," even though she was on Elm Street. She really believed she was somewhere far away.

My mother left and took up with an unkind man. We'd see her around town sometimes with fading bruises on her face and arms. We'd say, "Come home, Dad still loves you," but she always shook her head, smiled softly. She'd say, "You are too young to understand the pleasures of penance." Her boyfriend broke her; she ended up in the hospital. I sat by her side and asked, "Have you had enough penance?"

My mother left with great fanfare. After dinner, spaghetti, she called the entire family into the living room. She pointed her finger at my father, her hand shaking. "You too," she said. We sat quietly as she explained why she was leaving in exacting detail. We were all culpable she said, to one degree or another. I asked what that meant and my brother jabbed me with his elbow. Later, I looked it up.

My mother left quietly but even before she left it was like she was already gone. She rarely spoke to us, always looked right through us. When she disappeared it was like she had never been there, like we were miraculous accidents who showed up one day, hanging onto my father's legs with sticky hands as he stared down at us in wonder.

My mother left and took the younger set of twins. There was still a chance, she said, to help them become something. The rest of us were hopeless, I guess, even though I was the youngest and thought by her reckoning I could still become something too. She moved to the other side of town with my brothers, even changed their names, taught them to ignore us if we saw them around.

My mother left and took the older set of twins, said she had known them just long enough to love them instead of leaving them behind. We watched as they packed. They were smug and made a big show of packing their things. They even stole one of my action figures. We'd visit them on Saturdays and they'd brag about how they were the ones my mother truly loved. We shrugged.

My mother left and took me with her, said a girl needed her mother and boys needed their father and sometimes mothers and fathers no longer needed each other. The night she told me we were leaving we sat in the backyard, on the cement wall along the edge of the property. The moon was high and full, but an ugly color, not the color to mark a leaving. "We'll have an adventure," she said.

My mother left because my father drove her away. He didn't hide his philandering, that's what she called it, always came home reeking of cheap sluts, their drugstore perfumes and tacky lipstick clinging to his dress shirt collars. Enough was enough, she said, so she left him and left us because he deserved to know exactly what he lost. It didn't take him long at all to miss her, to want her back but she refused.

My mother left because my father threw her out. She didn't hide her philandering, that's what he called it, always came home reeking of cheap sluts, their drugstore perfumes and tacky lipstick clinging to her blouses and dresses. He demanded she stop and get right with God and their marriage. She insisted she was as right with God as she ever hoped to be. She moved in with a lady named Nancy.

My mother left because my father was too kind, an uxorious man who adored her morning, noon, and night. It was impossible to breathe around a man like that, my mother said. It was too much to be with someone who was unable to see her flaws. There was, she said, one afternoon in her new apartment, such a thing as being loved too well. "Can you breathe now?" I asked. She inhaled deeply.

My mother left and we never knew why. We spent half the week with her and half with my father. We lived two extraordinarily ordinary, nearly identical lives, always wondering why my mother one day woke up, packed a suitcase, kissed us on our foreheads, and said she'd send for us soon. When we asked my father why they were divorcing he said, "I will never know."

### What Happened When the Glass Broke

The twins, the younger ones, started bruising all the time. A doctor looked them over, said, "These boys are sick." Before long they were in the hospital and we sat by their sides, bored, watching them die, not understanding they were dying until it was too late to care as much as we should have. I moved into their room, after, and smelled them all the time. My parents became quieter, sat side by side, muttering, "Our boys." We might as well have all died.

The twins, the younger ones, were walking home from school when they disappeared. For months, neighbors swore one minute those boys were there, swinging their backpacks as they shuffled their way home, and the next minute, they vanished into thin air. The police looked for them. We spent night after night bundled up in our warm coats, walking through frozen, empty fields with flashlights, two feet apart, looking for those boys. Then most people stopped looking because they were sure there was nothing left to find. My mother set their places at the table night after night. She put their favorite foods on those plates. Each morning, she set out new outfits even though they wouldn't fit anymore, not years later. One day, there was a knock at the door. I answered and these two young men were standing there, well-dressed, nice haircuts. I recognized the freckles on their left cheeks. "We're home," they said, and walked into the house like they never disappeared. They would never tell us where they got off to or what happened, not ever. Whenever they were asked, they just smiled like they knew the best secret in the world.

The twins, the younger ones, started getting in trouble at school and then they brought that trouble home, fighting everyone who tried to say a word to them. My parents eventually got fed up, said there wasn't enough love in the world for a parent to put up with their kind of trouble so they sent them away to a camp that had nothing to do with camping. Every three months we'd visit the boys who always wore gray sweatshirts and khaki pants and canvas sneakers. They were still a whole lot of trouble but it didn't matter so much. I know we were supposed to miss them but none of us did.

The twins, the older ones, were playing in the street, some silly game they had invented involving lying in the street to feel the rumble of cars on the next street over, a busy thoroughfare. They didn't see the old Charger, didn't hear the pistons sliding or the roar of the broken muffler, the Skynyrd blasting through the open windows. I like to think they turned to look at each other just before their bodies were crushed beneath the hot rubber of that muscle car. I like to think they knew they would never be alone.

The twins, the older ones, were out at the overlook with friends, drinking, dancing around a bonfire. One of the twins went to the car to make out with some girl who wore a lot of eye shadow and chewed gum all the time. We called her Bit because she always looked like she was chomping at the bit. The other twin, he got the idea he wanted to fly so he tore off his shirt and ran off the cliff and for a little while he flew but then he hit the outcropping of rocks below. That stopped his flying but good. In the car, with Bit, his brother suddenly grabbed his chest and all his bones started to ache like they meant to come apart. He started trembling and Bit thought that meant something about what her hand was doing in his jeans. He pushed her away and stumbled out of the car his dick hanging half out, calling for his brother like a crazy man and all those kids out there drinking with them, they just stood and stared. They didn't know what to say.

The twins, the older ones, didn't want to be bothered with anyone else in the family. One morning we woke up and they were gone. Their room was immaculate, probably even cleaner than the day we moved in. Their clothes were gone but everything else, they left behind. On the lower bunk of their bunk beds, there was a note. All it said was, "We don't belong here." It was hard at first. The house was quieter, emptier. We had more room to be ourselves and we didn't know what to do with that. Eventually, though, we realized, those boys were right. I saw them once, in Vegas with my husband many years later. They both wore expensive-looking suits and walked in lockstep. I saw them making their way toward us and raised my hand to wave, could feel words hanging from my lower lip but they stared right through me and kept walking on by.

My father had a temper. He and the older twins were out late drinking, or what my mother called catting around. Another drunk said something to the twins my dad didn't appreciate and that got my father in some kind of rage. He broke a glass bottle over the bar, like it was something he did every day. He said, "Don't you talk cross about my eldest boys." He lunged forward and he did not blink. With one slash he cut that other drunk's throat and blood started streaming down that man's neck, staining his shirt. He fell to his knees holding his throat, the blood oozing between his fingers. When the man finally fell all the way down, my father nodded, dropped his broken bottle, wiped his hands on his jeans and sat back down at the bar with his boys. He ordered everyone a round of drinks. It was some time before the police were called and everyone swore they did not see a thing.

My mother loved to find trouble. She'd go looking for it any old place. She also had a thing for knives, kept a real sharp blade in her purse. One day she went walking on a rough street in a bad neighborhood. She held her purse tightly against her body and kept one hand in her purse, fingering the handle of that knife. One way or another that blade was going to find flesh. That night it did. She was taken to jail and my father went to visit her. She was still waiting in an interrogation room. It's a small town; they let him talk to her. She sat quietly staring at her hands. There was a crimson droplet on the collar of her blouse. "I hope it was worth it," my father said as he sat down. My mother looked him in the eye. "Oh yes, it was," she said, and then she resumed staring at her hands.

My parents weren't much for abiding the law. When they wanted something they took it. If something got in the way of what they wanted, they got rid of it. I don't think they loved a goddamn thing but each other and maybe my brothers and me. They saw a movie and got it in their heads to rob a Triple-A baseball park so they donned a pair of ski masks and took my granddaddy's Colt and stole a little more than $13,000. It wasn't that we were embarrassed by our parents when they came home and told us what they did. It was their lack of ambition that bothered us.

Dogs in the neighborhood started to disappear. It was the strangest thing. It used to be that some days there were so many dogs, all of them yapping and barking and chasing their tails making everyone crazy, you couldn't even think clearly if you were walking down the street. The streets got quieter and quieter and soon, the last dog alive in the neighborhood was our dog, Rusty. People started to talk. I didn't see it happen but my brothers did, the older twins. One night, they heard growling in the backyard and so they ran downstairs and out onto the patio. There our father was crouched real strange, growling, his lips wet with spit dripping down his chin as he and Rusty circled each other like only one of them was going to get out of the fight alive. Only one did. A girl down the street, only fifteen, went missing the other day.

None of us were surprised when we heard what happened. I always saw how my father looked at my friends, how he sometimes looked at me. There was something in his eyes, some kind of hunger that seemed to tear at him. When my friends and I were watching a movie or sunbathing in the backyard, I'd see him, standing almost out of sight, his hands shaking like he was trying to hold himself together, his lips shiny and wet.

My mother and I were home alone and a man walked into our house, real natural, like he belonged there. Terrible things happened to us both. We were witnesses for each other. My father took us to a doctor friend of his, *a discreet man.* "It's a little late for discretion," my mother said.

My mother and I and the younger twins were home. My father and the older twins were at the park. I wore a training bra and lip gloss. I was young but not young. A man walked into our house, real natural, like he belonged there. My mother stood in front of us like that would stop him, her arm iron-straight across our bodies. She gave him a look that should have scared him but it didn't. The man had a gun in his waistband. He tied up the twins. He grabbed me and she clawed at him. She told him he wanted a woman not a girl. He threw her into a wall and she slumped to the floor. He took me into my parents' bedroom and when we were on the bed, I thought, "I am on my parents' bed." He broke me but I didn't know how to explain it so I stopped talking, started hiding in my room and then I left home, moved in with my aunt. I didn't want to live in that house anymore.

My mother and I were home alone. I don't know where the others were. A man walked into our house, real natural, like he belonged there. My mother knew what would happen before I did. She looked at me real hard. She said, "Baby girl, you fight no matter what." He put us on the couch and sat on the coffee table tapping our knees with the barrel of his gun like he was deciding where to start. He had me tie my mom's wrists with a lamp cord. I sat next to her holding onto her arm while she whispered things to me. He found the liquor cabinet and started drinking. My mother said, "My husband will be home soon." The man laughed. I started to understand what would happen.

I've seen movies. He took me first. I did what my mother said, fought like holy hell. I looked into her eyes the entire time. She did not look away.

My mother and I were home alone and a man walked into our house, real natural, like he belonged there. Terrible things happened to us both. My father found us, in their closet, holding on to a pair of his slacks. We were both shaking. He wanted to call the police but my mother said no. I said no. He asked what happened. My mother couldn't speak so I said, "Nothing." That lie was easier for him to believe. We followed my father through the house as he checked every room, made sure the windows and doors were locked. I took a long shower. I didn't sleep for a long time after that. I didn't feel comfortable in any room where that man touched me which was nearly every room. One day, my mother told me to pack my things. She packed her things. We got in her car and drove far away, moved into a house in a gated neighborhood with a fancy alarm system. We were very quiet but we were always alone together.

My mother and I were home alone. She had been drinking and was on the couch wearing a thin nightgown that went just past her knees. I was in the kitchen painting my fingernails purple. A man walked into our house and from the set of his face it was clear what he meant to do. When he grabbed my mother, she pointed at me, said, "She's younger. What would you want with an old lady?" The man laughed and shook his head, shoved my mother to the couch. He said, "You're a real piece of work, one hell of a mother." He took a sip from the bottle of wine she was drinking from then came for me. When he grabbed my arm, he looked at me almost like he was sorry. Then he dragged me into my bedroom and kept me there for a long time and touched me almost like he was sorry. I didn't make a sound. I wasn't going to give my mother the satisfaction.

My mother and I were home alone. She had been drinking but she looked real pretty, her skin flushed, her lipstick a little smeared like some man had been kissing on her all night. I sat next to her, watching an old rerun of *I Love Lucy*. Two men walked into our house like they owned the place. When one of them grabbed my mom and pulled her to her feet, twisted her arm behind her back, she gasped and suddenly she didn't look real pretty anymore. It scared me to see her like that so I stood up and I put my hand on that man's wrist. I said, "Please leave her alone." I slid my hand up his arm in what I hoped was a way that let him feel calm, maybe a little less mean. His friend laughed and took a sip from a flask. My mom sank back into the couch, pulled her knees to her chest. She looked so small, so young. It was strange though. She didn't do a thing to help me. All I wanted was for her to look pretty again.

## *Who We Are Beneath the Glass*

My mother and father are older now. Their skin hangs loose from their bones. They move slow. They eat canned food and wear loose clothes. They sit on the couch and watch television. When they fall asleep, their bodies refuse to touch. They repeat themselves, telling the same old stories to each other or anyone who will listen. No one wants to listen. They talk too loud. They say too much. They never say enough.

My brothers are older now. They are tall and broad. Two of them have bellies hanging over their pants. Two of them have bright red cheeks, a fondness for gin. They are all married. They live in the same town, on the same street. One of them has a lover who looks just like him. His wife doesn't know. One is married to a woman who looks just like me. His wife has to know. They have jobs. They have children. They have houses and lawns. They say nothing about who we were. Even that is too much.

I am older now. I live in a big city in a tall building. I have an important job with an important title. I have a walk-in closet and a bathroom I share with a man who is my husband. We have his-and-hers sinks. We have floor to ceiling glass windows we pay a brown-skinned woman to clean. At night, the lights of the city stretch around us in every direction. At night, I often stand and stare into that glass, past the faint edges of my reflection. I rarely recognize myself. Once a year we visit my family even though they only live an hour away. It is too much. We always stay in a hotel. We fill our days with them so I don't have to find what's left of myself, of us, of who we were. My husband asks, "Why do you keep them at such a distance?" I tell him, "There is no other way."

That is to say, we all lived happily ever after or we didn't.

# Roxane Gay Is Feeling Ambitious

The author of *Difficult Women* talks about putting in the work
and following her "very dark imagination"

## By Mensah Demary

Few contemporary writers are called upon to render opinions
more often than author Roxane Gay, a consequence of amassing
a readership through, among other ways, critiquing the culture
at large with generous, entertaining essays, independent of the
topic. To Gay, the *Fast and the Furious* movie franchise is as wor-
thy of intellectual consideration as any obscure tome exhumed to
brace esoteric points. Gay is always relevant and often correct,
which not only explains, to some small degree, her popularity
among fans across genres and aesthetics—from her new *Marvel*
comic to co-writing a film adaptation of her debut novel—but
also makes her opinion a highly-desired commodity, even if the
matter at hand is of little significance or relevance to Gay. This
leads to miscommunication, for lack of a better word, played out
within Gay's Twitter timeline, where fans and trolls alike commune for kind words or invective or impromptu requests for some

kind of labor—intellectual, literary, even emotional—offering to young writers a glimpse of what literary stardom looks like, the necessity to remain, with restrictions, accessible to fans while protecting one's private life.

Difficult Women is a collection of short fiction that solidifies Gay as a writer just as committed to technique as she is to storytelling itself. The book includes the seminal stories "North Country," "I Am A Knife," and "Break All The Way Down." Each word and every sentence in Difficult Women invites instead of repels the reader. Her erudition and ardor always strive for connection, and her blunt stories are anchored by curiosity and emotional depth while avoiding the maudlin, or needlessly grotesque plots. I spoke with Gay for Electric Literature about Difficult Women, the short story form, her writing life, and the challenges of memoir.

Mensah Demary: "I Will Follow You," originally published by West Branch, and again in Best American Mystery Stories, begins Difficult Women, a collection of realist yet vibrant stories of women and their lives, seen from their perspectives, told in their voices. It's a disquieting story about two sisters and the trauma they both shared and endured. Why are they difficult women who, as written in the epigraph, "should be celebrated for their very nature"?

Roxane Gay: I don't know that they are explicitly difficult women. The collection gets its title from one of the stories and certainly, many of the women in the book are difficult in one way or another, but not all. The protagonists in "I Will Follow You," are, more aptly, women who have faced difficulties.

Demary: Many of these stories were published prior to your debut novel *An Untamed State*, soon to be adapted into a film, and *Bad Feminist*, the *New York Times* bestselling collection of essays. The stories are fresh and relevant to readers, and you've written quite a bit since they first appeared. Do the stories still feel fresh and relevant to you, the writer? Should such a question be of any concern to a writer?

Gay: I've long thought that most writers write the same story over and over, and certainly, in my fiction, there are some prevalent themes. When I re-read the stories in *Difficult Women*, there is a sense of being at home. I know these women and I know their hearts and in that, they are always going to feel fresh and relevant to me and hopefully my readers. The question I concern myself with is not if a story is relevant, but rather, if a story is both timely and timeless but that concern comes when I am revising. When I sit down to write, I just sit down to write what's burning in my fingers.

Demary: *Bad Feminist* introduced your nonfiction to thousands, but many readers will be introduced to your short fiction for the first time with *Difficult Women*. Often, readers presume fiction to be a set piece for actual memories, or lived experiences. To what extent does this presumption prevent the reader from experiencing a short story as art, that is, as valuable independent of the story's materiality relative to reality? Have readers forgotten how to enjoy a short story for its own merits, its imagination?

Gay: I'm not sure I understand the question. Readers often assume fiction is thinly veiled autobiography. They assume there is no art or craft to fiction. Those presumptions make for an impoverished reading experience. I cannot imagine thinking so little of a writer's capacity for imagination. Alas. Some readers have forgotten how to enjoy a short story without obsessing over a story's "truth," but not all, and it's our job as fiction reminders to continue to remind readers that fiction is fiction is fiction. The story is not about the writer at all.

Demary: *Difficult Women's* titular story succeeds as it plays with roles assigned to women: "Loose Women" and "Crazy Women" act as sub-classifications further explored via vignettes entitled "What a Crazy Woman Eats" or "How She Got That Way." The story is disinterested in edifying those who perpetuate these roles, caring more for reclamation and redefinition of language as it relates to women. The titles of your books make the same in-roads to this reclamation. Can a difficult woman be a bad feminist; do the ideas intersect in your mind? How should fans of your previous books approach *Difficult Women*?

Gay: Certainly, I am challenging the traditional idea of a "difficult woman," much in the same way I challenge traditional notions of feminism with the phrase "bad feminist." There are all kinds of intersections at play here. I don't have any prescriptions for how fans of my other work should approach *Difficult Women* other than to read the stories with an open mind and an open heart and to recognize that as a writer, I contain multitudes and a very dark imagination.

Demary: "Bad Priest" is a memorable story, and one of the earliest collected in *Difficult Women*, dating back to 2009, now a suddenly distant era. Father Mickey, a Catholic priest, and Rebekah, "a perfume girl in a department store who still lived with her parents," have an affair: "The first time they fucked, they were in the church, and it was late—two in the morning." Rebekah falls in love with Mickey but Mickey is preoccupied with himself, that is, with his soul in the eyes of mother and god. Mickey uses Rebekah to offload his shame. At what point does Rebekah get to deal and be present within her own life, absent the burdens of others, men, such as Mickey? When does a difficult woman get to drop her guard?

Gay: Why do you assume Rebekah isn't dealing with her own life? In love, people often tolerate all kinds of bullshit. In "Bad Priest," Rebekah is willing to tolerate Mickey's self-absorption because she loves him and because, perhaps, she enjoys the taboo of having an affair with a priest. Rebekah isn't passive in their relationship, nor is she naïve. I think Rebekah and Mickey see each other exactly as they are. Sometimes, that's a relief.

I don't know that a difficult woman ever drops her guard. She knows better.

Demary: Do you still write short stories? Are there collections you've recently enjoyed, or those that remain memorable to you?

Gay: I still write short stories. I will always write short stories. I've got a few I'm working on right now but sadly, I always have to put them at the back of the queue of what I'm working on. No one is ever clamoring for short stories from relatively unknown writers but that's okay. I write them anyway. I recently enjoyed *Always Happy Hour* by Mary Miller and *Homesick for*

*Another World* by Ottessa Moshfegh—both dark, strange, a bit uncomfortable, sexy. One of the most memorable collections remains *How to Suffocate Your Own Fool Self* by Danielle Evans. Each story in that book is exquisitely crafted. Whew. That woman can write.

Demary: You have been writing a *Marvel* comic, *Black Panther: World of Wakanda*. What has been the response, the feedback, from your readership, now larger and all the more diverse as many comic book fans read your words for the first time? What is it like to write a world populated and influenced predominately, if not entirely, by black women?

Gay: The response, so far, has been overwhelmingly good. I was really nervous about *World of Wakanda* because I am new to comics and I was writing into a really established canon but readers have been very generous. It's exhilarating to write a world dominated by black women. We need more work like this, work where whiteness isn't the default, and where it isn't even something of relevance to the stories we tell.

Demary: In *GQ*, an article in conversation with John Malkovich advised against ambition as a motivating factor in every day life, and in art, dismissing it simply as "the need to prove something to others" and "a need for rewards outside of the work." You've written about ambition before, and it appears as a theme more than once in *Difficult Women*. Can ambition distract at times from the work, in this case, the writing? How much does ambition motivate you toward new challenges, writing a comic book for the first time, for example?

Gay: Eh, people have strange ideas about ambition as a dangerous thing because they only want certain kinds of people (ahem)
to be ambitious. I vigorously encourage women and people of
color to be ambitious, to want and work for every damn thing
they can dream of. We're allowed to want, nakedly, as long
as we're willing to put in the proverbial work. Ambition is a
distraction if it's the *only* motivator. I am ambitious because
I love what I do, not simply for ambition's sake. Ambition is
what allows me to take creative risks and try things I never
thought I could do. Ambition makes me a better thinker and
writer. Ambition makes me.

Demary: Do you maintain a writing routine, a regimen perhaps
forced due to workload, and if so do you work in time to write for
yourself, to write something other than work assigned or com-
missioned by third parties? How often do you read for pleasure
these days?

Gay: I have no real routine or regimen. Because of a very hectic
schedule, I write when I can, where I can, as often as I can. I am
writing this at 2 am at my parents' house. My brother is snoring loudly two rooms away and I can hear him. Before I started
tackling these questions, I finished the first draft of the screen-
play for *An Untamed State* which I mostly wrote on a couch in Los
Angeles and finished up here. Tomorrow, I'll finish revising *Hunger*
and work on my anthology *Not That Bad*. I don't really write for
myself as much as I want but when I do, I write fiction. I try to
make the time at least once a month. I read for pleasure quite a
lot, pretty much on a daily basis, before bed, in the morning. I
read a lot on airplanes.

Demary: Your first memoir, *Hunger*, is highly anticipated; you revealed via Twitter some struggles in completing the book, and I imagine there was some trepidation in being so revealing of yourself for art's sake, which makes me think you decided to write *Hunger* for reasons beyond yourself, for a goal other than personal catharsis. Should that be the goal of all memoirs, the reach toward the outside, toward other people, in spite of the form's inherent insularity?

Gay: The vulnerability demanded by *Hunger* terrified me so I dragged my heels quite a lot. It delayed the book a year when all was said and done. I am, in fact, a very private person but I think it is absolutely necessary for more people to write about different kinds of bodies, the truth of living in those bodies, without necessarily framing those stories in narratives of triumph and conquer. So, yes, I absolutely wrote this book not just for myself, but for anyone, and especially any woman, who has struggled with trauma, being overweight, the cultural expectations we place on bodies, and the perpetual diet so many of us are on. Personal catharsis had nearly nothing to do with it. This was my first memoir so I would not presume to declare what the form should do but I believe all great writing looks both inward and outward.

# ACKNOWLEDGMENTS

Versions of these stories have appeared in *Best American Mystery Stories 2014*, *Best American Short Stories 2012*, *NOON*, *Barrelhouse*, *West Branch*, *Monkey Bicycle*, *Night Train*, *Oxford American*, *Twelve Stories*, *Collagist*, *Hobart*, *Acappella Zoo*, *Annalemma*, *Pear Noir!*, *Word Riot*, *Storyglossia*, *Minnesota Review*, *A Public Space*, *American Short Fiction*, *Literarian*, *Normal School*, *Copper Nickel*, *Joyland*, and *Black Warrior Review*. I am grateful to all the editors who originally published these stories. I want to especially recognize Elizabeth Ellen, who picked my story "North Country" out of the submission queue at *Hobart*, making it possible for that story to be included in *Best American Short Stories*.

Amy Hundley is the gracious steward of my words. Maria Massie is the agent who asked me what my writing dream was and has made it come true. To say thank you to her would not begin to be adequate. Nonetheless, thank you. John Mark Boling is my beloved publicist at Grove and I am always grateful for how he gets my fiction out into the world. I would also like to thank Amanda Panitch, Clare Mao, Jami Attenberg, Lisa Mecham, Mensah Demary, M. Bartley Seigel, Alissa Nutting, Aubrey Hirsch, Devan Goldstein, Tayari Jones, Brian Leung, Krista Ratcliffe, Trinity Ray, Kevin Mills, Sylvie Rabineau, Terry McMillan, Channing Tatum (with particular appreciation for his neck), Beyoncé (with particular appreciation for the *Lemonade* album), and *Law & Order: SVU*.

I am grateful for my immediate family, who are my most ardent cheerleaders and keepers of the real—Michael and Nicole Gay, Michael Gay Jr., Jacquelynn Camden Gay and Parker Nicole Gay, Joel Gay and Hailey Gay, Mesmin Destin and Michael Kosko, Sony Gay, and Marcelle Raff.

Last but never least, I thank Tracy, my first and last reader, best friend, motivator, secret keeper, heart holder.

# CREDITS

The following stories first appeared in these publications.

"I Will Follow You" originally appeared in slightly different form in *West Branch* 72, Winter 2013; and in *Best American Mystery Stories 2014*, copyright © 2014 by Houghton Mifflin Harcourt Publishing Company.

"Water, All Its Weight" originally appeared in slightly different form under the title "The Weight of Water" in *Monkeybicycle* 7, copyright © 2010 by Monkeybicycle Books.

"The Mark of Cain" originally appeared in slightly different form in *Night Train*.

"Difficult Women" originally appeared in slightly different form under the title "Important Things" in *Copper Nickel*, 2013.

"FLORIDA" originally appeared in slightly different form under the title "Group Fitness" in the *Oxford American* Issue 80, Spring 2013.

"La Negra Blanca" originally appeared in slightly different form in *Collagist* Issue Three, October 2009.

"Baby Arm" originally appeared in slightly different form in *Rick Magazine*, formerly *Mississippi Review Online*.

"North Country" originally appeared in slightly different form in *Hobart* 12; *Best American Short Stories 2012*; and *New Stories from the Midwest 2012*.

"How" originally appeared in slightly different form in *Annalemma* Issue 6.

"Requiem for a Glass Heart" originally appeared in slightly different form in *A Cappella Zoo* Issue 3, Fall 2009.

"In the Event of My Father's Death" originally appeared in slightly different form in *Pear Noir!* #3.

"Break All the Way Down" originally appeared in slightly different form in *Joyland*, 2013.

"Bad Priest" originally appeared in slightly different form in *Storyglossia* Issue 34, July 2009.

"Open Marriage" originally appeared in slightly different form in the *Minnesota Review* Issue 80, 2013.

"A Pat" originally appeared in slightly different form in *NOON*, 2012.

"Best Features" originally appeared in slightly different form in *Barrelhouse Online*, November 2010.

"Bone Density" originally appeared in slightly different form in *Word Riot*.

"I Am a Knife" originally appeared in slightly different form in *Literarian* Issue #4.

"The Sacrifice of Darkness" originally appeared in slightly different form in *American Short Fiction* Vol. 15, Issue 55.

"Noble Things" originally appeared in slightly different form in *A Public Space* Issue 21, Summer 2014.

"Strange Gods" originally appeared in slightly different form in *Black Warrior Review* 37.2.

"Pilgrims" originally appeared in *Annalemma*, 2009.

"We Are All So Happy Now" originally appeared in *Cream City Review*, 2011.

"Glass" originally appeared in *Atticus Review*, 2012.

"Roxane Gay Is Feeling Ambitious," an interview by Mensah Demary, originally published in *Electric Literature*. Copyright © 2017 by Mensah Demary.